A NEW ENGLAND BILLIONAIRES BOOK

Tangled Heirs:
Book Three of the New England Billionaires Series.

Copyright © 2025 by Odessa Alba

Rusty Ogre Publishing
www.rustyogrepublishing.com
Casper, Wyoming, USA

All Rights Reserved.

Cover Art by Erica Summers

For Fran, Olivia, & Cindy

*Some losses cut deep, but in the end, I am grateful
for the permanence of the scars.*

Layla

"Just wait. My lawyer is going to eviscerate you and whichever Collins whose dick you're sucking to make them take on your case for cheap. Spend as much money fighting me as you want. It's not gonna matter. Danny is staying with me."

Alan's voice seethes through my dashboard via Bluetooth, a molasses-thick poison oozing into my cochlea through my lymph system, detonating into every extremity.

Another dark bend in the unfamiliar road rushes at me hard, fast. The tires of my sedan squeal as I whip right to stay on the asphalt, hugging the striated rock wall. Hitting that would be better than going off the sheer edge on the other side into the frigid woods below.

"Look at the fucking facts, Layla. He's in a fucking magnet school now, getting the best grades of his life. He's in sports. He already has friends. And he's financially taken care of in a two-parent household."

"He was in a two-parent household!" I snarl. "Until you walked out!"

Alan doesn't dignify that with a response. He wouldn't dare admit fault aloud like that. "Point is, Layla, he loves it here. There ain't a court in the land that's gonna make us share custody after they find out what a hot-fuckin'-mess you are."

I bite my lip, gnawing so hard that I can taste the metallic tinge of my own blood. "Alan, how the hell do you expect me to watch you and your little side-piece raise him from afar?"

He laughs. "Side-piece? No darlin'. She's an entree now. Or did you forget that she's got a ring on her finger? I know sometimes the booze makes your memory fuzzy."

"Alan, why would you say that?"

"You're a drunk. Remember when you were late to Dan's birthday because you were sleepin' one off?"

"I wasn't sleeping one off! I told you, I was taking a fucking test. I have to stay up on my certifications to keep my damn job."

"It's always an excuse. I'm tired of hearing it. But no one's more tired of it than Danny." He sighs. "Save us all the money and energy, and don't fight me on this."

"I'm not backing down, Alan. Fucking me over in our marriage is one thing. That, I can handle…"

"Apparently not," he says with a hearty laugh.

I growl into the night air, my breath visible inside the car because the heater hasn't worked for about a year.

"That's right. Yell. Scream. Throw a useless tantrum. Whatever makes you feel better." He sounds so callous when he says it.

"I am not rolling over about Danny without a fight! You'll get sole custody over my dead body, which I'm sure you'd prefer right now."

"What? You being gone for good?"

"Yes!"

"Yeah, I wouldn't mind it if I'm being honest. You'd kinda be doing us all a favor, Danny included."

The comment sends me into a dazed state of shock, cut too deep to react. This from a man who promised a decade-and-a-half ago to love, honor, and cherish me until my dying day.

What a fucking fool I am to ever believe the sack of shit meant it.

"I think we're done here, Layla. Next time, whine to your lawyer, not me. I don't give a shit about what you want anymore."

"Pfft. Like you ever fucking did."

"Aww, sounds like someone's still jealous."

"I'd rather drink drain cleaner than ever be with you again. You were a terrible husband and, frankly, a lousy fucking lay."

The second I say it, I realize it's stupid, this wounding him in retaliation. His pride is delicate. No one knows that better than I do. A verbal assault like this will be construed as an act of war.

He groans. "Layla, do the world a fucking favor. Go crawl into the bottom of a bottle somewhere and fucking die."

The connection cuts out abruptly. I bite again. My front teeth pierce flesh with a pain that is far preferable to that of Alan's request.

The path before my bumper reveals itself in the darkness a foot at a time around the mountainous wall, one whose jutting ledges are capped in the dirty-white remains of last week's snowfall.

I'm in the center of the road, straddling the solid yellow line, trying to lessen the severity of the turns, hoping no one else is on these back roads, too. With another twenty-five minutes until I'm home, I stare out at the icy curves, searching for the slightest sign of headlights around each blind corner so I don't end up in a head-on collision.

As miles pass and my bald tires chew through icy fingers creeping away from the rock wall, Alan's callous words echo in my brain. The threat of my only child becoming a stranger to me suddenly feels more real than ever before. As an engineer, Alan has the money to afford phenomenal lawyers. Deep down, with everything he's got on his side, I'm almost certainly fucked.

Do the world a fucking favor. Go crawl into the bottom of a bottle somewhere and fucking die...

I wish it was that easy.

For Danny's sake.

For Alan's.

Hell, even for my own.

If I died, my problems would be over. No more selling everything I own to pay Bart Collins. No more waiting by the phone for Danny to call. No more birthdays, Mother's Days, and Thanksgivings alone. No more tears. Heartache. Hangovers. No more faked smiles at office Christmas parties, watching lawyers flaunt their money. No more waiting for people to die, just to keep a meager amount of food in my fridge.

It could all just… be over.

Once and for all.

My burial costs, the font on my headstone, and filling my shoes at the firm would all be someone else's problem.

I am so fucked my body can't even feel anything beyond despair. Tonight happens to be my anniversary. Not to the night Alan and I said 'I do' ten years ago, a night where I wore a lace floor-length veil and an ivory satin gown with a cumbersome train, a night I hugged some sixty strangers that Alan insisted on inviting.

No. Tonight is the anniversary of the death of our union. Two years ago today, our divorce was finalized. It would only be another week after the judge banged that gavel that Alan would announce his new engagement to Kayla, his Rubenesque co-worker and the woman my son promptly started calling 'Mom.'

My sedan hugs another tight turn of the New Hampshire road, weaving past the faded yellow stripe of paint, tires chewing the raised bumps on the edge with a loud, low warning growl.

The thought of permanently losing Danny to Alan somehow makes every muscle in my body ache. It sucks the air from my lungs and wrenches my stomach, the stomach riddled with stretch marks and a C-section scar that incubated him for three-quarters of a year.

With Danny gone, part of myself is missing. His absence left a void I can't seem to fill, one that seems to only be soothed by distilled spirits whose bitter aftertaste lingers on my tongue.

Yes, I drank tonight.

I understood everything I'd lose if anyone on Alan's legal team found pictures of me downing eggnog in the background of someone's online selfie. But the thought of being erased from my son's life was too much to bear. *I'm fucking human.* The burn of alcohol warming my throat was the only comfort in a room full of ugly sweaters, fuzzy Santa hats, jovial laughter, and plastic mistletoe.

As anger and disgust pulse through my veins, I ease down on the accelerator until I'm careening around the next blind curve. I just want to get home, soak in a hot bath with a bottle of Stoli, and let Calgon take me away.

I don't see the fawn until it's basking in my headlights, frozen, a mere fifteen feet from my high beams. Out of sheer reflex, I spin the wheel to miss it and instantly realize that I've jerked too hard. My left front tire bypasses the raised bumps and speeds right off the cliff's edge. I try to over-correct back toward the rocky wall, but my rear left tire slips off next, and my right tires lose their grip on the road.

My car thrusts off the edge, slipping off the perilous cliff's face. I snap through saplings and bushes like a hot knife through butter. In a disorienting flash, I am off the edge, powerless in the unforgiving clutches of gravity, no longer supported by the hard road and snow beneath my tires. My stomach lurches at the weightlessness, muscles clenched, bracing for a cataclysmic impact with the forest floor that will be my end. The sedan is in free-fall, tires revolving through the frosty air, a metal comet hurtling toward the leaf-covered ground far, far below.

I don't even have time to scream.

And then I see the tree. Massive and stately, its sprawling arms welcome me home like a loving mother. I'm nose-diving straight toward it, too shocked to scream, too dizzied to move. Limbs assault the chassis as it careens, graceful, like a bird through the winter air.

The violent sound of the smash echoes into oblivion. In a harrowing final moment, there is bark everywhere. Scraping. Tearing. Swatting.

The tree pierces through metal and glass like the vehicle is a mere ghost. There is a crunch and judder as the car accordions. Loose items smash with violence against the dash, the windshield shattering. The blur of the steering wheel coming at me is the last thing I see before I blink out.

The obnoxious sound of my cell ringing rips me from a relaxing dream in which my head was in Sydney Sweeney's lap. Her hands stroked my ginger hair lovingly, something I've not felt since I was a kid. My mom used to do it until I fell asleep.

The third ring is met by my guttural groan. I claw blindly through the darkness to answer it.

Andromeda's name is splashed across the painfully bright screen. I roll my eyes. If my sister needs to borrow money, can't she at least have the decency to beg during business hours?

I get a mental image, a flash of her in jail, fake Gold Star nails clenched around grimy iron bars, in for something she didn't realize was even illegal.

She's blissfully ignorant, naive, and spoiled. Her mother turned her and Leo into privileged little monsters before I ever came into the picture.

I hit the green circle to answer and grimace. "Jesus, Andromeda, somebody had better be dead."

There is a long pause. A pause so long I feel my pulse quicken. It isn't until I hear the pained hitch of her breath, the squelched cry that escapes her throat, that true panic oozes in.

"It's… dad," she finally manages through the wails. I can hear the wetness of her mouth, the long, damp drag of her nostrils struggling to take in enough air, the judder of her tone.

Andromeda's on far too much Xanax to emote like this. And, unlike Leo, she's never been partial to pranks.

I rise from the clutches of my Egyptian cotton sheets and remind myself to stay calm.

"What about dad?" My heart thuds hard against my ribs. "What's wrong?"

"He's… gone, Orion."

"What do you mean? Where would he go? It's," I look at my watch, "two-forty in the morning. Did you check the observatory?"

"No, Orion!" she cries loudly. "He's not missing. He's… *gone*."

"I don't understand."

That's a lie.

I do.

But I need to hear the words, or else I won't believe it. I… can't.

"Orion… he's not fucking breathing!"

Andromeda explodes into a chilling wail of pain.

I am too stunned to say one damned word. I am filled with panic and denial, with rage and horror. My father, my best friend in the world, my closest confidante…

No goodbye.

No last words.

He's just… *gone*.

3

The second The Birdie has touched down, I am scrambling out the door, jogging around the side yard, and skidding along the icy edge of the long, curved drive, seemingly hitting every patch of black ice lying in wait at the edge of the brick. In my haste to leave, I didn't think to wear shoes with tread or even a heavy coat.

Twirling beacons of red and blue revolve atop Deputy Glenn's squad car near the steps. I recognize it immediately, not from the number emblazoned on the fender near the New Hampshire state seal but from the silhouette of the stuffed piglet dangling from his rearview mirror.

The deputy's eyes meet mine with a sorrowful, apologetic look. Beside him, Andromeda is wrapped in another officer's arms, rail-thin body shuddering with every sob, muffled by the man's department-issued windbreaker.

I slow as I approach as if making it all the way to them will somehow make the news of this all suddenly true.

"Orion," Glenn says before his eyes cast down to one of the evergreen holly bushes flanking the snow-dusted steps.

He doesn't say anything else. Just my name in the form of a condolence.

"Can I… see him?" I finally manage to get words out, still standing on the lower ground level, feeling like a frightened little boy again despite being six-foot-two.

Glenn looks like he is going to deny me the morbid right to seal Dad's fate, to add some finality to Andromeda's declarations.

"I don't know if that's a good idea," he finally murmurs.

"I need to see him, Glenn." I say it as if it is a favor. It is. I need to see him for this to be real.

Glenn thinks for a moment and then yanks his head sideways toward the foyer of Dad's sprawling manor. "C'mon."

I follow up the steps and inside, where air from the frigid winter wasteland outdoors melds with the warmth of my childhood home, one full of memories.

And I'm about to add one more to that pile.

We pad beneath one of the home's more modest chandeliers up the sweeping staircase toward the second floor, leaving snowy shoe prints along the ancient runner. I follow Glenn down the hall, my gut-wrenching, cinching itself into a tight bowline knot.

"You're sure you need to go in there?" Glenn asks, trying to talk me out of it.

I nod and swallow painfully.

Glenn pushes Dad's bedroom door inward, staying next to the jamb like a sentry, reluctantly granting me access. I've so rarely been allowed in this room that it almost feels foreign to me.

I take a few steps in, shoes squishing into the plush scarlet carpet that adorns so many of the rooms in this house. Dad's favorite color. Inside, half of the window dressings have been yanked off the bronze curtain rod. It lays askew, cocked diagonally like a brown line graph of the Dow Jones stocks slowly plummeting. The curtains, heavy and ornate, lay rumpled in a gold-and-sangria-colored wad near Dad's outstretched hand.

A white blanket is down, the shape of a body beneath. Still.

"Last chance to change your mind," Glenn warns quietly.

I nod, and he pulls the sheet back reverently.

I kneel, trying to contain my tears, my rage, my panic. Trying to remind myself to keep breathing.

It's him.

I recognize the hard angles of his wide-set jaw, that shock of silver hair atop his head that resembles Leslie Nielsen's more than mine or Leo's. His eyes are lifeless and open, deep-set in their sockets. His thin lips are twisted into a grimace. He looks like a statue, his features frozen for eternity like this.

I nod, trying to see Glenn through the blur of tears that his stocky figure is now muddled by.

"I'm sorry, Orion." He means it. He and Dad have been friends for decades.

I wish I hadn't seen my father like this. I wish I could erase this final image for good, wipe it from the very recesses of my brain with a scrub brush and bleach. Among all of the memories I have of Alexander Stone, this one will forever bob in the water among them, this rotten razor-blade-filled apple in a bucket of sweet Jonagolds.

4

Layla

Gary Collins looks tense. His brother, Ed, looks disappointed, as if he's just found out his wallet has been robbed of all the cash in it.

"Alan's attorneys are going to have a fucking field day with this." Ed's eyes finally meet mine.

Gary pipes up. "She's lucky she didn't freeze to death out there. We're about to have another Nor'easter. She could've been dumped under a foot of snow."

"I know," I murmur quietly through my busted lip, feeling the sound of my own voice rattle behind my bruised ribs. Pain flashes through me in the shape of a seatbelt as I try to adjust myself in the hospital bed.

"They found you in a *tree*," Gary exclaims. "Like a fucking baby bird."

"I know." I'm starting to get perturbed now at all the anger he's laying on me.

I'm still feeling disappointed for even waking up at all. I shouldn't have survived the crash. If I hadn't, all of my troubles would have been over. My son wouldn't feel pulled in two directions. Alan could save all the money his attorneys are draining from him in an effort to ruin my life. And two-thirds of the lawyers at the firm I work for wouldn't be lecturing me in my hospital room.

"How many drinks did you have at the Christmas party, Layla?" Gary whips his hand up. "No, fuck it. Forget I asked. I don't want to know. If I end up having to represent you in this…"

"I didn't breathalyze. They tried to check my BAC in the ambulance, but I refused."

Ed breathes a sigh of relief. "Well, that's something, I guess."

Gary starts in on me again. "Yeah, we can fight a DUI if you get charged, but if we lose, they're going to take your license. And I don't mean your driver's license."

"I know."

He means my assessor's license, the credentials I need for the career I've worked my ass off for.

I take my lashings. They're just, overdue because I'm one massive fuck-up after another for the last two years. Still, it doesn't take the sting out of hearing them. It doesn't salve the pain.

"This'll be fine," Ed says, ever the optimist. "You didn't blow. They can't prove shit. The roads were slick. They found you off a tight curve. You hit a patch of black ice. End of story. Happens all the time."

"Yes," Gary agrees, lightening up. "Plus, your car was that ancient old beater, so we don't have to worry about them pulling any camera footage from it. So that's a positive."

"There was a deer," I mutter, every syllable exhaustive. "A baby one. Stepped out onto the road. I swerved."

"Okay," Gary strides toward me, his long legs closing the gap from the hallway to the bed in two aggressive steps. "That's good. That's very good. Did you hit it? Would there be any evidence? Blood, hair?"

"No, I don't think I hit it. I think… I swerved in time."

"Okay," he wags a finger at Ed and chews his lip. "This is good."

"No," I say, my head pounding, "they revoked my license because I refused to blow."

"Oh fuck, that's right. A hundred-and-eighty days. Fuck." He smacks himself in the taut forehead, one I know he gets injected with Botox on his lunch breaks a couple times a year.

"I'm sure the car is totaled, but now I can't even drive a rental." I grimace as I palpate the bruises on my forearm that look like I was trying to shield my face from the steering wheel.

"It's fine." Ed shakes his head. "I'll see what I can do about getting you set up with Uber rides or something or paying Chris to scoop you up on his way in so you can carpool. We'll get this handled, one way or another."

After a long silence, I have to ask Ed the question lingering in the air. "Are you going to fire me?"

Ed shakes his head, and I feel relief. "No."

Gary interjects again. "You gotta promise us that until we find out for sure that you're not going to be charged with a DUI, you're not gonna touch another goddamned drop of that shit."

I nod, but he doesn't believe me. I don't blame him. I am not even convincing myself at this point. Acting was never my strong suit.

"I mean it, Layla."

"Okay!" I put my hands up in the air, eyes suddenly glimpsing the IV in the back of one of them. "I won't drink."

As if it were that easy.

As if it were some declaration I could simply make, some firm action I could will into existence if I only believed it enough.

But it doesn't work like that.

The effortless ability to turn my brain off to the reality of the mess my life has become with a couple of drinks is insidious, beckoning me, bending my will like a reed with its magnetic pull.

If it were that fucking easy, I'd have quit right after I started. Right after the divorce. I wouldn't have dug myself deeper into a world of hurt. I wouldn't have given Alan the fucking custody ammo.

I press my throbbing head back into the cheap hospital pillow, feeling the ache in my neck, my shoulders, the sting of the glass cuts on the side of my throat and cheek.

Why did I wake up?

My life was ruined *before*. Now, I have a possible charge and revoked license to add to the pile? Is this some kind of sick joke? I feel like I'm tied to a slab with a sharpened pendulum lowering toward me, swinging so close that I can feel it tickle the fine hairs on my throat.

Waking up when the paramedics pulled my limp body out of a tree like a rescued kitten felt like a cosmic fucking slap in my face.

The pain could've been over.

This mess I've made of my life could have been straightened out… *forever*.

But instead, I had to open my fucking eyes.

5

Leo

My father's skin looked pallid and waxy as two old men wrapped him in the *Tachrichim* and doused him with water for the *Tahara*.

Let's call this supposed time-honored tradition what it is: a bizarre Jewish ritual where people dribbled pots of water over his fabric-swaddled corpse. It's weird. They did it to Mom, too.

I didn't understand it then, and I sure as hell don't now.

Rabbi Rosenberg says a prayer, but it just sounds like phlegm-ridden gibberish through all the ketamine right now.

It all happened so fast. Andromeda found him dead last night, and they're already putting his un-embalmed ass in the ground some twelve hours later.

The irony? He had enough money to purchase a small Midwestern city outright with no bank loan, and yet, they stuck him inside a plain, cheap pine box that looks like some kids whipped it up in shop class in an hour.

In front of the Torah Ark, the Rabbi stands atop the *bimah* and addresses all of us in the curved pews around it, filled mostly with my late father's friends. Men on the left, women on the right.

The Rabbi speaks for a bit in Hebrew and then, unfortunately, repeats the entire *El Maleh Rahamim* in English:

"Oh, God, who is full of mercy," he says, "and dwells on high, provide a true rest on the wings of the Divine Presence among the holy and pure ones who shine as brightly as the brilliance of the sky to the soul of Alexander Stone, son of Ezra Stone, who has gone on to his eternity. The Garden of Eden shall be his resting place. We beseech the Merciful One to shade him forever with divine wings and to bind his soul up in the bonds of life. The Lord is his heritage, and he shall rest peacefully on his bed. And let us say, Amen."

I itch the *kippah* on my head, the one mashing down last week's two-hundred-dollar haircut. I shift against the wood, wondering what we would have done if Pops had kicked the bucket on a Friday night since, according to Jewish law, he can't be buried on *Shabbat*.

So many rules. So many traditions.

And yet… we all are reduced to a pile of goddamned bones in the end.

It's Andromeda's turn at the podium. She delivers a dramatic eulogy that her dumb-ass television producer friends would be proud of.

Even as I listen to her drone on about what a *mensch* our father was, bringing up all of his philanthropic *mitzvahs* like she's giving potential investors some kind of strange PowerPoint presentation, I feel strangely disconnected from it all.

Instead, I think about what I want for my own funeral one day. I don't want this kind of humble *dreck*. I want fanfare. An extravagant event. An elegant spectacle. I want excess and bloat. I want perfectly good timber, shellacked to hell, with accents of chrome, lined with yards of premium ruched satin. I want to be buried in a fucking suit that costs more than some poor *schmuck's* community college tuition.

I find my lips turning down at the sight of Orion in the pew to the left of me, *futzing* with the synagogue-provided basic-bitch *yarmulke* pinned in his ugly-ass orange hair. Fucker looks like a burger-slinging clown.

This service… death. It's all such a waste. A waste of everyone's time. A waste of wood. A waste of tears and sentiment. Life fucking goes on for the rest of us. Half of these people haven't even talked to my father since his last heart attack, the small one. I don't understand why we couldn't just cremate his ass, dump him in the water at Rye Beach, and be done with it all.

Andromeda wraps up her eulogy, blubbering and barking her last few words like some kind of communicative seal. I sigh and stretch, glancing around as she sits her narrow ass down across the aisle.

The Rabbi says something in Hebrew that releases us all from this stuffy stained-glass hell with marching orders to follow each other to the Temple Israel Cemetery. I rise and crack my neck, thinking about what my father's house will fetch on the market. This all couldn't have happened at a better time, financially. Plus, the three-way split of the six million dollar house plus all the shit he's got in it might just be enough to get me out of fucking debt once and for all.

6

Orion

"I thought it was a nice service," Andromeda mutters, shoulders raised like skin earmuffs as she adjusts on her low stool in the den. "Didn't you think so?"

I fluff out a black sheet from the linen closet and fold it neatly in half so that it's more manageable.

"The turnout was fucking terrible," Leo finally mutters, more of a petulant growl than anything.

With all of the philanthropic work Dad has done over the last few decades, Leo and I agree on something for once. I sure as hell would never utter that aloud, though. He's narcissistic enough without any additional fuel.

"Yeah, well, it was also very last minute. This time yesterday, Dad was alive, probably playing chess with Wanda," Andromeda says with a sniffle.

I catch a glimpse of my tired, red-ringed eyes in the mirror before I cover it with the jet-black fabric. "That's the last one down here. I'll do all the ones in your rooms and bathrooms on the second story next."

"Thanks," Andromeda says, wiping tears from the corners of her hickory-colored eyes. "You can probably leave the third floor alone. Doubt Leo and I will be going up there."

Leo doesn't look at me. His suit-clad elbows are on his thighs, head dangling, gaze affixed to the maroon-and-gold Oriental rug on the floor.

A loud, insistent knock at the front door startles us all.

"I got it," I say. For the next week or so, I'm my siblings' butler, cook, and personal assistant while they take part in this seemingly archaic grieving process. I am suddenly elated that I was given the choice to choose my mother's religion as a young boy instead of the alternative.

I pry open the heavy front door. Light dapples the wall behind it, diffused by a colorful window of stained glass.

On the front stoop, "Aunt" Kay greets me with a sad smile.

"Kay, so good to see you," I say, whisking her inside the foyer. She peers up at the dark walls and glittering chandelier as she shoves a casserole dish into my hands. I can smell the cottage cheese and sour cream of the traditional Ashkenazi dish through the loose foil top.

"I brought *kugel*," she says to the ceiling in her raspy voice, ignoring my greeting, treating me as if I'm staff. She's had an issue with me for as long as I can remember, most likely because I don't subscribe to her family's religion.

Kay drifts into the living room like an old butterfly, spine curved like a shepherd's hook. She wraps her arms around Andromeda and squeezes her tear-streaked face against the breast of her black turtleneck.

"It's so good to see you, *Bubbe*."

Kay is Andromeda and Leo's aunt on their mother's side, their oldest living female relative, hence the moniker.

"It's good to see you, too. So sorry it's under these circumstances." Kay pulls away and wipes both wrinkled eyes with the pads of her prune-ish ring fingers. "How are the babies? Are they here?"

"No, they're back in Wooster with Dale," Andromeda says. "One of the nannies will FaceTime me in a bit with a progress report, but they're in good hands."

"Nannies? As in plural?" Aunt Kay looks like she just caught a whiff of body odor.

"Yes, we have three now. One for the cleaning, one for the cooking, and then one who does their hair and picks out their outfits and stuff."

Andromeda shrugs like it's no big deal to have three women raising her children, as though every modern mother has an entire *fleet* at their beck and call. I suspect that it's because their mother, Bambi, was aloof and uninvolved, often shirking parental duties. I, of course, only know this from the stories I've heard from them over the years. I have a feeling neither of Andromeda's kids will even notice she's gone much this week.

Aunt Kay laughs in a way that suggests she's oddly envious. "I wish I could afford my own personal stylist."

Andromeda chuckles, humoring the comment like a princess who won't apologize for being born into royalty.

"What's left at the end of the day for *you* to do with them?" Now Kay seems passive-aggressive.

"I work a lot, Aunt Kay. We've been trying to get the new press-on line off the ground. We've been shooting ad spots *and* print work. My schedule's *meshuggeneh*. Don't worry… they basically get the joy of four moms instead of just one who's frazzled all the time."

She's referring to her line of beauty products. Gold Star Cosmetics, a cruelty-free brand she pioneered after she starred on a season of a now-canceled reality show in her early twenties about eight whiny little rich kids with petty upper-upper-class problems.

It was an embarrassment for the family to watch her air her, and therefore *our*, dirty laundry for the world to see. But, to her credit, once things quieted down, she took the money she made from the season and a handful of guest appearances while she was still relevant, combined it with her inheritance from Bambi's passing, and parlayed it all into a moderately successful lifestyle brand. At least she didn't piss her inheritance away like Leo did.

As Aunt Kay makes small talk, I whisk the *kugel* to the kitchen and tuck it in one of two fully stocked fridges before returning to the parlor, lingering in the archway.

"I was shocked the man, Eduardo, from the cancer foundation came," Kay says in her very New York accent. Sometimes, she sounds like the old Mike Meyers Coffee Talk character on SNL.

"Why? Our father funded an entire oncology unit for him. Shit, he *owed it* to Dad to come," Andromeda says.

Kay wipes a finger across one of the glass-top coffee tables, checking for dust and wincing when she finds it. "That man and your fatha' had a falling out a few years ago when he announced they were gonna discontinue clinical trials. That pissed ya fatha' off *royally*."

Andromeda shakes her head and scoffs. "He had some sort of delusion that if they put enough patients in remission, he could somehow make up for being powerless with mom."

"I know, doll. I know." Kay waves Andromeda away with a handful of clunky rings, the diamonds and emeralds dulled in the dim glow. This house never did get adequate light. The place has the vibe of a lavish funeral home, dated decor, luxurious textures, and sunlight choked off by all the oddly small windows and their sheers.

I remember Mom trying to keep plants alive here, an impossible task.

Everything here eventually dies.

"Your father neva' did get ova' the death of ya motha.' Everyone knows that," Kay says as if it is a fact and not simply her opinion. I know it to be false, though I would never be so callous as to say it to her. He loved my mother, Aria, too. But like most people in this family, Kay brushes their twenty-plus-year relationship off like some kind of extended fling, like he never *really* gave his heart to her because it still somehow belonged to his first wife.

There is no denying that Dad loved Bambi. And I know there were lingering regrets. He didn't push Bambi harder to get checked out when she first had the inkling that something might be wrong.

Having almost fourteen-and-a-half billion dollars of liquid assets and still being powerless to save either of his wives… it ate at him. He always thought if he'd done things differently, one or both might still be alive. But if Bambi hadn't passed, Dad never would have met my mother, and I wouldn't have been born.

"What are you guys doin' with the house? You gonna sell it?" Kay eyes the detail on the ceiling panels and strokes the textured wallpaper on the walls.

That perks Leo up. His head raises like a curious prairie dog. "You in the market, Bubbe?" He straightens on his low stool. "I actually know a *very* good-looking Realtor who'd give you a great deal on the place."

He means himself.

The women snicker, and then Andromeda's face wrenches into an expression of disgust as another bout of tears forces its way to the surface.

"Fucking-A, Leo. Dad hasn't been dead a full twenty-four hours yet, and you're already trying to unload our childhood home. Give it a rest," Andromeda says before her head droops, eyes tearing up.

Kay waltzes to Andromeda's side and strokes her straight, dark hair lovingly.

Leo rolls his eyes at the ceiling as if to silently ask Dad if he's witnessing all this. "Christ, it was a joke."

But everyone here knows he wasn't joking. I wouldn't be surprised if he'd been lining up potential buyers for the estate after Dad's last heart attack.

"Leo's right, though," Aunt Kay says, shocking us all. They rarely agree. She starts to scrounge through the contents of her Prada purse in search of something. "When my father-in-law passed, it was a nightmare. Our first probate lawyer didn't know what the hell he was doing, and the appraiser they hired wasn't worth a damn. He kept undervaluing everything, trying to sell it all for cheap."

Leo, Andromeda, and I have all found ourselves hanging on Kay's every word, though probably for wildly different reasons. I'm not ready to sell the home we all grew up in. Dad's bed isn't even cold yet. Leo has dollar signs in his eyes already, and Andromeda's tears mask a slightly hopeful expression.

"Ah, here it is." Kay hands a business card to Leo. "We fired the first lawyer and then did some digging and went with this firm."

"Collins, Collins, & Collins," Leo says, reading it off the card.

"Yeah, one does probate, another criminal, and I think the third does, like, family law. We used one of them, Gary, for my grandson Billy's case last year. Little shit stole a car and went joyriding around in it. I could have *strangled* him. Lotta *chutzpah*, that kid. My son is too lax with him. Anyway," she realizes she has digressed and waves that thought away, "the one you want is Ed. He's excellent. He and his appraiser handled everything. Settled the estate. Went through his bank accounts with a fine-toothed comb. My father-in-law, not Billy. Ed got all his debts handled and everything. Even filed his taxes, which I didn't even know you need to do with a dead person."

Kay lifts a lamp, adjusts the crocheted doily beneath, and sets it back down. She waves again, her long gel-tipped fingernails clawing limply through the air. "Ed went through the will and all that. And his appraiser lady ended up getting us a lotta money just selling his old, useless antiques and all that. Half of that stuff, I was just gonna donate to the Goodwill. Tell him I sent you. Who knows, he may give you a discount or something."

Aunt Kay looks up at me but doesn't say a word. It's the first time she's acknowledged my existence since she forced the *kugel* into my hands.

The moment is fleeting, her attention quickly back on my siblings. "Well, I have to run. Salon appointment." She playfully crunches some dyed brown hair in her hand as if she's hoping we'll tell her she doesn't need it. No one does.

"It was great seeing you, Aunt Kay. Thanks for coming by," I say, forcing a courteous smile, the same one I'd give to a stranger in public.

"Call Ed," she says to Leo. "I'm serious. He's a *mensch*. You'll love him." She points up at the chandelier in the foyer. "You're all gonna make a pretty penny off this place."

Great. They're probably still shoveling dirt in on Dad's casket at the cemetery, and Aunt Kay is congratulating us for how much richer we're going to be once we dump the house.

I grew up here. I took my first steps in the den in the left wing into Dad's open arms. I took my hideous prom photos on the stairwell landing beneath the split. I got drunk for the first time in my life in the basement. Green-apple Pucker. Two bottles and five hours later, I swore it off for life in the *en suite* bathroom attached to my room. I won my first game of chess in Dad's study, finished Tolstoy's *War and Peace* in the library, and made Mom weep in the yoga studio when I handed her my acceptance letter to Yale.

I haven't lived here in over ten years, but every inch is still rich with memories. I'm sure for

Leo and Andromeda as well. The thought of it all vanishing as suddenly as Dad makes my heart feel like a heavy stone encased in tender meat.

Aunt Kay kisses Andromeda on the head and then Leo. She waves before slinking out the front door, barely able to pull the cumbersome thing shut behind her. It surely weighs more than she does.

"Yeah, always so nice to see you, too, Aunt Kay," I say to nobody at all.

Leo holds up the business card.

"The old bat made a point. We should start the probate bullshit sooner rather than later." He sets it on the glass top table beside him, one of six in this room that match as some absurd set, all dated cherrywood and lacquer.

I raise my hand, unable to hear it, unable to participate in the scramble over Dad's belongings. It is a greedy cash grab, this not-so-silent auction of a lifetime of stuff.

Just a few hours ago, he was here.

He was *alive*.

"What? I'm just being practical." Leo feigns innocence. As if he hasn't been thinking about it since Dad's collapse in his planetarium years ago. As if he didn't mentally divvy everything up after the last time Dad ended up in the hospital tied to tubes, pumped full of blood thinners.

"Leo, you're sitting *Shiva*, for God's sake. You're supposed to be here to mourn, not fucking lay claim to Dad's shit." I rub my forehead, worry wrinkles suddenly creasing it.

"Look, *you* can sulk and cry and do whatever you gotta do to get yourself through this. Dad and I haven't exactly been close the last, I don't know, *four decades*. I'm sitting on this uncomfortable fuckin' stool out of the small goddamned shred of *respect* I can muster, not because I need to sit in the corner and boo-hoo like a bitch for a week. If you don't want to call the lawyer, that's fine. *I* can be the executor and handle all the tough decisions while you and Andromeda sob into your little matching hankies."

"Jesus, you've always been such a venomous *prick*," I say, stating the obvious. "Must've gotten that from Bambi. You sure as hell didn't get it from Dad."

Leo barks out a laugh and rises to his feet. He waltzes over in silence, smile fading. The second he is in arm's reach, he shoves me violently toward the wall, toppling me over the rounded side table behind me. It clatters to the floor, dumping the lamp and crystal bowl of wrapped candies on it into the corner.

"What the fuck?!" I growl.

Without thinking, I launch back at him, a pissed-off Jack-in-the-box on a spring. My palms slam against the lapels of his Armani suit, and the piece of shit stumbles backward into the middle of the room.

He holds his arms out wide, begging for a full-blown fight. "You wanna go, Annie? Let's fucking go!"

"Leo!" Andromeda shoots up from her stool. "What the fuck is wrong with you? Chill out! Leave Orion alone!"

Annie.

I knew it was only a matter of time before it resurfaced, the shitty nickname he gave me when I was just a kid, one likening me to the orphan in the musical due to my red, then-curly hair.

Thank God Andromeda taught me how to use a fucking straightener…

I approach, fists clenched, shoulders back, chest broad, the expression on my face a furious one.

Leo's eyebrows struggle against his Botox to rise. "C'mon, you ginger bitch. I will *destroy* your ass!"

My vision darkens around the edges until all of Leo's smug face fills the narrow pinholes. I don't know if he remembers -- or ever cared to learn -- that I'm a fucking black belt.

"Fighting won't resolve this shit," Andromeda says, a look of disgust on her porcelain face. It is a face that has seen a thousand mud masks and facials and buzzing neon wands to keep her skin youthful.

I choose my words to Leo carefully. "After Dad's first heart attack, he made me executor of the will."

"Who gives a fuck?" Leo's stance suggests he's still ready to pounce. "Do the job he fucking gave you then!"

"Christ, Leo, his body is barely fucking cold! Can't we just fucking… focus on *him* today?"

"What good does all the crying and sniveling in the world do, Annie? Is it gonna somehow resurrect him like Lazarus?"

"He was our fucking *father*." My voice cracks as I say the last word. "Show some goddamned respect."

"You can't be the gatekeeper between us and *our* money. I swear to God, Orion, I will fucking *take you down* if you drag your feet on this shit."

I am appalled by Leo's words, by his reduction of Dad's life to some fucking payday like he's somehow owed reparations. His insulting, gauche cash grab is really pissing me off.

"Fuck you," I say firmly, wishing I could deck him right now. I hope to God Dad's spirit isn't lingering where he can hear this heated exchange.

"Fuck me? Fuck *you*!"

It's not his best retort, but then again, I can never expect much from the overgrown frat boy. He was always all looks and no goddamned *brains*.

"No, thanks. I heard you have hookers to do that," I say.

It's a cheap shot, one that refers to Leo's brief arrest for the solicitation of a Manhattan prostitute that happened during a slow news cycle and -- much to the Stone family's misfortune -- got a surprising amount of media attention.

Mysteriously, the charges were dropped, and Leo only spent a few hours in a holding tank for it, but it has been a point of contention for a long time, a soft wound I can jab a thumb inside to make him howl.

And howl he does.

Right on cue.

Leo roars like the fucking animal he is. He snatches a vase from the fireplace mantle, one Dad got on a trip to Rome years ago, and hurls it at the burgundy and gold damask wallpaper. It explodes, spraying shrapnel at me like fragments of a grenade.

"What the fuck, Leo?!" Andromeda screams, cowering, protecting her face with her forearms.

"What? You guys don't care about getting money for any of this shit, apparently. So you don't mind if I destroy it, right?"

"That was expensive, I think!" Andromeda shouts. I realize when she says it that everything around us is really just dollars and cents to her, too.

"Some of this has sentimental value," I yell to both of them.

Leo flips one of the coffee tables over with a growl. The protective glass layer atop it shatters. One of the legs of the table bends inward, collapsing in on itself. "I'm sorry, Annie. Was that imported matching set *sentimental* to you?"

His chest heaves with deep breaths as he waits for an answer, though he should know by now that I won't dignify it with one.

The truth is, it *is* sentimental to me. I was present at the time of its purchase. The light dappled Mom's pretty copper curls through the shop window as she chatted with the artist, arranging payment so the whole set could be shipped back to America. I still remember the way the words '*It's truly divine*' rolled off her tongue with the faintest remainder of her Scottish accent every time she looked at it.

I also remember, during this crystallized fragment of time, the way Dad was grinning at her over his shoulder, his body filling the open doorway of the studio. Despite miles of stunning landscape before him, all he could see was Aria and the joy the pieces brought her.

I feel pity for Leo. He probably rarely bore witness to that kind of love or adoration. Dad told me in confidence over a number of lit cigars through the years that my mother, Aria, was the true love of his life. While he cared deeply for Bambi, he claimed she became cold and materialistic in her later years. He said he imagined that was how Leo and Andromeda became the way that they did.

When my mother died, Dad was destroyed. For weeks, he was convinced he would soon die, too. She was the oxygen he needed to breathe. It took a while to get him to a place where he realized life simply had to go on.

And now that's how I feel about him. No matter how shaken my foundation, how choked the air in my lungs is from losing my best friend, my mentor, my idol... I still have to take that next breath.

Dad wouldn't want us to rip each other to shreds. He wouldn't want me to hit Leo in the throat so hard that he might need surgery to speak normally again, even though I fucking *could*. I'm sure he doesn't care that his firstborn is destroying material things. They are of no use to him now.

...Wherever he is.

Every fiber of my body wants me to knock out Leo's front four, but I knew Dad better than anybody on this earth. He would want me to show my half-brother patience and empathy, two of my personality traits he often praised. If Leo needs money so bad he's willing to parcel out a loved one's life like a butcher would a cow, then so be it.

I lock eyes with Leo. They're dark and steely, with pupils nearly the same color as the irises. Eyes like a shark. Merciless.

"Give it to me." I extend my hand toward the business card Aunt Kay left. It sits on the side table near Leo's beveled crystal glass of Glenfiddich, a liquor Dad always kept around in case Leo came to visit, which was rare... unless he needed an infusion of cash in his account. Dad always gave it to him, too, despite the jaw-dropping inheritance money Leo got at twenty-five from Bambi's death. Money he promptly squandered on a house his first ex-wife won in their divorce, a yacht that his friend sunk, and several failed business attempts.

Leo looks at the card suspiciously and then at me. He probably doesn't trust my change in demeanor, doesn't believe that real men are capable of deescalation. He fishes his phone out of his suit pocket and snaps a picture of the card before handing it to me, presumably in case I shred it like his petulant ass would if roles were reversed.

Finally, he places it in my hand. I tap the corner of it against my palm and frown. As much as it pains me to give this place up, I have no plans to buy Leo and Andromeda out of their share and keep it for myself. I have a home. A nice one, albeit not nearly as expensive. But I don't want Dad's place. The memories I have in it are more valuable than the estate and all of its contents.

"I'll… get things started," I finally say.

A smug smile creeps onto Leo's face, a face he made often after he dropped out of the Ivy League college Dad called in favors to get him in so he could have a somewhat successful foray as a model. Being attractive is the only thing that has ever brought Leo positive attention, especially during the three-month stretch when he was on a bunch of billboards near Times Square. It was an exciting flash in the pan compared to the rest of adulthood for him.

"Glad you came to your senses, Annie."

I could *easily* knock the smirk off of his face from where I'm standing. Instead, I turn on my heels and leave before I say something unforgivable.

I see that my mourning for my father will have to wait until the forty-four-year-old baby has been pacified.

7

Layla

My bruised ribs and waist make me wince as I bend to wave through the open door.

"Thank you," I say briskly to the driver as I exit an almost brand-new Honda Civic.

Why am I thanking him? I'm seven minutes late, thanks to his little *detour*. I suggested that Washington Road would be much faster. He ignored me, and we ended up behind an overturned truck on Interstate 1. We got stuck in a full mile of standstill traffic thanks to a bunch of rubberneckers hoping to catch a glimpse of vehicular carnage.

The Uber driver nods and takes off the second my door clicks shut. I step back in a hurry so the guy doesn't run over my foot in his haste to pick up another fare.

I make my way up the short set of concrete stairs into the building, careful not to catch my heels on any ice. Once inside, I breeze past the secretary seated at his squat desk in front of a giant blue-and-white billboard on the wall with the company logo for Collins, Collins, & Collins.

He is a fourth Collins. Lyle Collins. The fuck-up of the family. The too-casual charity case. The nepotism hire no one speaks about around the firm.

Lyle runs a tattoo-covered hand through the near-black roots in his short frock of bleach-blond hair. Then, he itches his dark mustache, listening to someone on the other end of the phone yammer on.

I offer a half-assed wave as I pass, but he isn't paying attention to me or even the caller. His eyes seem locked, instead, on the GameBoy Color atop his appointment book and the Mario game that's on pause.

"Layla," Bart sees me from down the hall and hoists his charming Dunder-Mifflin coffee cup in the air at me.

"Hey." I force a smile and adjust the sunglasses on my face, a gold pair that draw attention from one of the blackened eyes beneath.

"Gary and Ed told me about the accident. So glad you're okay."

Although the sentiment is nice, I'm not okay.

In fact, I'm very *deeply* not okay. My life is being systematically dismantled and destroyed one day at a time, and instead of digging myself out of this hole, I only seem to tunnel deeper. Every inch of my flesh aches. The last time I saw my vehicle, it was hanging like an ornament from a tree. My license is in the possession of the New Hampshire police. I'm not in the clear, DUI-wise. My bank account is drained. And my ex-husband is probably going to end up with sole custody of my only child, who is now calling another woman 'Mom.'

So yeah, not okay.

I want a real drink to start this day. One that is far more Bailey's than coffee. Or a shot of vodka. Anything to numb the gamut of pain I'm feeling. Just thinking about how much I want a drink right now, I'm itchy in my own crawling skin. My mind and body are tired. I woke up in the middle of the night twice last night, my heart racing. In my dreams, I kept careening off the edge of that curvy cliff, weightless, the ground and trees flying at me from a wrong angle. I should've died in that accident. Maybe if I had, Danny would've remembered me as the mother who fought valiantly, taken from this world prematurely instead of a floundering screw-up, stripped of everything, including a stupid driver's license.

"Whittaker, yo, in here," Ed hollers through the open door of his office, snapping his fingers at me like I'm some waitress he's trying to get the attention of instead of a certified, licensed professional.

"Yes… okay… I'm going to put you on speakerphone, Mr. Stone." Ed scrambles to press the right button on the phone before setting it back in its cradle. He yells at the machine like he's talking to an old person with impaired hearing. "Still there, Mr. Stone?"

"Yes. I'm still here." The voice on the other end is smooth and deep, one that commands attention.

"Great." Ed punches the air, excited he transferred the call successfully this time. I can't even recall how many people I have seen him accidentally hang up on.

"Mr. Stone, I've got Layla Whittaker here in my office. She's our certified appraiser. She works in tandem with my office for probate cases like this. She's who we send out to do the full evaluation of a decedent's assets and property for the estate and death appraisals."

Ed urges me to say something, putting me on the spot.

"Hello, Mr. Stone."

"Hello."

After a brief but awkward pause, Ed jumps back in. "Now, it's Ms. Whittaker's job to evaluate the fair market value of all property for an executor. This kind of assessment can help us with the fair division among the decedent's survivors. Sometimes in probate cases like yours, Mr. Stone, there can be an almost overwhelming amount to divide. Layla makes that all really easy. Plus, she also has relationships and a rapport with auction houses across New England for the high-end valuables to be sold."

"Sounds like exactly what we need."

"Layla, would you like to take it from here?" Ed asks, putting me on the spot again.

I lean down toward the phone. My knees throb, and my shoulder aches so much it feels like my collarbone fractured when I careened into that tree.

"S-sure," I stutter and narrow my eyes at Ed. My hand trembles, and I can't tell if it's from my jangled nerves or the stark sobriety. "Mr. Stone, it's a pleasure to make your virtual acquaintance."

"Likewise."

Ed mouths something positive at me and rubs his fingers together, indicating this client is a financial whale, a fat payday for a firm like this.

"Mr. Stone, just to let you know a little bit about what I do, I work on the firm's behalf to do thorough assessments. I typically come out to the home of the decedent and do a complete inventory of any valuables and research them against the item's condition and age before assigning them a value based on the current market demand."

"I see… I think."

"I'll evaluate everything of value on the property. Collector's items, jewelry, coins, stamps, artwork, antiques, *et cetera*."

"Okay."

He sounds hesitant, on the fence about having someone rooting through his dead loved one's things. It's common in my line of work. Ed looks at me expectantly, urging me to quell the man's fears and give him the rest of the spiel.

"I'm certified for valuations of items in the home, vehicles, the home itself, any other structures or parcels. I can handle all of it for you."

Ed interrupts, dissatisfied with my efforts. "Mr. Stone—"

"*Orion*, please." It is less a polite request, more of a demand.

"Yes, certainly. Orion, I'll be happy to guide your family through the legal process from start to finish, ensure your father's debts are settled, and go through bank accounts and other real estate holdings. I can start with the last will and testament once you fax it over, and that'll help me get the ball rolling. This appraisal Ms. Whittaker will spearhead is something we could use for the settlement of the estate, sometimes called a Date of Death Valuation."

"I hate to ask this. What happens if, say, one of my siblings doesn't..." he hesitates, and it almost sounds like he's trying to compose himself in a moment of anger even though he's been eerily calm thus far. "What if one of my siblings doesn't agree with something in the will or claims he was promised something he wasn't?"

"Allow me to put your fears about that at rest," Ed says, fidgeting with the gold pen on his desk. "I have a reputation for resolving probate disagreements and discrepancies between beneficiaries quickly and amicably should any challenges arise, especially to the will."

I lean forward and speak. "You're in good hands, Orion. I promise."

"Look, Orion, it's no secret that Alexander was a billionaire. Let us do the heavy lifting so you and your family can focus on moving through your grief."

Stone. Alexander Stone? That Alexander Stone? Jesus Christ. I didn't even realize that's who we were talking about!

"You handle a lot of wealthy cases like this?" Orion asks. I can't tell if he thinks the concept is dubious or if he's genuinely asking.

"Absolutely," Ed assures him, despite it being a bald-faced lie.

The truth is, business has slowed lately. Ed hasn't had anyone retain him with a net worth of even a million since the summer. Much less billions. Plural. Most of his clients this fall were middle-to-lower-class people feuding over who gets their dead father's pickup truck or their mother's jewelry.

I think at one point, around Halloween, we even had a large family from a trailer park arguing about a dead cousin's amassed shotglass collection. There was one for every one of the fifty states from various road trips and vacations. The family refused to divide them up. It got surprisingly heated.

"We are a full-service firm, Orion. We can even assist with the filing of the inheritance taxes for your family members as well. Ms. Whittaker would be thrilled to assist with all the on-site work. She's great. You'll love her."

"Well, you've sold me, Mr. Collins." Orion sounds like he is smiling on the other end when he says it.

Ed rises from his seat, veins popping from his neck excitedly. He extends a hand. I weakly high-five him, focused more on the shallow cuts on the back of my hand than his morbid excitement. Thin streaks of red mar my skin like the tails of maroon comets hurtling through space. I am suddenly there again, cradled in the arm-like boughs of a leafless maple, broken glass fragments glittering from the sun-cracked dash to the forest floor like snow.

"That's fantastic, Orion. I'd like to send Layla out as soon as possible to start her inventory and evaluation."

"My siblings are here at the house sitting Shiva. They're fairly limited to the parlor and bedrooms right now, so you can start evaluating the rest as soon as possible. I'm not taking part in the tradition. I'm working remotely from Dad's house the next few days to help them out, so I'm available to assist or offer support wherever needed."

"Wonderful." I manage a smile. I know how he *meant* it, but the offering of support makes me feel like a rope ladder has been tossed down into the depths of the dark well I've been trapped in.

"We're tucked out of the way a bit down here in Rye. The house is an eight-bedroom, and there are only three of us, so if it makes your life a little easier while you're doing the audit... or inventory… or whatever you call it, you're welcome to stay in one of the guest rooms as long as you need. Might cut down on your travel time."

Or my outrageous rideshare fees.

"I appreciate that." My cheeks bloom with a bit of warmth.

I'm not sure how Ed is going to feel about it, but my heart leaps a little at the money and time it would save. Not to mention the change of scenery from an apartment full of memories of an ex-husband who probably never really loved me and a son living half a country away.

Ed is busy pretending he's a locomotive chugging excitedly in place, the long sleeve of his button-down shirt making a quiet, rapid *swish* against his side as he celebrates the influx of money the firm is about to have after landing this account. I'm sure with Christmas just around the corner and the dwindling clients these last few months, this news pleases him even more than normal.

"Ed, I'm going to have the assistant from my office overnight you a copy of the will. Is the mailing address on your website correct?"

"Yes! Absolutely," Ed blurts, overzealous. "Make it care of Edward Collins, and I'll make sure my guy at the front desk keeps his eyes peeled for it."

"Will do. I'll shoot an email over to you in a few with the address of the estate and my contact information. Feel free to forward it to Ms. Whittaker."

"What would be an ideal day and time to come by?" I ask.

"Today. If that works for you. If not…"

"Today works for her," Ed hurriedly interjects. "She can be there this afternoon." Then, he looks at me as if to say, *'Don't blow this for me.'*

"Uh… yes." The abruptness takes me off-guard, but I welcome the excitement after spending the last few days counting the ceiling tiles at Portsmouth Regional. "I can start this afternoon."

"I appreciate you being available on such short notice."

"My pleasure," I say, forcing a cordial smile down toward a telephone that can't see me.

The tension in Ed's shoulders visibly loosens. "Okay, Orion. You have my number. If you need anything in the meantime or have any questions, give me a ring. Two karat or higher grade, preferably." His dumb joke lands like a clumsy elephant. He scrambles to reverse course. "Just kidding, Orion. Sorry. Little probate humor. My apologies. I've been dealing with jewelry appraisals all morning."

"Sure." Orion isn't amused.

Frankly, neither am I.

"Thank you for putting your faith in us, Orion. We will get everything handled for you," Ed says.

I speak up. "I'm deeply sorry for your loss."

"Thank you." He sounds like he's smiling a little again. "See you soon, Ms. Whittaker."

The phone goes dead on the client's end.

Ed presses the button to end the call before erupting into another flurry of bastardized karate punches aimed at his bronze sculpture of a cheetah, his self-proclaimed 'spirit animal.'

"Oh, Layla!" He spins comically on his heels and presses his hands together like he's about to pray. "It's a Christmas-frigging-miracle."

I force a smile. I don't feel much like celebrating. We are still, after all, profiting off of death.

"When would would you like me to go out there? First thing tomorrow?"

"What? Are you kidding?" Ed looks surprised. "Layla... *today*. I want to cinch this deal. I'm not giving him any time to waffle or shop around. I swear to God, if I lose another one to Trammel and Tarantolo's firm, I'm going to scream." His eyes lock on mine with a sudden seriousness, eyes pleading. "Go now. Get this thing locked in, Layla. Milk it a little. The Stones have *money*. Go through every damned junk drawer in that place. Be thorough."

I nod dutifully to assure him.

I hold out my hand. "Can I get a company credit card for incidentals and expenses?"

"No, Chris fucked up and lost his. Someone found it and started buying shit. So now they're issuing us new cards. Probably won't be in until after Christmas. Just send me an invoice along with your hourly, and I'll reimburse you."

I don't want to argue, but I also don't have enough left in my account after the barrage of recent expenses and deductibles to avoid over-drafting.

"What'll I do about the rideshare fees and food?"

"You don't have enough to cover them until you get your next check?"

I don't bother to dignify that with an answer. He knows damn well his older brother is squeezing me like a mafia Don. The divorce and custody case weren't just ugly and contested. They obliterated me financially.

"Well, shit. I guess… pack a bag. He wasn't kidding. The guy's got *plenty* of room. It'll be like a paid vacation."

Ed twists his PC monitor toward me and lifts the polarized security film to reveal a behemoth manor on a map on the internet. I can't believe its sheer size. It's got the footprint of a castle with enough acreage to build an adjoining shopping mall.

"After all," he points to the monitor, chuckling, "when's the last time you got to stay in a mansion like *that*?"

8

Leo

Orion sets another double of Glenfiddich twelve single-malt on the table beside me and takes my old glass like a *good little maid*. Why we ever had a butler growing up when we could have just slapped an apron on Orion is beyond me. Probably could have saved the family a fortune if we just had the little ginger bastard serve us all the time.

Leaving the parlor, he steps over the ruins of the table I destroyed in my fit. It makes me smile. I love seeing him inconvenienced by the tacky piece of furniture his *mommy* picked out.

He returns a few moments later with two tiny plates of lukewarm *kugel* and forks for Andromeda and I.

He doesn't look me in the eye during either trip.

"You're not eating?" Andromeda asks him.

Orion glumly responds. "No. Not hungry."

He sniffles, and I roll my eyes. *It's just us.* He's not at the synagogue anymore. So, I don't know who this pathetic show of emotion is for.

As he hands Andromeda her napkin, the doorbell chimes. He swiftly makes his way into the adjoining foyer and opens it, having a brief exchange with our mystery visitor.

A woman from the sound of the voice. Thirties maybe. Soft. Unfamiliar. I wonder what kind of homemade slop she's brought to offer her condolences.

Futilely, I lean forward to see who it is, but soon, I drop the two rear feet of the low stool back down. Whoever she is is blocked by a wall filled with vintage books, useless *tchotchkes*, and dusty bric-a-brac.

Orion leads the woman in, takes her coat, and says something to her that makes her laugh. The sound of it is almost musical. Melodic and genuine. Consider me intrigued.

Orion enters the parlor's opening with a black roller suitcase gripped in his left hand, one with rollers that people who fly commercial might use as a carry-on. Strangely, in his right is a black laptop bag, not a casserole dish.

Now I'm thoroughly confused.

A moment later, she comes into view, a fox with wheat-blonde hair shimmering beneath Aria's hideous mini-chandelier. Her black dress is slinky. A wide band of silver hugs her tapered waist. There is a delicate gold chain of pearls around her throat that I immediately imagine replacing with a warm string of my own.

She's a fucking knockout.

"Ms. Whittaker, this is my sister, Andromeda."

"How do you do?" the woman coos, sliding a hand out to shake my sister's. Andromeda eyes her with suspicion.

"I've... been... better." She looks at Annie. "Orion, you dog."

"Excuse me?" Orion looks annoyed.

"I didn't even know you were seeing anyone." Andromeda laughs at the woman. "Finally! It's about damn time he found someone."

There's no fucking way Orion is scoring with this chick. She'd be a punch *miles* outside of his metaphorical weight class.

"No, this is Layla Whittaker. From Collins, Collins, and Collins."

"Wow, that was fast," Andromeda balks.

The smoking-hot *shiksa* peels her eyes from the shattered remains of the end table splayed across the rug.

"I'm..." She gawks at her surroundings. "I'm the licensed appraiser from the firm. I'm here to start an inventory."

She drifts past Orion to the pile of busted wood and bends down, studying it. I can smell her perfume from where I'm sitting. She smells good enough to eat.

She kneels in front of the destroyed piece and fingers the detailing on the side. While she is deep in thought, I stare at the two-inch purple bruise where her neck meets her collarbone. The hand she's touching the wood with is slightly cut up, like she was protecting her face from the claws of a pissed-off cat.

"This is a Theodore Alexander. Flame-veneered mahogany. Brass mounts. Frieze drawer. Fluted legs. This… wow… is a nice piece."

"*Was*," I joke with a chuckle. But the gaze she flashes at me as she stands isn't one of mutual amusement.

Let's face it… that thing was fucking hideous. And the ornate keyhole for a drawer that doesn't even have anything in it… how fucking pretentious.

"The last time I saw one of those was at an auction house in Vermont a few years ago. It sold for forty-two hundred. Per table." She glares at me. Then, she looks over at Orion. "They go for more if the set is complete, obviously. Which, now… it isn't."

My stomach churns a little at the thought of lighting four thousand bucks ablaze with the current state of my finances, but then I'm reminded that everything this chick sells for us gets divided three ways, so, really, it's money out of Orion's pocket, too. That is of some genuine consolation to me.

"Forty-two hundred?" Andromeda parrots it in disbelief.

"Well, I'll try to throw that hideous Ming vase next time you infuriate me instead." I point to the ugly-as-sin white vase on one of the knickknack shelves. There's a blue line drawing of a bird on it.

The woman laughs again and walks over to it. "*That?*"

I nod.

She smirks a little. She looks downright naughty when she does it. "That's not a Ming."

"Yes, it is," I reply confidently.

"No. *That* is a vase from the Japanese Meiki Period. It's not a bird. It's a phoenix."

"Bird, phoenix. Who cares?"

"Well, there's kind of a big difference in the two, actually. A Ming is a dime a dozen these days. You can even find them at Goodwill sometimes for twenty bucks or new for fifty to a hundred. This Meiki phoenix is… it's worth over twenty grand."

I try not to let my surprise show.

She's in awe as she takes in the decor of the remainder of the parlor. "Your father had expensive taste."

"Yeah, well, Encyclopedia Brown, this has been fun." I sarcastically raise my Glenfiddich to cheer in her direction, not allowing her seemingly accidental one-upmanship to get the best of me.

Orion gestures in my direction. "This is Leo. The family asshole."

"Orion!" Andromeda whacks him in the thigh with the back of her hand. It pleases me to see little sis come to my defense.

Layla nods cordially to acknowledge me and takes the laptop bag from Orion's hand. "How about you take me to wherever I'll be staying and give me a little tour of the place so I can decide the smartest place to start?"

"Absolutely," he says.

She turns back to me. "Don't worry. I promise I will stay out of your hair. You won't even see me while I'm here."

"Well, *that* had better not be true," I ooze, dragging the rim of my glass along my bottom lip. It is a pose that made me famous in SoHo in the late nineties when I was in a bunch of print work for Guinness. In the back of my mind, I am holding out hope that she will remember me from the ads.

She smiles courteously and turns to Andromeda. "Lovely to meet you. Truly sorry for your loss."

"Oh… thanks," Andromeda says, seemingly taken aback by the stranger's genuine condolences.

Orion motions for her to lead the way up the staircase that splits toward each wing halfway up. As Layla ascends, my half-brother fires a vicious warning glance my way. If looks could kill, they'd be dropping my ass in the worm-ridden soil right next to Dad.

Orion shoves open a heavy wooden door at the end of the hall and motions to it with my laptop bag. "This is the most spacious of the guest rooms. Full walk-in closet. It doesn't have an *en suite* bathroom, but that door right there," he motions to a room two doors down, "is a full bath.

I enter the guest room, trying to suppress my awe at the grandeur. Everything in this mansion is lavish, large, and rich in its palette and textures. Real wood adorns every room. There is ornate crown molding and textured ceiling tiles in every room. Velvety crimson damask wallpaper adorns many of the walls. French-inspired gold and brass flourishes punctuate nearly every piece of furniture in every room. Small amounts of filtered light seep in through romantic sheer curtains throughout. I feel like I'm in an old Broadway theater, one with a storied history. My guest room reminds me of the Dutch Golden Age painting wing in the Louvre.

A spacious suite like this at a hotel would cost nearly a grand per night, I'd imagine.

I've never stayed anywhere close to this opulent. Immediately, I have the feeling as my heels squish into the luxurious carpet that I don't belong. I don't deserve even a temporary respite here.

"I can show you the other available rooms if you'd like, but they're in the other wing by *their* rooms." By the phrasing, I assume he means the rooms in which his siblings are staying.

"No." I turn to him with a smile. For a split second, I feel a glimmer of hope that my luck is finally changing. This all seems way too good to be true. "This is perfect."

Orion manages a smile, and it is the first moment in this flurry of introductions that I'm finally getting a good look at him.

He's… striking. His styled hair catches the diffused glow from the window in a way that makes it look like warm copper, polished and vibrant. His eyes glint, bold jade with a ring of emerald shavings near the centers. His jaw is angular, posture impeccable, height looming over me even in heels. A smattering of freckles lightly graces his rigid cheekbones.

I've never seen anyone like him.

His brother, Leo, seems oddly familiar, like someone I'd see in a commercial or a Calvin Klein ad in his briefs. He, too, was devastatingly handsome. But it was clear that he's well aware of it, a personality trait that doesn't really appeal to me.

Orion, on the other hand, strikes me as the kind of guy who has no idea just how fucking handsome he is.

Our gaze has locked for what feels like a second too long, and I avert it, glancing down at the bed's expensive comforter. I know from the brand embroidered on the bottom that it is Buxton white goose down. The divan is cashmere. One pillowcase sham probably costs more than my mattress and box spring back home.

"Thank you so much for the lodging. This really makes things convenient. I can work later and be out of your hair much sooner."

"No problem. As you can see, there's plenty of space."

"That there is." I laugh and take my suitcase from his hand, laying it gently on its side on the bed.

"Don't work yourself to the bone. I'll be here through the first of January at least, working remotely. I'll be around to assist with anything you need for the appraisal process. The maid will be back in a few days. Until then, I'll be ordering meals for everyone, so if there's anything in particular you would like to eat, let me know. I'm more than happy to accommodate."

"The only place I've ever really been to around here is Petey's. A client took us there for lunch once."

"The seafood place on Ocean?"

I nod, finding myself once again locked in the beam of those green eyes.

"Did you like it?"

"Oh God, I *loved* it."

"Best lobster roll on the coast, in my opinion. They've got a bisque that's amazing, too."

"Do they? I've never had it."

He nods with control and smooths his tie against his chest. "I do believe dinner is decided then. I'll order a variety for everyone."

"They don't keep kosher?" I point to the floor.

He shakes his head and scoffs. "I'm surprised they're sitting Shiva, honestly. I don't expect them to last the full seven days, either. Not this close to Hanukkah. Andromeda has kids and a business. And Leo… well, Leo gets bored easily."

"So, you don't practice that stuff?"

"Hanukkah?" He shakes his head. "Their mom was Jewish. Mine wasn't."

"So, did you guys do that blend of the two holidays like they did on the O.C.? Chrismukkah, or whatever?"

"The O.C.? Was that… a show?"

"Yes." I laugh. "Show about rich kids. Very popular when I was a little kid."

"Afraid not. As big as this place is, I'm sure you'll soon notice there aren't a lot of TVs."

"Of course."

He smiles again, and I resist the urge to blush. I feel like his eyes pierce right through me. "And to answer your question, no. There wasn't really a blending of anything around here. Quite a bit of separation, actually. Hell, I didn't even grow up in the same wing of the house they did."

"Interesting."

"Is it?"

I nod. Then, another brief silence lingers between us.

"Well, I should give you a tour, shouldn't I?" he finally asks.

"I'd love that. One second." I reach into my laptop bag and grab a legal pad and pen.

"Alright, I guess we'll start on this floor for the sake of convenience."

He starts back toward the split staircase, the stunning focal point of the home.

"While we're here, we're all staying in our old bedrooms." He points to the door next to mine. "I'm in there. Feel free to do whatever you need in there while I'm working elsewhere. It's just you and I in this East Wing."

He leads me down the long corridor past the stairwells. "Here in the West Wing, the first two on the left are more guest rooms. You have full access 24/7 to those. Next to that is a door to… I don't know. We call it a den."

I scribble notes on the pad, drawing myself a crude map with messy lettering.

"Next one's another bathroom. The door straight down at the end is Andromeda's. The one after that is the elevator."

My eyes bolt wide as I follow him toward the West Wing. "An elevator?"

"Yes," he says casually and then points to the next door as if it's not strange to have an elevator in a home. "The one to the right of that is Leo's room, although, during the day, I'm sure that entire wing will be vacant."

I peer inside the wing's massive bathroom, where a black sheet covers the mirror. He continues the tour before I can ask about the sheet. If the mirror beneath is broken, I'll want to notate that.

"There are several more bedrooms downstairs, including the master suite."

"This place is huge," I say, despite it being painfully obvious.

"It is. Dad really wanted more kids, but I guess it wasn't really in the cards."

Same, I think to myself. I nod, refusing to pry. Instead, I motion to a small staircase across the hall from the lower-level ones. "What's upstairs?"

"The office and the observatory. Although the observatory is locked. I gotta track down the key for you. It's around here somewhere."

"Annie!" I hear Leo's voice hollering from downstairs. Orion's expression turns to one of obvious disdain.

"Annie? Is there someone else here?"

"No," Orion grumbles. "It's just a stupid nickname."

"For you? He calls *you* Annie?" I'm confused. I assume that it has to do with his hair, with living in this gigantic mansion.

"Just ignore him. He has the attention span of a gnat. In two minutes, he won't even remember that he called for me."

"Annie? Annie, hun, big bro needs a refill!" Leo chuckles in the parlor.

Orion rubs the bridge of his nose, biting his tongue.

I fight the urge to chuckle. "He can't refill his own drink? Is he… injured or something?"

"No, waiting on the mourners is a Shiva thing, they both assured me, but… I have a feeling he's abusing it. Or maybe they're both just… pranking me. I don't know anymore."

"Annieeeeeee…"

"Do you need to go to him?"

"No, it's fine," he says, running a hand anxiously through the side of his hair.

"Annie, don't ignore me." Leo laughs harder now.

I point to the door of my room. "Actually, if you need to tend to him, I can take some time to unpack and get settled."

"Carrot Top, you're being summoned!" Leo barks it, slightly more annoyed.

Orion sighs and stares at me, his green eyes dazzling even when his expression is soft. "Yeah, let me go tend to the infant. Go ahead and get settled in. Whenever you're ready to see the rest, just come and let me know, and I'll take you. There are several other buildings on the grounds, too."

"Thank you."

He starts to walk away. Once he reaches the banister to descend the East stairwell, he turns. "Oh, the Wi-Fi is 'Stoneresidence.' And the password is Callisto_1."

I smirk a little. "What, no love for the other Xena characters?"

"Xena?"

"The… warrior princess?"

"Oh," He smiles a little. "Callisto is one of Jupiter's moons. Fun fact, Xena is the name of a dwarf planet, and Gabrielle is the name of its moon."

I smile. He's a handsome nerd. It's honestly a little… endearing.

"Sorry, my inner geek is showing. Dad set the password, though. As you'll surely notice when you walk around, his life revolved around astronomy."

"The fact he gave you names like Orion, Andromeda, and Leo were a bit of a dead giveaway if I'm honest."

He can't manage a smile this time. A flash of pink rips through his cheeks, nose, and throat. His eyes fill with tears, and he gazes at the runner beneath his feet. After taking two seconds to compose himself, he looks back up at me. "Thanks for coming, Ms. Whittaker."

I nod. "You can call me Layla, by the way. If you don't mind."

I hate the sound of my ex-husband's last name being associated with me. I only kept it for Danny's sake, for school paperwork, and to save the money it costs to change it for the custody case. The second the battle with Alan is finally over, I plan to change it back to my maiden.

"Layla. Sure. That's pretty." He says it innocently, but it still makes me blush a little. Without another word, he descends.

10

Orion

"No, he was on season three, and he's a total douche. I met him on the reunion special," Andromeda says two rooms away to Leo at a volume far too loud for their ten-foot distance.

I don't care about the ludicrous reality show she was on. I don't give a damn about the answer to any of Leo's questions.

I suppose there is a little bit of jealousy in my anger, too. He has always taken such an interest in her life. He's never talked to me that way, never cared enough to ask anything about my life. Even now, as adults, they're part of some little exclusive club I've never been a part of: the Little Rascals' *He-Man Ginger-Haters Club*.

Leo mutters something mindbogglingly stupid about one of her co-stars, and they both explode into a fit of giggles…

As if our fucking Dad hasn't just died.

Gone for-fucking-ever.

It is as if we aren't recently orphaned adults now without a single parent to guide us.

It disgusts me to see how unaffected they are by his passing. It is business as usual in that parlor.

Not a single anecdote or kind recollection. No grief or mourning.

Meanwhile, I feel like my goddamned heart is missing from my chest. I feel panicked. Nothing is ever going to be the same again. Could I have done something? Should I have been here? Could I have saved him? Will I ever see or sense him again?

As my siblings' laughter grows, I regret leaving my noise-canceling earbuds back at my house. I debate ordering another pair to be delivered stat, but I decide against the frivolous expense. This place is three stories, and there are plenty of places that I can go to focus on the documents that Duane, the V.P. of Dad's company Aspect Technologies, just sent me containing stock holdings and asset information for Dad as well as a whole slew of questions about our future plans for the company that I don't yet know how to answer. I suppose we should have had a contingency plan in place for all of this, but I thought we had a lot more time.

In the corner of my eye, I see Leo in the other room acting out some story he's telling with sweeping arm movements. Something about sport fishing, I think. A tale of something that transpired during his comically brief time aboard his yacht, one promptly docked on the floor of Ipswich Bay.

Part of me is worried he's going to break more valuables with all that gesticulating. He's disrespectful and irreverent, with no regard for Dad's things.

I'm sickened by how hard he and Andromeda are laughing less than twenty-four hours after she brought over a Hanukkah present and saw the disturbing expression on the face of Dad's corpse. I can't get the image of it out of my mind. Every time I blink, I see the ghostly imprint of his silent scream, his hand clenched into an outstretched claw, scrambling to right himself, the synapses in his curious mind no longer firing. There, on the floor, it was as if his being was instantly reduced to an itemized list of coldly divisible assets, this curious astronomy-loving tech giant, reduced to a bullet-pointed email about stock holdings from his second in command. A loving husband and a supportive father remembered with little more than a casserole dish of *kugel* and a rectangular pit in a Jewish cemetery.

My nose sparks with the feeling that I am going to lose it. I cannot let Leo see me emote. I'll never fucking live it down. If he says one cross word or calls me a pussy, I'm liable to snap and make that pretty boy's face unrecognizable.

I stand, eager to escape his field of vision, opting for the long way around the house so that I don't have to walk past them. I carry my laptop through the kitchen, past the walk-in pantry, and to the elevator. It's like a phone booth inside. I jab the button for the second floor. As it lifts, I recall the day Dad announced he was having it built.

The stairs were hell on his knees after his second meniscus surgery. Standing in it, I'm grateful for the silence and the privacy. My eyes begin to well. I feel overwhelmed, surrounded -- *literally* -- by memories of him.

When the elevator creaks open, I rush through both wings to my room. The second my door clicks closed, it all hits me at once. A boulder dropped on my chest.

It hits me that I can never talk to my father again. About *anything*. I'll never be able to discuss the vastness of the cosmos... or chess opens... or the timeshare we used to own in the Bahamas... or Mom.

We will never have another discussion about Gordon Lightfoot's best album or argue over who has the best cheesesteak in Philly. We will never chat about politics or debate ethics. We will never discuss how prolific Catch-22 and 1984 were at length again. We'll never smoke another Churchill while drinking booze older than Leo's latest girlfriend while musing about religion, climate change, or the newest, most worthwhile philanthropic endeavors.

I want him back. I want to play chess with him or take him up in The Birdie. I want to stargaze with him or have him regale me with stories and coordinates to some new nebula he's just discovered.

I need to know that he isn't scared anymore, that his frozen expression of pain won't last for eternity.

All the air is gone from the room. I feel like I'm in the vacuum of space, unable to breathe, bones under implosive pressure. My chest feels like it's caving in. The seal shatters, and my tears are unleashed in a vicious torrent. I struggle to restrain the guttural wail building inside of me, one aching for a release. Gut wrenched, I collapse into a silent scream and cover my mouth, fist balled so tight my nails threaten to pierce palm skin.

A noise hisses out of me like a percolating teapot. A pained squeal. The ruthless sound of bottomless hurt, of unrelenting agony.

I struggle to imagine what profound wisdom about grief and the Garden of Eden my father might offer in a moment such as this, but I can't hear him despite my best attempts.

He has only been dead for hours, and already I can't remember the sound of his voice.

I am filled with a sense of undeniable panic. Twisting tension. Blasts of dread radiating from my belly, flickering in my brain.

Life will never feel the same.

I bellow sincere and unintelligible apologies, gibberish words coming out as mushed and soggy as the skin around my eyes.

I am so sorry, Dad.

Sorry that I wasn't there.

Sorry that I couldn't save you.

Sorry I saw your face like that. Sorry for robbing you of dignity, allowing you to be lowered into the dirt with that image brutally emblazoned on my mind.

Sorry that I'm the only one who seems to be in pain.

Sorry that your firstborn sees your death as a payday instead of a fucking crisis.

Sorry that I didn't get to say goodbye.

Sorry that I couldn't do more, that I couldn't save you.

I'm just… so fucking sorry, Dad.

||

Layla

"What, no *latkes*?" Andromeda scoffs as she looms over a dining room table filled with white foam boxes full of steaming food. "This isn't Hanukkah food, Ry."

"Look, I never claimed to understand the customs of the holiday, Andromeda. I observe Christmas," Orion says, seemingly annoyed. "If you wanted *latkes*, you should've said something earlier." Orion crumples up one of the paper bags the food arrived in and disappears into the kitchen.

Leo swishes through the fronds of a seven-foot palm and digs in a drawer beneath the lit menorah on the buffet table, pulling out a gold coin and pointing to one of the white containers with it. "There's cod over there, sis. Just… pretend it's *gefelte* fish."

Andromeda rolls her eyes playfully.

"Here." He flicks the coin in the air, and she catches it. "For dessert."

"Oh shiiiiit. I haven't had *gelt* in a minute. My kids swarm them like hungry piranha any time I bring these home." Andromeda takes a seat with a turquoise Royal Crown salad plate peppered with a couple of clams and little else. The plates are ornate with gold flourishes, something I've only seen online due to their exorbitant cost. A service for eight usually runs around thirty grand, about two years' rent for my apartment... for *dishes*.

While the seafood all smells incredible, I stay standing for a moment to gaze in awe at the dining room table beneath this insane spread. It is an eleven-piece Carlene with ten deep-button tufted leather chairs, each with scroll work across the top and down the tapered legs. Both leaves are in, making it one cohesive, stately piece of cherrywood artistry. New, it typically goes for somewhere around ten grand. Probably more than all the furniture at my home combined. And here it sits, covered in sweating Styrofoam and a vase of peace lilies on a crocheted doily. The graceful white flowers fit the somber occasion elegantly seated beneath a three-tiered Allegri Rondelle wide-ring chandelier with Firenze crystal squares along all three chrome belts. The bulbs inside glimmer off every inch. I've seen one like it go for thirty grand at auction.

Andromeda is indifferent to her plate as if it could be a disposable paper one. But me, I've never before eaten off such lavish things. I feel like a phony who doesn't belong, a fraud about to be discovered.

"Help yourself. Eat up," Orion says, leaning against the kitchen doorway, refusing to let his eyes meet mine. They're lightly ringed red, matching the swath of pink crawling up his taut, muscular jaw. I heard the soft sounds of pain oozing through his bedroom door. I feel for him.

Even though I wouldn't dare, part of me wants to give him a hug, wants to tell him that I, too, am secretly in pain, grieving my own form of loss. This morose solidarity, our bond of shared misery, would strangely be a comfort.

He watches quietly from the corner, arms crossed, the faintest trace of a smile light-years away.

I focus my attention on my plate, placing a lobster roll on it. I hoist it toward him. "Thank you for this."

He nods and tries to force a smile, but it comes out flat and strange.

Leo brushes against me as he walks to his chair, craning his face down to my ear and cooing in a velvety voice, "Mmm. Delicious."

I want to assume he is referring to the food, but I'd be lying if the softly groaned words didn't light a fuse deep in my body. I have always had a weakness for a man's moans or good dirty talk. And thanks to Alan destroying my life, it's been over two years since I've been pursued, since I've heard a good-looking guy groan in my ear, since I've been touched…

I laugh the comment off and catch a glimpse of Leo's eyes, piercing with irises so dark they nearly match the pupil. They're dangerous and unrelenting. He has a certain mass appeal. His naturally tanned skin makes his dark features captivating.

"Petey's has the best steamed clams and lobster tail this side of Maine," he finally says with a John Stamos-like smile, one that jellies my knees a little. Both of these brothers are so goddamned handsome in their own right.

He shifts his plate into his right hand and takes one of mine in his left as I reach for the fried calamari. "What happened here?"

His thumb softly swipes across the back of my hand, rife with minuscule cuts.

"Car accident," I say quietly.

"Recent?"

I nod, my mind's eye replaying the image of the tree smashing through my windshield before the stranglehold of my seat belt carried me off into the darkness.

"I was wondering why you showed up in a Lyft or whatever. Now it makes sense."

I don't know what to say to that, so I smile and nod… and then I wonder why the hell I just smiled. Knee-jerk reaction, I suppose.

I take a seat at the far side of the table, and, despite all of the empty seats elsewhere, Leo takes the seat directly next to me, flashing that charming grin as he scoots himself in.

"You married, Ms. Whittaker?" Leo just comes right out with it. No filter. No trying to disguise his interest. His dark eyes flit up and down me.

"Divorced." It's a bitter pill, a hard word to say aloud.

"Same," he says before popping a piece of calamari onto his tongue. I get a glimpse of his nails, buffed and manicured, every inch of him preened and pampered. His hands look strong, and for a split second, I imagine what they might feel like slipping between my bare thighs, eager fingers exploring.

Orion approaches on my other side, offering two wine glasses. The look in his eye silently asks, "Is *this fucker bothering you*?"

But his lips say something different.

"Chablis?"

My eyes affix to the wine in his hands, neither glass containing a modest pour. I desperately want to drink them both, to chug until I'm once again numbed to all of my problems.

Leo extends a hand to grab one. I can smell some kind of lotion on it, something with cucumber. "Yeah."

Orion hands him one of the Waterford Crystal glasses.

Leo swirls and sniffs the alcohol, then allows some to slip across his tongue. "Is this the Christian Moreau?"

"It is." Orion seems supremely annoyed that Leo has such a refined palette.

"The '22 from the rack in the kitchen?"

Orion nods.

Leo is instantly disgusted. "Aw, come on." He hoists the crystal goblet back up in the air.

"It's a holiday, and we have a guest. Don't dishonor her with that fucking *swill*. Go fetch a 2015 Rothschild from the wine cellar."

Leo smiles at me as if to make sure I know he just defended my honor like a chivalrous knight instead of an entitled trust fund snob.

"I'm not a golden retriever," Orion says with a thousand-yard stare.

"You're a fuckin' Vizsla, if anything. Goddamned *Clifford* with that red hair…"

I gently take the other glass from Orion's hand. "Please, don't trouble yourself. This is phenomenal, I'm sure."

He offers me the faintest hint of a smile. Even for that briefest moment, it changes his whole face, his emerald eyes suddenly more striking than normal.

"You always have had shit taste in wine." Leo takes another sip despite his apparent disdain and skewers a clam with his fork.

"I never claimed being a *sommelier* was part of my skill set," Orion says, taking a seat at the end of the table near the kitchen, like he wants to be able to leave quickly should the need arise.

"There are a lot of things that were never part of your skill set. Right, Annie?"

Anger flashes across Orion's eyes at the mention of the nickname, but he remains silent, caressing the rim of his own crystal glass until it hums.

"What's the deal? You got this huge feast for everyone, and you're not going to eat?" Andromeda rolls her eyes.

"I'm not hungry." Orion's voice is unyielding, like a man who is aware of his worth but doesn't need to throw his weight around to be heard.

"Pfft. *You're* one to talk. You've got, like, what, a couple clams and three shrimp?" Leo motions to her plate, speaking through a mouthful of half-chewed food.

"No. Too much *kugel* earlier. All those carbs have me feeling like a whale." Andromeda makes a sour face and plays with one of her remaining clams, tapping it around the plate with an expression of boredom instead of eating it.

"You look like a skeleton. It's not cute, Andromeda. Men like curves. You're starting to look like Ariana Grande, all Ozempic-scrawny. Your bones are jutting through your skin." He stabs a hunk of breaded cod with his fork and voraciously chews. "Just… do what I do. Eat what you want and spend more time in the gym."

"When I want your advice, I'll ask for it," Andromeda says, looking like a spoiled kid, waiting to be excused from the table, head sagging into one propped-up hand in a way that mushes her gaunt face like a skinny Shar Pei. She forks a piece of a buttered lobster tail out of one of the containers and pops it in her mouth with a cast-pewter dinner fork, part of an Italian Valpeltro Alton flatware set. Then, she glares at

Leo and speaks through a mouth of it. "Happy now?"

Leo smirks. The man is used to getting his way.

"Thank you for the meal," I finally say to Orion. He nods a little, then mindlessly strokes the table with his middle finger, deep in thought. For some reason, I can't look away from the soft circles he's making on the lacquer. The combo of the Chablis and the visual makes me feel like the heat in the house just cranked up to eighty degrees.

He catches me staring, and my heart feels like it has skipped a literal beat. We stay locked in our gaze for what feels like a moment too long before I chicken out and glance back to my food.

"So, Layla," Leo says, completely oblivious. He swigs a gulp of Chablis to wash down the fish. "How long does your inventory typically take?"

"Well," I take a deep breath. "It really depends on what I find. Normal-sized houses can take anywhere from a couple of days to a few weeks. But a property *this* size, with the amount of valuables it contains, it could be anywhere from a couple of weeks to a couple of months."

My eyes flit back to Orion to see if he is still staring at me, but he's deep in thought, eyes locked on the doily beneath the peace lilies.

"Can't you just, I don't know, haul some of this stuff to an auction house or something and be done with it?" Leo seems testy about the proposed timeline.

"Certainly. Some of this will go to various ones in New England that I have built a rapport with. Additionally, I can also gauge whether auctioneers would like to host one here, but I still need to research a lot of the items so they can advertise accordingly to draw the right kind of purchasing power to this sort of estate. There is also the matter of the building itself as well as the others on the property and the land that all needs to be appraised. It takes a little bit of time."

Leo nods curtly. "What if we sweetened the pot a little?"

"What do you mean?"

"I mean, is there anything we can throw in to get you to work longer than the typical nine-to-five to get this over with? I saw you eyeing that vase with the dumb bird on it."

"Phoenix," Andromeda corrects.

Orion is silent, just soaking it all in.

I nibble off a bite of my lobster roll and wipe my mouth with a luxurious cloth napkin. "I'm not sure taking a vase as a tip would be entirely ethical, although I'm happy to work overtime if you're willing to approve the fees with Mr. Collins."

"Done."

Leo waves his hand. No need to hear the cost. Whatever the number it is, it would surely be a pittance to this man. I imagine it must be nice to be able to chuck cash at your problems.

"Great. Well, I assure you all that I'll work tirelessly to expedite this process for your family."

12

Leo

My muscles burn as I push through my reps on the weight bench. Afterward, I shakily put the bar back in its hooks with a metallic sound that rings out through the basement gym. Sweat pools in the hollow of my neck as I suck in deep breaths, feeling every inch of my aching biceps tingle from the fibrous shred. I sit up just as the door opens. It's Orion. There's an apologetic look smeared across his pale face and a monogrammed towel slung over his shoulder.

For a split second, as he notices me, he looks like he's going to flee but quickly decides against it. He straightens his back and enters fully. I stare, watching him wordlessly as he makes his way over to the treadmill across the massive room.

"How many miles do you do?" I bellow, nodding at the machine he's on, trying to lessen the awkwardness.

"Usually five. You?"

I chuckle. "Zero. Reminds me of being a hamster on a wheel. I do weights like a big boy."

He jabs at the control panel, raising the incline and speed with a series of beeps.

"You know, that's part of your problem. Women don't really give a fuck that you can run like a gazelle, Annie. They want muscles. They want a set of abs they can eat lunch off of." I pat the eight-pack beneath my tank top.

"You mean like these?" Jogging, Orion lifts the bottom of his white T-shirt to reveal a surprising set of his own.

God damn. Didn't think he had it in him.

He drops his shirt and continues running, beeping the interface until he's full-blown running. "Just because I'm not… on a forty-foot banner… selling shitty cologne on Broadway… doesn't mean… I'm some troll. The difference between us… is that… in another ten years… when you're, what, fifty-five… and I'm forty-four, I won't have a portfolio… of print work… reminding me that… I used to be… *just* a pretty face."

Hearing him say it in that *I'm-better-than-you* tone pisses me off. "I may be in my forties, but I could still get any woman I want."

"I hate to break it to you… but… with a fat bank account… even *ugly* guys can get laid."

He doesn't even know how much that one stings. I've been very private about my staggering financial losses. In recent months, the hemorrhaging of the S&P wiped out half of what little I hadn't already squandered. Plus, there's the alimony. To *both* ex-wives. Still. And the slowing drip of commissions… The truth is, my account is no longer "fat." In fact, my house, my car, and the future of everything teeters, leveraged on tanking stocks, dangerously close to collapse. With Dad dead now, I just have to hold out for my inheritance, whatever that ends up being.

Anxious to change the subject off my financial crisis, I pivot. "Layla's hot."

Orion turns his head to look at me, and it suddenly occurs to me that I might be dancing near a slight nerve. It isn't the first time we've both wanted to actively pursue bedding the same woman.

"She was putting out some vibes," I say, prodding for a reaction. His face betrays him, and I receive one almost instantly. The muscles in his jaw tense, face returning to the bouncing tits of the instructor displayed on the screen of the Peloton.

"Leave Layla alone," he finally grumbles.

"Why? You think you can just call dibs, Annie?"

"I'm not calling *dibs*. She *works* for us. You think a few weeks for inventory is slow? Wait until there's a sexual harassment lawsuit on top of that."

"Eh. I think I'll take my chances." I shrug.

"You always do," he mutters in a pissed-off tone.

"Sorry. I just have no interest in being a lonely incel like you, jerking yourself off every night because you're too scared to talk to girls."

I know it probably isn't true.

He probably gets laid at least a couple times a year. He's a Stone, after all. He's been featured on Forbes lists. There was some truth in what he said. The fatter the bank account, the wetter the snatch. Plus, he's been the keynote speaker at enough events for Aspect Technologies that he probably has a harem of geeky little astrophysicists clamoring for that fucking fire-crotch of his.

He laughs at the absurdity of my comment, but I can tell I'm in his head. I've known him three-and-a-half decades. He's so easy if you know the right buttons to push.

"Yeah, too bad I'm not like you," he huffs with a shrug, legs moving like an antelope on the open plains, "An aged-out model and a stellar *husband… oh… wait.*"

The jab about my failed marriages enrages me. I rise and walk across the squishy floor mat to him.

"That's okay," he continues. "You may have alimony payments… instead of wives… but… at least… you know… you've got… your *yacht.*" He turns to me. "You know… the one you spent your mommy's inheritance on. The old S.S. Edmund Fitzgerald…"

He's grinning now at my embarrassment, tennis shoes rhythmic on the moving belt. His reference to the boat is the last fucking straw. This rage-and-testosterone cocktail makes me want to yank the freckled fuck off and smash his face into the ground until he resembles a wad of ground hamburger and orange hair.

"Say something else. I dare you." It's all I can think of. Fury has clouded my vocabulary. I want to hurt him, to make him pay a price for the shame I feel.

"You've always been able to… dish out the insults… but you sure as hell never could take them."

"You run your fucking mouth like your whore mother," I say.

His head whips, looking at me as if he'd just been slapped in my direction. I knew that would get him. He always was a bleeding heart when it came to that bitch.

His smile vanishes. He pushes the emergency stop button. In a matter of two seconds, it slows. Without a single word, he jumps off and steps to me. Our bodies are like atoms colliding.

There is suddenly a flurry of smashing fists, wrenched arms, banging foreheads. His and mine, a mess of limbs flying with vigor and prejudice. I feel pain in so many different places it isn't even registering. I sock him so hard in the rib that it leaves him breathless.

I shove Orion far enough away to get leverage so I can deck him, but he takes the space back and hits me in the neck so hard that I can't breathe.

What the fuck?!

It is everything I can do not to drop to my knees and hold my throat. As I clutch my trachea, hearing the singular wheeze of my own gasp, he twists and lands an elbow right in the side of my neck.

Before I can react, his other elbow smashes against my nose. Searing pain radiates. I see stars, feel rage. I try to punch him in the ribs again, but his arm blocks, locking mine in place in a flash, his mouth expelling another aggressive grunt. I manage to wrench myself from his grip.

The pain in my head radiates like an earthquake, the epicenter being the bridge of my throbbing nose. My muscles sting, the struggle and workout compounding.

Somehow, Orion stands before me, looking completely unscathed.

I launch at him again, unable to let the piss-ant best me. I refuse to allow him to leave with bragging rights after such a smug verbal assault, as well. My pride simply won't allow me to back down.

As I pounce, there is another flurry of his tensed elbows and hard chops, hands grappling to retrain me. He roars and hooks his arm behind my head before delivering a knee forcefully to my side. Before I can react, his leg swings behind, sweeping me onto the floor with a painful *thud*. The fall rattles me, but my fire burns brighter than ever.

He's standing in some sort of fucking karate pose above me, legs wide, arms poised to attack again. Tasting blood from my nose as it dribbles to my lips, I smash my elbow into his crotch so hard it makes my own balls cringe in empathy. A cheap shot to the jewels.

The fucker left me no choice.

His arms drop, posture changing to cup his groin. I shoot at him in a werewolf lunge, tackling him backward, carrying us both through the gym like I'm playing offense for the Eagles with a Super Bowl on the line. I don't stop until he smashes shoulder-first into the wall of mirrors between the door and dumbbell racks.

The mirror he hits shatters into pieces, one large, jagged one still swinging from the mounting clips like a guillotine, poised to behead royalty. The sound he makes is horrific, and he leaves a blood smear on the wall as he struggles against me.

I shove myself away, pushing him back into the mirrored wall until I am out of arm's reach. My bloodied nose throbs. My neck aches. I struggle to stand, prepared for more retaliation.

Instead of lunging at me, he staggers away, blood drenching the sleeve of his shirt. He looks at me, eyes far more wounded than his arm.

"*I hate you*," he says with a grimace, his tone warbling in its blend of anger and pain. I notice rivulets of red racing down to his fingertips.

Fuck. I wanted to knock his smug, shitty ego down a peg, not leave him needing a goddamned EMT.

Orion's posture straightens. He lifts the sleeve to examine the wound, re-covers it, and then flashes a last vengeful glare. He hisses, cradling his shoulder in his hand.

"Do you want me to call an ambulance?" I ask, quieter now.

He whips his head like a snarling animal baring its teeth, a warning before the bite. "Fuck off!"

His voice is fraught with fury and pain. In the thirty-plus years I've known him, I can't remember ever seeing this much hate in his eyes.

Orion wipes his palm on his abdomen, opens the door, and thrusts himself through, feet pounding up the stairs. As the heavy door clicks back into place, the shard of dangling glass drops from the clip and shatters in the sea of busted fragments on the floor.

13

Orion

I turn at the top of the second-story steps and make my way toward the bathroom, trying my best to keep blood off the runner on the floor. It's some sort of huge custom one I've honestly never given a single thought to until now. I bolt through the door and find myself face-to-face with Layla, who jumps straight up off the damp tile floor like a frightened cat.

She's covered by a white towel… *barely.*

"Jesus-fucking-Christ! I'm so sorry!" I holler, averting my eyes behind my bloodied arm like she's Medusa. In the foggy mirror, as I turn to head out the door, I catch the blur of her form through a layer of steam.

"I wasn't thinking," I say, full of regret for the inappropriate intrusion, tacky hand fumbling the doorknob. "I'm so sorry!"

"Stop. You're bleeding," she murmurs with alarm.

"Yeah, I just… can you hand me the first aid kit beneath the sink?" My red-streaked arm shields my face. There is a soft pattering noise as droplets smack against the bone-white tile by my feet. "I'm not used to anyone ever using this restroom."

"It's alright." She kneels to get the kit, her face level with my throbbing groin. I step backward to give her more space.

"No, stay over the tile. It'll be easier to clean." She sounds so pragmatic and calm. As if I were a child dripping with hose water.

She retrieves the kit and sets it on the counter. I start to take it by the handle, ready to head to another room to tend to my wounds. She gently presses the door closed.

"No. Come here. Sit." She lowers the toilet seat and motions to it.

I stare at her for a moment. Confused.

"It's okay. Sit. Let me take a look. I'll get you cleaned up, and we'll see if it's bad enough to go to urgent care, alright?"

With reluctance, I take a seat as she opens the case. "Looks like it's coming from your shoulder. Can you take off your shirt? I need to be able to rinse it."

I nod, suddenly feeling strangely bashful. Minutes ago, I was lecturing my brother about avoiding a potential sexual harassment lawsuit. Now, I'm peeling my shirt off in a closed bathroom with her while she's wearing nothing but a damned towel.

How do I know this for certain?

Because her lace thong sits on the floor next to a pair of heels and a rumpled dress, all black, all of them sending a wave of arousal through my aching lower half.

My dick stirs at a momentary mental surge of imagery: her with her ribs against the bathroom counter, curvy thighs spread wide at the perfect height thanks to nearly three inches of heel, delicate hands expertly tied behind her, beautifully bound and writhing in eager anticipation. In this vision, the spank-able skin of her ass pinkens as she readies herself to loyally obey all commands, to comply faithfully with my stern order to spread herself wider, presenting her sensitive flesh for me to do with as I please.

The snap of the latex glove against Layla's wrist might as well be a hard slap in the face, ripping me back to the even more inappropriate scene happening in this bathroom.

"Orion?" She says my name so softly that it gives me a chill despite the room feeling like a sauna. "The shirt?"

"Sorry." I peel the fabric off carefully, easing it over my injury with precision. I ball it up and toss it in the dewy tub. It leaves a pink stamp on the porcelain. A wet cotton ball drags across my right deltoid.

"What happened?" She asks it so softly I almost don't hear it. "Did you trip? Or fall?"

"No." I don't elaborate. I'd like to leave it at that. Fortunately, she doesn't pry.

I try not to wince every time she gets near the incision. She leans in for another look, examining the area carefully.

"Was it glass? Or maybe a mirror?"

"The latter." I stare forward at the empty towel rod on the wall. "Does it need stitches?"

"Can't tell for certain yet. Maybe, maybe not. There's a piece still in there. Once that's out, I'll have a better idea. Got any tweezers?"

I nod up to the medicine cabinet. With haste, she retrieves it, uncaps a bottle of rubbing alcohol from the kit, and sterilizes the tool. With the seriousness of a triage doctor, she leans in again. Her wet blonde hair drags against my back. It sends another bolt of excitement through me. I have the urge to wind it around my fist and pull her down to me so that I can explore her mouth with my own.

I feel an acute pain in my arm, and I close my eyes.

"Sorry," she says apologetically, her hair still grazing.

"No need to apologize. Isn't your fault." I grit my teeth as the pain worsens.

"I've got the head of a pair of tweezers inside your arm right now. I beg to differ," she snickers a little. The sharpness eases.

A moment later, she announces, "Got it."

I look at the offending hunk of mirrored glass pinched between the prongs of the tool. It's not as large as I would have thought.

"You took that like a man." She smiles, her eyes flashing to mine for a moment. She seems a little impressed. "Most of the guys I know are giant babies when they're hurt. You didn't whine or anything. I guess it's not true what they say."

I look up at her, baffled. "What do *they* say?"

"That gingers are more... sensitive. That they feel more pain and pleasure than people with other hair colors."

"That's actually true. Scientifically, I mean." I look down, willing my jiggling knee to settle, commanding my body to compose itself from the adrenaline dump, from the anger and shot nerves, from Leo's words, from Layla's proximity. "We have to get more anesthesia during surgery and dental procedures. We have, literally, thinner skin."

"I *see* that," she says, pointing at my wound with the pinched mirror shard. "I'm actually looking right at it."

She leans across me to drop the glass in the trash can beside the shower, and I catch the faintest whiff of her body wash, something floral and feminine.

"You more sensitive to hot and cold, too?"

I nod.

"What about *touch*? Are you... extra ticklish and all that?"

I nod, fighting the urge to snicker at how strange this situation is.

"Cool."

Eager to change the subject to something other than my hair color, my body, and its odd peculiarities, I ask, "Was that piece all of it?"

"Yeah, I think so, but I'll rinse it with saline just to make sure."

She squirts solution into the wound and palpates the flesh around it gently with gloved fingers. She leans in, inspecting thoroughly. "Looks all clear. The bleeding has slowed. Not to diminish your pain, but that seemed like an awful lot of blood for such a small wound."

"I take aspirin." I feel embarrassed, though I don't know why. "As a preventative."

Just. Stop. Talking.

As Layla cleans the tweezers, I clear my throat. "Honest opinion, Dr. Whittaker. Do I need stitches?"

A laugh bursts from her lips. "If you want a second opinion, I understand, but with a wound this small, in this straight of a line, I think you could get away with some superglue."

"Superglue? Are you insane? You don't put superglue in a wound."

Her eyebrows raise as if I'm being absurd. "Yes, you absolutely can. People do it all the time. Vets do it for dog attacks, too. Sometimes you won't even get a scar if you glue it."

She hikes up the corner of her towel a little to show me the palest of white lines on her upper thigh. "This was glued."

I can't even focus on the almost imperceptible scar. All I can think about is how I want to nuzzle my face beneath that towel and let my tongue roam until she is moaning my name.

She lowers the terrycloth and digs back into the first aid kit. "Oh, there's Dermabond in here."

"What's that?"

She laughs, a whole-body laugh this time. "Medical grade superglue, basically." She holds it up. "Your call."

"I'll defer to my freshly-showered EMT." I shrug and lean my shoulder toward her. I feel her fidgeting with my skin, presumably preparing it for the glue.

"Is it going to sting?"

She laughs. "Apparently not."

I turn back to her, and she points to the wound. "Already finished. Just gotta let it dry for a sec."

She fans it with her blue-gloved hand and blows on it softly. Her eyes meet mine, catching me blatantly staring at her. She rights herself and removes her gloves with another rubbery smack.

"You did great. I wish I had a sucker to give you, like they do at the doctor's office." She smiles and tosses the bloodied latex in the trash. In my head, a crude comment rattles around about something else I'd rather have against my tongue as my reward.

She smiles, and I suddenly feel like a scumbag, or a pervert, or even worse…

Leo.

"Give it another minute or two to dry, and then you can shower off. When you get out, you might wanna put this on it." She holds up a large square bandage. "It's probably overkill, but it won't hurt to wear it to bed in case you start bleeding again. It'll help keep it clean, too."

I reach out to grab her hand to squeeze it in a show of appreciation, but then I see that it is caked in dried rivulets of blood, and I withdraw quickly. "Thank you, Ms. Whittaker."

"Layla." She gently moves a fallen tuft of hair from my forehead with her ring finger. It's a small gesture but an intimate one. Nurturing. I haven't felt anything like it in so long. I have the urge to lean in, to urge her to caress my jaw, a greedy dog seeking affection…

"Well, I'll let you get cleaned up," she says quietly, twisting her wet blonde hair over her bare left shoulder.

I nod with an appreciative smile.

She scoops up her clothes, carrying my fantasy away in a black fabric wad against her dampened towel.

"Goodnight," she says softly. The door closes, and I feel cold, as if all of the room's warmth has left with her.

14

Layla

I pad down the stairs, loving the feel of the stair runner beneath my bare feet. It's Persian, hand-knotted. Gold and burgundy. It feels like silk and wool. I'd have to check, but I feel like similar ones have gone for something in the neighborhood of ten grand.

That's more than my car costs. Well…

More than it *had* cost. Past tense.

I wonder if they ever fished it out of the tree or if it is still hanging there like some morbid Christmas decoration in the New Hampshire woods.

The foyer and parlor are dim now, lit only by the glow of the security floodlights outside. The stools and tables now cast long, dark shadows through a dwelling of ghostly memories destined to vanish after my inventory is done. Material things that once meant so much to Alexander Stone will soon host new memories across the globe.

The stench of fresh seafood lingers in the dining room as strongly as an aromatic cigar. I gravitate toward the light in the kitchen like a moth. I'm met with the cloying smell of chocolate cake and a shirtless male at the table in the attached breakfast nook.

"Jesus," I clutch at my racing heart. I'd expected the room to be empty, for everyone to be in bed for the night. But Leo is there, sliding a forkful of cake between his lips, abs for days on display, chiseled jaw tight, mouth cast into an annoyed grimace.

"I've been called a lot of things over the years, but as a Jew, that might be a new one." His nose sounds swollen when he says it, and his eyes lower to the slice on his plate. He stabs it with his fork.

"I'm so sorry," I say, crossing my arms in front of my satin pajama-covered breasts. Had I known anyone was still down here, I would have put on a damn bra. "I just came down for some water."

"In there." He nods at one of the fridges, and I see slight discoloration in his cheekbone, near the corner of one eye, as if he's been in a fight. Suddenly, I think back to Orion, to the shard of the broken mirror, to the avoidance of naming the injury's cause. Now, it all makes sense, especially since they've done nothing but bicker since I arrived.

I open the fridge to see bottles of Fiji, cans of flavored sparkling water, and green glass bottles of Perrier. I pluck a can out and hoist it in the air. "Thanks."

Just as I start to head out, I hear a "Huh-uh."

I turn around at the sound of the protest.

"Negative." He stands and cruises through the dim kitchen with the familiarity of someone who spent years in this home. He pulls a fork out of the drawer and steps close.

Wearing nothing but a pair of basketball shorts and a smile, he looks a little like a dark-haired Brad Pitt, four-inch strands of it dangling over his forehead. "You're not the kind of woman who'd make a broken man eat alone, are you?"

I snicker. The cake does look amazing. "Well, no. I'm not a *monster*."

"I knew it. You have an aura about you." He slides my silverware onto a napkin.

I smile, taking a seat. "Oh yeah? What does my *aura* say about me?"

By the time he answers, he has a bottle of whipped cream vodka in one hand and two shot glasses in the other.

My smile vanishes. "Oh no, that's nice, but—"

"Oh, come on," he whines playfully, deep brown eyes locking onto mine like a panther. "I'm in mourning. You're going to make me drink *alone*? I thought you said you weren't a monster."

My face feels like it drains of all color. Every fiber of my being wants a shot, wants to take the edge off of being in this foreign mansion full of strangers. But this shit has already robbed my life of so much, lowered my inhibitions, thrown my common sense out the window.

And a few days ago, *it damn near killed me*.

He plops into his seat, pecs flexed as he fills both glasses and slides one to me. He leans back, legs falling open wide in a cocky model's pose.

"*L'Cheim.*" He hoists his shot toward me.

My hand trembles as I pick mine up. "Ch-cheers," the stuttered word barely audible.

He swallows in one gulp, and I follow suit, taste buds alive and burning as it glides down my throat and warms my belly like a comforting hug.

Before I even set the glass down, he's pouring me another. I want to protest, but he wags his index finger at me.

"Don't fight it."

I suppose I'm not driving anywhere. Danny isn't around to see me tipsy. It's not like it's illegal for me to drink.

"Fuck it," I say quietly before slamming it, too.

"Atta girl," he chuckles, eyes sparkling with mischief.

"I think… I finally figured out where I know you from." I blush before tossing back a third shot that has almost magically appeared, each going down easier than the last.

He leans back in his chair, hooks his foot under the bottom rung of mine, and slides me toward him. The wood groans against the floor. His piercing gaze sends a rush of excitement through my body.

God damn, Alexander must have had some amazing genes. Both of his sons are just… gorgeous.

I think back to Orion in the bathroom, the color of his eyes like envy, flashing with lust, with need, staring at my mouth like I could satiate his deepest cravings.

And now, Leo is here, plying me with liquor, heat radiating from his ripped body, looking like if I followed him up to his room, he'd have my clothes off before the door even shut.

"It's the billboards." He lolls his neck back against the scrolled top of the chair's back. He's playing coy, pretending he's tired of talking about it even though he brought it up. Despite the humility in his words, his cocky half-smile says…

Keep going.

Adore me.

"Oh my God, Madison Square?"

He chuckles. "All over, darling. You'd have to live under a rock to have never seen one."

"Cologne, right?"

"Cologne. Underwear. Leather jackets. Motorcycles. You name it. I did print work for all of it."

I nod, unsure what to say. It explains the cocksure confidence, the arrogance, the privilege, and the unspoken expectation that things are owed to him.

He forks cake into my mouth, and I allow it, washing it down with another shot I think I poured for myself. It's a slippery slope, this seductive bitch. Every glass of it is like the Devil's finger beckoning me toward the gates of Hell.

...And I follow every time.

He bobs his head at me. "What're you doing tomorrow night?"

I blush, unsure how to answer that. I can't very well lie and say I have plans. I have no vehicle, and I'm staying in the same house he is.

I don't respond. I just eye the bottle, debating another ounce of that clear liquid heat for my mind and belly, bargaining that it will help me sleep better in these strange new surroundings.

Leo's eyes subtly drift down to my chest, the immodest peaks where my chilled nipples are trying to rip through the satin. I lean forward, curling my shoulders in on themselves, draping an arm across the table to cover them. I stare shamefully at the table, warmth blooming across my cheeks.

"So shy. I love it." Leo leans forward, speaking lower now, like he's letting me in on a secret. "What's your favorite kind of food?"

I pretend to think for a moment, even though I knew the answer before the last word was even across the threshold of his lips.

"Sushi."

He turns his head to think for a moment. The dimmed overhead hits his nose enough for me to see him better. It's cut, swelled, red across the bridge.

"Ever been to the Shokudo and Sake Bar down there by Fuller Gardens?"

I shake my head, feeling coy.

"It's fantastic. Be ready to go at seven-thirty sharp. I'll make a reservation." He stands, looming over me. He plucks playfully at the thin strap of my pajamas and leans close, close enough to feel his radiating warmth, to smell his spiced cologne. "It's an upscale place. Come in something… *tight*."

The way he utters the last sentence leaves me speechless, imagining something far less innocuous.

Come in something… tight.

These handsome, busted-up Stone boys are going to be my damned downfall.

Leo starts out of the kitchen, stopping at the threshold to stare at the framed picture near its entrance. It's of a man with dark brown hair and a woman with fiery copper curls in the middle of a flour fight, laughing like children. Leo flicks the woman in the face and leaves, plunging me into a slightly aroused silence with the remains of a vodka bottle and an icing-smeared plate.

15

I don't know where I am or how old I am, but everything just seems… accurate. I see my father on the brick-colored carpet, crowing, a swath of gray hair matted in the sweat on his forehead.

I can't hear what he's saying, but somehow I know it's my name.

It's so good to see his face again. I recognize us in his face. Leo's near-black eyes. Aurora's chipper smile. My angular jawline.

I open my mouth to speak to him. To ask if he needs help up. To ask why he is on the floor in the first place. Then, I see Mom on the bed beside me, staring down, her arm outstretched toward his. It's my first inkling that things aren't what they seem.

Dad's mouth stretches wide into a scream as he reaches for Mom. I race over, gripping him by the armpits to try to get him on his feet.

He decomposes in my hands, his body dissolving into loamy soil, his being reduced to sand between my fingers. A rectangular hole opens in the ground, deep and gaping, swallowing him into the bowels of its black abyss.

I look up and scream, but Mom has vanished. The wound in the earth heals like Dad was never here. Like he never existed at all.

***

I awaken, covered in sweat. Before I can wrap my mind around what I've just experienced, my eyes flood with hot tears, angry streams winding down the sides of my face, and pooling on the pillow sham beneath.

Dad is dead. It's real, this nightmare.

I look at my phone, full of lingering dread. I feel the burn in my muscles from my brother and I battering each other last night.

My lock screen confirms the date.

December 24th.

Christmas Eve.

Jesus Christ, this will be my first holiday without my father. Without any parents. *Little orphan Annie, after all.*

But this isn't just a fucking hard-knock-life. The sun *won't* come out tomorrow. It'll be bleak and wintery, snuffed out by the tiny fucking windows in this place.

I can't breathe.

The rise and fall of my chest is too fast, my crying mouth in a full pant like an overheated dog. I feel dizzy. Like I can't get enough air. My vision darkens. I feel like I'm joining Dad in that dark fucking hole.

I sit up, gasping. Stomach wrenching hard. Hands trembling. There is no air in here. No air at all. I'm in the vacuum of space. No helmet. No breathing apparatus. Only impenetrable darkness.

During all of this, one overwhelming thought stands out over the others:

I'd give anything to have him back. I'd trade my fortune for another day, another hour. Hell, even minutes. Long enough to let him know what he meant to me.

The air is thinner still. Lungs shriveling. Throat closing, but still, my cry escapes between gasps. The tears come harder now, unrelenting, pouring over the dams of my lids.

I try to breathe so hard I'm wheezing with each drawn half-exhale, teeth clenched so hard they could shatter. A growl seethes out of the tiny gaps between them. Then, a wail of pain. I feel a pickaxe slam through my abdomen, an elephant seating itself on my chest.

There is a soft knock at the door I can barely hear through my labored breaths.

"Orion?"

It's Layla. Feminine and angelic.

I'd be fucking embarrassed if I didn't feel like I was dying. The noises I'm making, these howls and whimpers between honking drags of air, they aren't by choice.

I hear my name again through the dizziness. I feel like I'm going to lose consciousness. I don't know how she transported there, but a second later, she's touching me, her forehead against mine, fingers slipping through the hair on the back of my head, her touch like the softest silk.

Her mouth moves, but her words don't register. Panic swells. My father's frozen expression in death is all I can see, shrouded by a curtain of darkness.

Layla's voice slices through the madness, an outstretched hand over the cliff I'm dangling from, trying to pull me back to solid ground.

Her lips near my ear. A shock runs through my neck into my torso, sparking something to life deep within me. Her hands cradle my jaw, forehead melding into mine like we are conjoined into one being at the skull. Her calm voice penetrates the chaos.

"Orion, tell me one thing that you can see right now."

What she says barely makes sense. My heart feels like a hand is squeezing it, and she wants to play *I Spy*?

"Just one thing."

I open my eyes, and they catch on the perfect curvature of her breasts peeking over a wall of charcoal fabric. They dart to the floor.

"Carpet," I finally mutter between gasps.

"What color is the carpet? Tell me about it. Give me a little detail."

Another squeeze of my heart sends more tsunami-sized waves of panic through me. I groan, gasping for air.

Her fingers caress the back of my head lovingly. So soothing. "Tell me about the carpet, Orion."

I stare at it again for a moment. The more I focus on the lush texture, the deep pile, the vacuum lines… the more the pressure slowly subsides. I gasp the air a little slower.

"It's… red. Dark red."

"And?"

"It's… soft." I must sound like an idiot, but her thumb caresses my jaw as a lover's would.

"Now, tell me something that you hear."

At first, it seems ridiculous. I am panting too hard to hear a goddamned thing. But then, as I concentrate, a sound cuts through, faint but distracting enough to slow my breathing a little more.

It's the tinkle of her long earrings. I twist to see one better. It's a three-inch string of connected butterflies, rose gold, each joined by the next one's wing tip. The soft chime would only be audible from this close.

"Your… earrings."

She smiles sheepishly, dragging her fingers through my hair, her French tips delightfully distracting my spiraling brain.

"You're doing great, Orion. Just keep taking slow, deep breaths. Just like that." Her hand slips to the front of my T-shirt, which is soaked with sweat from the nightmare. She presses against my heart, seemingly unbothered by the perspiration.

Slowing my breathing a little more, I'm able to take a few deep drags in through my nose.

"Good. Now, tell me something you can smell."

She pulls away, and I feel lost, lost in the vastness of space, adrift in an undiscovered galaxy, tumbling out of a black hole. She comes into focus, her hazel irises containing every color of the cosmos as they catch the filtered winter gloom oozing through the room's tiny window.

I smell something sweet. It's *her*. Shampoo or maybe body wash, I can't tell. She smells amazing. It's simple, feminine. It suits her.

"That's right. Keep breathing. What do you smell, Orion?"

I sit up straighter, my breaths slowing. Suddenly, I realize how embarrassing this all is. I feel resounding shame as my vision returns in full force.

"Vanilla." I suck in a deep lungful of air and settle myself. The panic is dissipating.

"You okay?" She strokes my hair a final time.

"I think so." I nod. "Where'd you learn that?"

"I… um, know someone with anxiety. It always works for him." She stands, taking that heavenly bit of vanilla with her. I get a view of her ass that I don't deserve as she walks toward the door.

She looks at me over her shoulder, an image of her that I won't soon forget. A classic regal pose, a queen deserving of worship. "I'll see you at breakfast."

I nod, unable to offer even a weak smile as she leaves. I feel a bit more of the panic ebb away, the wave flowing, returning with envy in its stead.

Part of me wants to know everything about the "him" she mentioned. The rest of me doesn't want to know there is a "him" at all.

16

Leo

Orion slides a plate of over-easy eggs and toast onto the table in front of me and sunny-side-up ones in front of Andromeda.

Neither of us thank him. This is the job he signed up for when he sent the staff home for the weekend, knowing my sister and I would be sitting Shiva.

"Wanda comes back tomorrow. I told her she could have Christmas Eve and Day off," Orion grumbles, giving off a pissy vibe.

"What about the driver and the other housekeepers," Andromeda asks. "And the chef?"

"No reason to keep them on the payroll. I let them go with a one-month severance yesterday afternoon. It'll just be Wanda until the place is sold."

Andromeda rolls her eyes and then casts them back down to the screen of her phone, the click-clack of her nails filling the silence between the three of us as her eggs grow cold. Orion watches her like a hawk, probably fuming over the sanctity of the dinner table being trampled upon by the use of her device. As soon as she sets it face down, it chirps. In a flash, it's back in her hands, commanding her full attention.

"Everything alright?" I ask, but I know it isn't. Her job is stupid, but she attacks it with the seriousness of someone about to launch a rocket into space.

"No. The dipshit I left in charge is having some sort of issue with our commercial shoot right now."

"Wow. Who'd have thought fake nails could be so stressful," I jest, scarfing down the last of my breakfast. After my morning workout, I'm famished. The whole time, I couldn't take my eyes off the busted mirror. Orion had it coming. He thought he was some kind of alpha dog. The bitch needed to be put in his place.

I glance up. He's staring right at me. Glaring, really. It brings a smile to my face to see him so aggravated by my presence. And still, he made me breakfast like a good little beta-bitch.

Mid-text, my sister's phone rings. She scrambles to answer like the cell magically transformed into a slippery eel in her hands. She slaps it against the side of her face and nearly topples the chair over as she leaves the table.

"What the fuck? Why aren't you shooting anything in portrait mode? You keep sending me fucking landscape. Yeah... it's fine for the web banner, but we need shit for social media reels, too!"

As she drones on, I reach over and steal Andromeda's toast, chomping a bite out of the buttered rye. I stare at my half-brother and his dumb fucking orange hair while I eat it. He looks like a clown. I don't know why he doesn't dye it a normal color. No one wants to fuck Ronald McDonald.

"What do you want me to order for lunch? We could do Hungry Lobster or Harborside…"

"Who the fuck are you mumbling to?" I ask, my unfiltered attitude flying in the ginger idiot's direction.

"*You*, asshole," Orion says, gritting his teeth so hard the right side of his face morphs.

I laugh. "Talking awful tough for someone who got his ass beat last night. Keep it up. There's a lot more where that came from."

"That wasn't a fair fight. You threw me into a fucking mirror." He leans back, tipping his chair on its rear legs. I have the sudden urge to kick the fuck out of his seat and topple him backward. I'd love to see him crack his ugly fucking head on the corner of the buffet table. But I think of how much less the dining set will sell for if it's a chair shy and decide against it.

"No one said I had to fight fair. You and I, we play by different rules."

"You're right. Should've known. After all, there's no honor among thieves, is there?"

"*Thieves*? Who the fuck are you calling a thief?"

Orion glares at me knowingly. I suddenly wonder how much Dad told him about why I lost my position at Aspect Technologies. Had I stayed,

I'd be head honcho there by now instead of Orion. He cocks an eyebrow smugly, and it's enough to tell me that he knows about everything. Misappropriated funds, vacations, lap dances on the company dime, the meager bonuses I was giving myself…

No one ever even missed it. The company grosses half a billion annually, for fuck's sake. The pittances I took were a drop in the bucket. I should have gotten a warning. Instead, I was hastily fired. Dad threatened to press charges if I didn't leave the company quietly.

So I did.

The look on Annie's face right now suggests he knows about what my father did to cover for me before booting me out to fend for myself with nothing but an inheritance to live off of.

What the fuck was I supposed to do with a measly three million dollars?!

"There's also Betty's and Sweet Chix," Orion grumbles.

"Are you still going on about lunch?" I feel irritated now, too. Looking at Orion's fucking mug does that to me. He looks like his mother, but he's twice the bitch she was.

"Just get me a Wild Dragon smoothie from the coffee place down the street, Common Ground, or whatever it's called. I'm staying light. I'm taking Layla out for dinner."

He doesn't respond to this new information, my attempt to remind him who the alpha is here.

I peel a platinum card out of my wallet and Frisbee it at him. "Here. Smoothies all around. Lunch is on me today."

Orion makes no attempt to pick it up off the floor behind him. He only glares.

"Is that wise?"

"Is *what* wise?"

"Taking the woman who is inventorying the estate for our family out to dinner."

I grin at how much I annoy him. I don't feel the need to dignify his question with an answer. So, instead, I ask my own. "How's the arm? End up needing stitches?"

Orion sets the chair back down, pushes away from the table, stands, and shoves the chair back in with a knock that rattles my watered-down screwdriver over the edge of the glass.

As he breezes past Andromeda, I chuckle and rise. I throw my napkin atop the remains of my breakfast, leaving everything on the table. Someone will clean it up. *Or they won't.* I really don't give a fuck. This house could go up in flames, and I wouldn't give a damn as long as the insurance paid out.

17

Orion

Rye looks different now. I take the same jogging route that I did when I was a teenager. Central to Perkins, through the canopy of trees, past massive homes with sprawling snow-dusted yards. Then, I take Perkins all the way down the boulevard. I travel along the beach, smelling the salty brine of the air. Then, Sea Road back to Central. One big loop where I can outrun my troubles for half an hour.

Only today, the thoughts are keeping up. I can't stop thinking about Dad's corpse doused with jugs of water in the synagogue, shattered mirror fragments all over the gym floor, the woman we hired helping me through a fucking panic attack first thing this morning, or how Dad's firstborn is parting out his home like a chop-shop would a car.

I jog faster, concentrating on the icy air blasting my face, but my thoughts quickly veer off-course again. I think about how my father will soon be reduced to nothing but numbers on a page, inheritance checks that fatten undeserving bank accounts, and a new round of toys for my asshole brother to fucking sink.

He and Andromeda hover around like vultures, half-ass pretending to uphold religious traditions. But they aren't even grieving. They are unaffected, as if Dad's death is just some pothole they can swerve around.

But Dad wasn't a pothole.

He was the Grand-fucking-Canyon. He left a deep, aching wound in my life.

The rhythmic synth of one of my favorite songs oozes out of the speaker of my phone, tinny and small in the noise-dampened snowscape around me.

"Is it an horrific dream?"

Yes, Tears For Fears.

I hope to Christ that it is. I hope this is all just some fucked-up nightmare I'll eventually wake from. But the suffocating pain tells me I'm wide awake, that this hurting isn't going anywhere. I wish there was a God I believed in, one that could numb me with blissfully ignorant thoughts of Heaven or Eden or some harem full of waiting virgins.

It isn't long before I return home and kick off my shoes, waltzing into the parlor where Andromeda and Leo are on their short stools playing chess on one of Dad's numerous boards.

"Where's Whittaker?" I ask.

Neither one bothers to look up. Andromeda finally announces, "Haven't seen her. Try upstairs."

"Why?" Leo somehow foolishly puts the 'rook in rookie' when he makes his next move. I cringe at how bad he is at the game. It's clear he and Dad never played much.

"I'm gonna get cleaned up and give her a tour of the grounds before it snows again. It's supposed to dump tonight."

Leo watches in shock as Andromeda takes the rook with her knight. I shake my head and make my way upstairs, checking the rooms in our wing. She's not in her room, the bathroom, or mine.

I find her down the other wing through the open door of the den, laptop open, phone in hand, snapping a picture of a figurine. I watch her for a moment, a peaceful slice of time I steal for myself. I soak it all in. The low heels, the curve of legs disappearing into the hemline of her charcoal dress, her elegant posture, the honey-blonde locks spilling over a zipper I want to tug down with my teeth until I'm worshiping at the altar of her ass… I commit the whole of her graceful image to memory.

She judders in place, scared as she notices she isn't alone. Fuck. I must look like a creepy asshole just standing here, sweating in shorts and a T-shirt in the doorway.

"Sorry! You scared me." She takes an earbud out of her ear.

"I apologize." I lean my head against the door frame, propping myself against it. "It's supposed to snow again tonight. Sometimes, the golf cart doesn't do well when it's fresh, so I thought if you were available in a bit, after my shower, I could take you for the tour of the grounds, give you all the access codes so that you can inventory them at your leisure. There's one unit that's literally just full of artwork that Dad loves to rotate—"

I catch what I just said, and I feel like Wile E. Coyote realizing he's completely off a cliff, defying gravity, his perilous plunge imminent.

"*Loved.*"

The word feels like an arrow through my fucking chest. Past tense.

Everything must be past tense now.

"He *loved* to rotate the art every few months, so it didn't get old. It'll probably be of interest to one of your gallery auctioneers."

She nods softly. "That would be great, Orion. Thank you."

The way she says my name gives me pause. "You should dress warm. It's pretty frigid out there right now."

She nods and smiles brightly. It's the last thing I see before I head to the shower and strip down, a mental image I cling to as I lather, a beautiful distraction from the lingering pain.

18

Layla

The air has a bite to it as we tour the grounds on the golf cart, bouncing across unseen pavers beneath an inch of white powder.

For the most part, Orion has been quiet, only speaking to point out structures as we cruise. We've driven past a romantic-looking gazebo, a rec-center-sized squash court, a long half-frozen reflecting pool, and the skeletal remains of a hedge maze gone dormant for winter.

"Down this path," he veers right down a wide walkway, the edges of which are obscured by lumped snow and ice, "is… *was*… Dad's planetarium."

The cart halts, and he's off in a flash, stomping the last few feet through the snow. He starts punching numbers into a numerical keypad. "Code to this one is 314159. It's just pi without the decimal."

I scribble the code onto my notepad and get out, following him up to the door. His slacks cling to every delicious inch of his butt. Beneath the black down jacket, the sweater he is wearing suits him. The olive green tone complements his hair, and hugs an abdomen that makes me salivate at the memory of it in the bathroom. The entire *Orion Stone package* is attractive.

He swings the door in, stomping his snow boots on the rug just inside. He leads me into the darkness and flicks on the lights to reveal a planetarium with movie theater-style chairs that recline back. The place is adorable and could easily seat thirty or so people at once.

"Oh my God," I say, in awe, staring up at the domed ceiling lit by a strip of LEDs. "Does it actually…?"

He laughs. "Yeah. Grab a seat. I'll show you."

I lower myself into one of the chairs on the end and lie back, peering up at the ceiling. Orion walks over to a tiny control booth and fidgets with some knobs and buttons. The LED lights dim, leaving us both in a pitch-black bubble.

A narrator's voice booms something about the Milky Way, and I am transported visually into space, flying through the ether on what feels like a solo journey. It reminds me of a school trip I had when I was younger to one in Concord. For a moment, I'm nostalgic, recapturing that youthful sense of wonder, that craving for knowledge about the cosmos.

"Cool," I utter.

The video cuts out, and the house lights rise until I can once again see the aisle and other chairs.

"I always loved hanging out in here, growing up." Orion tries to hide his grin as he makes his way into view from the booth.

I start toward the exit to continue the tour, wondering if Danny would find this as fascinating as I do, or if he has outgrown such things. Sometimes I feel like I barely know him anymore. It breaks my heart.

Before I know it, we are back in the cold, building locked, zipping across a field toward another structure.

"Final stop on this painfully boring tour," he announces once we park in front of an aluminum building, one large enough to park a deluxe RV motor coach in without even having to check the mirrors once.

"This is the storage unit where Dad keeps… where the art is stored." He corrects himself again, angry about the flub.

"It's okay." I turn to him in the golf cart, poking my face out from behind my scarf. "It's gonna happen for a while."

"Yeah, I know. I did the same thing with Mom."

"She passed, too?"

He nods. "While back."

"Mine, too," I add quietly.

"I'm sorry."

"Welcome to the Grieving Orphans Club," I say, with melancholy. "Not exactly the funnest club to be in."

"No, it's really not," he smiles a little at this strange thing we have in common, this kindred hurt. His visible breath dissipates, inadvertently drawing my attention to those emerald eyes of his.

"For the longest time, I thought grief was like a weight, but it's really not," I say. "It's a *hole*. You cared enough to carve out a space in your heart for someone. When they're gone, they leave a void where that spot was. Grief is proof that something *real* existed there."

His jaw flexes like he's struggling to keep his emotions at bay.

"Don't be frustrated with yourself for mourning a loss. Let it burn for a while. Give yourself the time you need. When you dust yourself off, you'll remember you have a lot more real estate in there." I press a finger to his chest.

He nods. "Thank you. That was… just what I needed to hear."

I step out of the golf cart and motion to the building with my notepad. "Alright, enough trite words of wisdom. I'm excited to see this art."

He nods and starts up the path to the door. As I approach him, I slip on the ice. Without thinking, I let out a Ric Flair-style "*Wooo!*"

To keep from falling, I grab his arm, nearly toppling him to the ground with me. He thinks fast, yanks me back to my feet. Even beneath the fabric of his coat, I can feel the power in his bicep, his forearm.

Jesus Christ, he could probably bench press me!

"You okay?"

"Yes," I say with a laugh.

He helps me to the door and opens it with the same code as before. At least two hundred paintings sit nestled in custom-built cubbies on one side of the climate-controlled building. On the other side is a row of twenty or more statues, some busts, some helmets and weaponry, some full human figures.

"Holy…" I let his arm go and cover my mouth with a gloved hand. I'm taken aback by all the ornate gilded frames peeking out of their wooden slots. It's enough paintings to fill a large room at the Louvre. Even if Alexander rotated paintings out of the house every two months, it might be five years before he ever saw the same one in rotation again.

"I think you have your work cut out for you," Orion says.

"I should say so." My eyebrows stay fixed nearly at my hairline. This type of wealth is insane. I'm living paycheck to paycheck, and this man hoarded a gallery full of artwork he'd probably barely ever seen.

"I'm going to head back to the house. My ringer's on. Call me when you want to be picked up. I'll be here in a flash."

"Thank you," I say, finally remembering to close my mouth.

"I'll text you a lunch menu. As soon as you know what you want, let me know and I'll have it delivered to the main house."

"Thank you."

"Sure." He bashfully plays with some snow on the doormat with the toe of his boot. "Need anything, just call."

"Will do."

He disappears out the door, and I hear the golf cart zip away.

Overwhelmed by where to start, my mind drifts to Danny. This'll be the second Christmas I haven't spent with him in a row. When I had him, I thought we'd celebrate them until he was eighteen. But the cold reality of being alone sets in. He's in Austin, probably getting ready to open presents with his step-mom, the woman who carried on a lengthy extramarital affair with my ex-husband.

It doesn't feel fair.

I pull out my phone, wishing I had a shot of alcohol to take the edge off the nerves.

I dial Danny's number. The phone rings repeatedly, each twisting my insides more with every unanswered chime.

Finally, I get his voicemail. *Again.* The familiar sound of it makes me want to cry. I talk to it more than I do to my actual child lately. The vague greeting makes me feel insignificant.

"Leave your message after the beep," his voice says.

"Hey… baby… It's me. It's Christmas Eve. I just wanted to call and see how you're doing. Getting excited about Christmas? I'm still curious what you asked Santa for this year."

I fidget with the corner of an antique American Gilt frame from the 1880s. The frame alone goes for about seven grand. As soon as I realize I'm even touching it, I pull away like it's scalding.

"Anyway, um… I miss you. Call me, please. I want to hear about your Christmas break and see how everything's going… Love you."

I feel so fucking awkward. I hit the end call button quickly. Without skipping a beat, I dial Alan. It rings and rings. It never goes to voicemail; it just says the mailbox is full. I want to hurl my phone across the room, but I can't afford to replace anything in here if I break it. I settle for a scream, one that is guttural, emanating from deep within, raising my blood pressure as it releases.

Angry, I dial again, this time it's the contact of one of my auctioneer friends who specializes in fine art. He answers on the first ring, and it somehow negates some of the stress from being ignored by the men in my life.

"Hey, it's Layla Whittaker. I'm working a probate case for a wealthy client in Rye."

Wealthy is an understatement. If I had any doubt before, it's gone now. Alexander Stone was a full-blown *billionaire*. There's probably twenty million dollars in art just in this building alone.

"If I send you some photos of some of the pieces, can you start gauging interest levels with some of your high-end collectors?"

"Absolutely," he says. It's a relief.

"Fantastic. Photos incoming."

"Sounds good. Send them to my email and I'll put out some feelers."

"Great. Thanks."

I end the call and tug one of the pieces carefully out of its individual cubby. It is an oil painting I recognize immediately. A Marc Chagall from the 1950s. Last time I saw a Chagall for sale, it went for a million-and-a-half. I pull it all the way out and prop it against the cubbies. I snap a photo and eye the vast wall of remaining pieces. This is going to take a while.

19

Layla

"Bring us… a Magaro blue-fin tuna roll, a Hotate seared scallop roll, you know, with the pears and shit. Let me get one… no, two spicy tuna rolls, an eel-avocado roll, one of those Dynamite rolls, four of the Temake hand rolls, a yellowfin jalapeno roll, the seared Wagyu small plate, one of those Unagi Gohan plates, um, a side of Japanese pickles, and sake. The… Chokaisan." Leo grins at the waiter. "Bottle, not the cup."

"A water for me, please," I add quickly, trying to do a mental tally of what is sure to be an astronomical bill, praying to God that Leo doesn't ask me to split the tab. I'd laugh because of our financial disparity, but then I'd cry because it would almost certainly max out my last credit card.

"Awww, come on. Water? Don't drink water. Fish fuck in that."

I laugh. It takes me off guard.

"You gotta have the sake. This place is literally known for it. Prepare to have your mind blown."

"I'm okay with water," I say timidly, the lure of anything alcoholic strong. This dinner is already awkward. Leo spent the entire Uber ride to the restaurant telling me about different supermodels he met in the early 2000s. I won't lie. He has a face worthy of painting. Hardened jaw, handsome, proportionate features. Looks-wise, he's expensive filet mignon. But his personality is… stew meat. Cocky and even boorish at times.

"Bring her a bottle of the Chrysanthemum Meadow," he says to the waiter. "If she doesn't drink it, I will."

The waiter nods and retreats.

Leo adjusts his body toward mine, dark eyes glinting. "I'm friends with the owner," he volunteers. "We used to go to synagogue together. He's not Asian. Some Jap broad runs the day-to-day and all that. He's just the money guy. He owns a fuck-load of other places around southern New Hampshire, too."

I smile and nod, never having asked the question I just received the answer to. The walls are exposed brick, elegantly industrial, lit dimly by dangling glass-globed pendants. There's a chalkboard behind the sushi bar, everything written solely in Japanese. In front of it, three Asian men in tall hats and white coats work enthusiastically on our outrageous order.

This place *is* upscale. The few people who are here are all dressed to the nines in bespoke suits and tight cocktail dresses. I can barely breathe in mine. If he plays his cards right, I'll be tempted to let him take it off me later just so I can take a breath again.

"Can I ask a question?" I'm desperate to have an actual conversation. "If it's too personal, you don't have to answer."

He chuckles. "Proceed."

"What was your father like?"

The question shifts his mood into something less jovial. He locks onto me with those warm brown eyes, the ones that made love to the camera in all of those forty-foot billboards in SoHo.

He smiles a little, as if he's about to utter something patronizing. He shrugs. "Alexander was an empathetic sap. A bleeding heart. That's where Orion gets it from… the *putz*. Every time you turned around, the ol' man was opening up some library or wing of a goddamned cancer hospital, donating telescopes to colleges, having those little snot nosed grade-schoolers from that disgusting public school by the house over to his planetarium. He spent like two straight years throwing thousands into high school astronomy programs. Always giving his damn money away to strangers."

He pulls his glossy set of chopsticks out of his napkin roll and shines them.

"It wasn't enough that his head was in the clouds, or the fucking *stars*, rather, but he wanted *everybody* infected with his obsession with outer space. Growing up, I got so sick of looking at the goddamned planets. I could draw you the surface of the moon from fuckin' memory. I don't even look *up* at night anymore."

The waiter returns with the chilled sake and Leo wastes no time pouring it into the small porcelain cups, shoving one my way.

"Your father sounded passionate," I say, twirling the cup in a circle, fighting the urge to toss it back, feeling my will weaken with every revolution.

He shrugs. "All the Stones are. Andromeda can't even get through breakfast because she's so involved with her stupid press-on nail line. And Orion… hell, that little suck-up became dad's Mini-me. He's basically a carbon copy, only half-gentile and with that fucking hideous orange hair."

The comment irritates me. Orion's hair is one of his most striking features. The color is vibrant, and the texture is soft. When he was having his panic attack this morning, I must confess that I jumped at the first chance I had to run my fingers through it. It didn't disappoint. It was even softer than I'd imagined.

"I kept telling my father to stop giving all of the family's money away, to reinvest in the company, or stocks, or to use that money for a fishing trip in South America… anything. But he never listened to me."

I shrug again, unsure what response he's seeking with his patriarchal complaints. "I think that kind of generosity is sweet. It feels underrated these days to see a billionaire giving back. In the media it's always these greedy damned CEOs who won't pay their workers a living wage and whatnot."

"Pfft. The first year or two, it was sweet. After that, he just had *sucker* stamped on his forehead. Everyone started coming to him, hands outstretched. He was a total pushover, more so after he met Aria. My step-mom turned him a big ol' pussy. Then, when *she* died, he ramped it up even more like it was some bullshit way to honor her memory. Layla, you wouldn't believe how many sharks start circling once Dad started chumming the water with charitable donations. God damn, anyone who started talking to him about black holes or moon cycles, before they knew it, he'd be writing them a fat ol' check for whatever stupid space shit those dickheads wanted."

He downs a small cupful of sake and points to mine. "You pregnant or something?"

The question jars me. Being pregnant would be a less embarrassing reason to not drink than the real one: *I don't know how to stop, and I'm slowly ruining my life with it.*

Fuck it.

I gulp it down in one swig. It's cold and smooth. The familiar burn of alcohol on my tongue relaxes me like a tranquilizer dart, even though the liquid hasn't hit my stomach yet. Psychosomatic relief before the real thing comes.

"'Atta girl."

He pours me another before I can protest, *as if I had the will to.* I'm angry with myself. Disappointed that I folded like a lawn chair.

Before I even think about it, I down the second cup, too.

"I just think," I start to speak so that I can keep my mind off the sake he just poured a third time, "that there is more to life than how much money one can amass by the end."

He chuckles, but there's something a little nasty about it. "Spoken like every poor person I've ever known."

The comment pisses me off a little. It feels like he just likened me to trailer trash. My apartment might be modest, but I still have a decent job. Maybe not compared to this privileged nepo baby, but still, decent by many *poor* people's standards.

"Let me ask you this." I sip from the cup, each mouthful easier than the last. "When they buried your father, how much *cash* was in the casket?"

"*Excuse* me?"

I worry that I've gotten a little too feisty, a little too riled. Perhaps I just jeopardized my job. If I'd have placated him, I'd have gotten free dinner and possibly a make-out session with an attractive model -- albeit one in his mid-forties, no longer commanding massive billboard space.

"I just..."

Our waiter appears with two cumbersome plates elegantly packed with rolls of freshly made sushi. I make space in the middle of the small table while Leo watches, leaning back, getting a little kick out of us both accommodating him.

"Wow, this is… a *lot* of food," I mutter, scrambling to make enough space so the man can set them down. Once he does, he returns what feels like ten seconds later with two more rectangular plates of food. Once we have crammed them all on the table, he promptly disappears behind the counter to start making rolls for other patrons. The rice rounds sit in front of us, much of it topped with vibrant slivers of fresh fish. Some are drizzled with spicy mayo or eel sauce, some are topped with unagi and roe, and some with thin-sliced avocado and a smattering of sesame seeds.

"Ladies first. I insist." He motions to the plate.

I pluck a piece of spicy yellowfin and chew it, groaning with satisfaction, flattened hand hovering in front of my mouth. "Oh my God, this is delicious!"

He smiles. I know deep down, he isn't as callous as he acts. Somewhere in that well-toned chest, beneath the tailored suit, beyond an aura of cologne that suits him so well it should be illegal, I sense that there might be a real person. The problem is, it's buried below a mile of hardened crust and fine trappings.

"You were saying," he says.

I wash the piece down with more sake. The first few cups of it are starting to warm my belly with that faux confidence.

"I asked how much *cash* Alexander was buried with." I pluck a piece from a roll on his half of the table.

"None. And… that's offensive."

"Offensive?!"

"It's antisemitic."

I squeak out a small laugh, covering my mouth. "How on *earth* is that antisemitic?"

"You're perpetuating the stereotype that Jews are so fuckin' greedy they'll take their cash to the grave."

"That is not at *all* what I was saying!" I laugh harder now at the ridiculousness of the accusation. "I'm making the point that *no one* is buried with their money. What good would it do the deceased? What's the point of hoarding it, dying with a mountain of wealth? Your father was trying to share it, to inspire youth, to give people access to something he was passionate about."

Leo is silent. I know this cannot possibly be the first time he's thought of this. He's bright, despite his shallow trust-fund pretty-boy persona. This has probably just struck a nerve because I made a point.

I eat another piece of sushi. It's so good it makes my eyes momentarily flutter.

"He could have given it to *us*. His fucking kids."

"So, let me get this straight… You wanted your father to hoard his money throughout his life so that you and Orion and Andromeda could have a fatter check at the end?"

"How many children do *you* have, Layla?"

The question makes my casual smile evaporate, my eyes lowering to the food. Suddenly, I no longer feel famished. I feel like taking the container of sake and drinking straight out of it.

"Don't say none because that's a lie. I know you have at *least* one. A *boy* would be my guess."

"Why do you say that?" I study his features, wondering if he did research before hiring me.

"Well, you just gave me the *I'm disappointed in you* mom-eyes, for one. You probably have a rambunctious boy who draws that look out of you on the regular."

"I don't have any kids," I lie.

Even if he *has* done his homework, I have no desire to let him jab at a festering open wound, no desire to air my dirty laundry to someone who doesn't give a damn right now about anything beyond getting laid.

"You're lying," he announces through a mouthful of jasmine rice and nori. "It's alright. I lie. Game recognizes game."

This makes me laugh, this brutal honesty. It disarms me for a moment.

His face morphs, changing from a playful expression laden with lust to one of complete disgust. I feel the presence of someone behind me before I hear her voice.

"Oh. Hmmm. Wow. You really do have a type, don't you, Leo?"

I turn in my seat to see a woman who looks vaguely familiar, but I have no clue from where.

Leo rolls his eyes. "Yes, Gwen. The sky is blue. This is sushi," he stabs his chopsticks at a piece of spicy tuna encrusted with panko, "and you look fucking bloated despite having liposuction. These are all facts."

Gwen tsks with her tongue and shakes her blonde head, pulling her leather jacket tight around her rather large breasts. "Are you ever going to grow up, you constipated man-child?"

There's hurt in her eyes. A man approaches from behind, rubbing her shoulders, a passive attempt to get her to leave. I recognize him from television. He's a… meteorologist or something. I feel like I can picture him waving his hands in front of a map of New England.

Then it dawns on me that Gwen is an anchor. Local channel 8. She's like a regional celebrity.

"Hi." I drop my sticks on the table and jut my hand out to shake hers.

She looks at me like I'm radioactive for a moment before shaking, unable to hide the disdain in her face.

"Layla Whittaker. I watch you on the news all the time."

Leo groans. "She's not Taylor Swift. She's a fucking nobody, Layla. Nobody outside of a half-hour radius knows who the fuck either of these losers are."

Gwen doesn't blink. "Look, Layla, you seem nice enough. Lemme offer a bit of advice, from one woman to another. Don't get mixed up with this narcissistic sociopath. *Run*."

"Come on, Gwendolyn," the meteorologist pleads, nudging her away from our table before she makes a scene.

"Seriously." Her eyes pierce. The man tugs her harder. "Worst sex I've ever had."

"Baby, *stop*," the meteorologist whispers.

Several patrons within earshot have already turned to gawk. One man is even recording the exchange.

"My jaded ex-wife, everyone," Leo exclaims, clapping loud enough for everyone to hear. "She'll never win a fucking daytime Emmy, but she did win Miss Wet-T-Shirt-2005 on our honeymoon while blackout drunk, so that's gotta be some kind of consolation. Isn't it, whore?"

"*Whore*?" She jolts at him like she wants to rip his head off with her bare hands. The man she's with whisks her toward the door. Her eyes stay locked on Leo. At the exit, she shouts. "Don't say I didn't warn you!"

The bell chimes, and they disappear beneath the amber streetlights into the evening's snowstorm.

Leo groans quietly. "Ugh. The ex-wife, obviously." He bobbles his head. "*One of them anyway*."

I pick up a piece of the yellowfin jalapeno roll. Despite the drama, I haven't been able to afford sushi in a long time. Seeing as though this is my first -- *and last* -- date with Leo, I'm not leaving until my dress is splitting at the seams.

"You're kind of a mess," I say with a laugh.

He hands me another full cup of sake and shrugs, seemingly without a care.

I take it and hold it up to cheers. "To messy lives."

He nods. "*L'Cheim.*"

***

We burst through the front door into the darkened foyer, snickering like two teenagers sneaking in past curfew. The Uber driver's high beams cut through the wall of large flakes that blanket the night sky in opaque gray. We stomp the fluff off onto the mat. The heavy door closes behind me, and Leo presses me against the wall just inside, both of us delightfully tipsy from polishing off both bottles of sake.

In the car, he kept telling me about people's houses that we'd pass, who lived there, random factoids about their net worth, and their family drama. With every tidbit, he leaned closer until his nose was in my hair, the alcohol on his breath overpowering his cologne. He's attractive enough to be plastered on Times Square billboards. I also imagine that in his mid-forties, he's probably got the body count of a rock star. He's one-night-stand material at best. If it hadn't been so long since I've been laid… as in *properly* laid… I wouldn't even be *considering* it.

Plus, after what Gwen said, there's a high probability that Leo's all looks and no talent in the bedroom. Some people say bad sex is better than no sex, but after being with Alan for so many years, I *wholeheartedly* disagree.

"What do you say we take this party up to my room?"

"I…" I hesitate, turning my head away to avoid the kiss I know is coming next.

The tip of his nose drags along the shell of my ear. The bulge of his cock strains against my thigh through his slacks, a heat-seeking missile searching for its target.

"I… don't think that's a good idea," I finally manage, Gwen's words echoing in my head.

"Boo," he says so softly it gives me goosebumps. "You're no fun." He pulls away, granting me enough room to shimmy out.

But I can't seem to will myself to move. While I don't like him as a person, another part of me longs to *feel something* right now. I'm horny and God, it's been too damn long…

The chandelier overhead flicks on, searing my eyes. Orion stands on the landing wearing only a pair of gray sweatpants and no shirt. His straight posture and wide stance exude a subtle big-dick-energy. The sight of him makes my pulse race.

"You know, there are bedrooms for that. Right, Leo?" He addresses his brother, but his green eyes are locked on me. He crosses his arms, his bandaged bicep bathed in the chandelier's glow. His arms are firm, muscular, and deliciously perfect. I wish with every fiber of my being that I'd been invited to *his* bed tonight instead.

"Thanks, Buzz-kill," Leo snaps back at him with snarky attitude, pulling away from me.

"It isn't what…" I start and then stop, realizing my words are futile. Not only am I a grown adult, single, able to make my own decisions, but it's not like I had an offer from him *first*. Orion's been difficult to read. I can't tell if he's been behaving chivalrously or if he just isn't interested.

"I need a fuckin' drink." Leo storms toward the kitchen, pissed off, pride wounded.

Orion stares at me for a moment and points in Leo's direction. "Are you okay? Was he…?"

He doesn't finish, but I know exactly what he is asking. Part of me is grateful that he cares enough to ask. The other part of me is embarrassed, unable to tell him that I yearn to be touched right now, that I'm aching with need. It feels like a weakness, like it's clouding my judgment. I am ashamed of how close I was to settling for what I'm sure would be ten minutes of sweaty writhing with the attractive scumbag in the kitchen.

"I'm fine. Thank you for asking." I ascend the stairs and pass him on the landing.

"Sorry. I didn't mean to ruin your fun," he says.

"You didn't." I turn on one of the steps and drink the whole of him in. That striking complexion, bright hair I long to stroke again, green eyes ringed pink by grief, the muscles of his chest bathed in Rembrandt lighting…

"Somehow," I flash a flirtatious smile, "I don't get the sense *he's* actually the fun brother anyway."

I don't know if it's the sake or the fact that I desperately want to know if Orion's interested, but I wink.

He smirks, fair cheeks blushing through his light freckles. He fidgets with the base of a stone bust on a pillar. "Right now, I suppose I'm a little less the *fun* brother and a little more the *envious* brother."

When his eyes return to mine, I feel my own face bloom with heat.

"For the record, a woman like you deserves so much better than Leo," he says quietly.

I chuckle. "You think so?"

"Mmm-hmmm." He holds up the middle three fingers on his right hand. "Scout's honor."

"Hmmm. *Got anyone in mind*?"

He laughs, covering his lips with his knuckles. Then, he runs his fingers over the statue again.

"Careful." I motion to it. "Neptune there. Roman God of Commerce. He's a John Flaxman Jr. made out of black basalt. Probably will fetch ten grand just for the head alone."

Orion takes his hand off the sculpture and smiles. "You really know your stuff."

"I'm *full* of surprises."

"You sure are." He bites his bottom lip.

"Sweet dreams, Orion." I grin and wink again.

"They sure as hell will be," he almost growls it beneath his breath.

I smile, every inch of my body warm and fuzzy from receiving some long-overdue male attention. I start up the rest of the steps giving him a perfect eyeful of ass packed into this suffocating cocktail dress.

20

Layla

This morning I feel rough and ragged, head thrumming from the alcohol, mouth dry, body sluggish. I remember Christmas Eve vividly, though. Much to my misfortune, my memory does not weave in and out like many who overindulge. No, I am typically left with the shame of my actions, often embarking on an apology tour the following day.

As I pull my skirt over my hips and thighs and zip it, I remember Orion on the stairs, tension thick between us, desire in his gaze.

Today is a new day. *Christmas.*

Though it doesn't feel right without a single decorated tree in sight. No string lights or presents. Just a colossal estate full of worldly collectibles and three people dealing with death in different ways.

I pull on my blouse, preening in the giant Victorian mirror over the seven-foot-wide bureau. I am not even sure how they get half of this furniture up here with that split staircase, much less the third floor. It's all so cumbersome and stately.

I slide into my heels and look at myself in the mirror from every angle. I think I'm ready to greet the day, and I know exactly where I want to start.

Orion's room.

I must admit, after getting the confirmation I needed last night, I'm curious to get to know the man through his things. I grab my laptop and phone and step into the hall. It's quiet, though I can hear chatter seeping up the stairs from the parlor on the first floor. Andromeda and Leo are having some kind of lively exchange, though grief and mourning don't come to mind. I thought that was the whole point of sitting Shiva.

I waltz to Orion's room. The door is ajar. I knock anyway. No answer. Judging by the aroma of blueberries and pancake batter wafting up the stairs, I imagine he's down there making breakfast.

I enter the room, eyes drifting to his now-made bed where he was when I walked in on his panic attack yesterday. He looked wrecked. I felt horrible for him. Thanks to self-medicating with my three favorite prescriptions, Skyy, Absolut, and Stoli, I haven't had one myself in a long time. That said, I can vividly recall how much they suck.

I set my laptop on the bed and awaken it. My various inventory spreadsheets pop up on neat tabs with various other resources like art auction sites, New Hampshire appraisal resources, and eBay, all running in the background for reference and estimations.

I wander around the room, looking for an appropriate place to start.

There's just one small window casting a soft beam of gray through thin sheers. There is just enough light cast inside that overhead fixtures would be redundant, a strange wash of yellow in the gray without actually brightening anything. The sun feels suffocated throughout this house. So much space, yet so little light. The storm clouds aren't helping matters. It feels like Christmas, like the description of it in an old Germanic folktale about Krampus, like there should be a fire roaring in every room, stockings tacked to the hearth, cider brewing.

I slide open the mirrored closet door to find a deceptively deep closet behind it. It's mostly bare, save for a few suits, a couple of dress shirts, and two pairs of dress shoes. On the shelves, some slacks sit, carefully folded with rolled ties atop them, shiny and constrictive, coiled like sleeping snakes.

I close the door. His room might be easier than I thought. It doesn't appear to have much of value. Nevertheless, I continue my search in an effort to be thorough.

I traipse around, getting a glimpse of Orion at his core through relics from his formative years. There is a framed photo of Jupiter, a painting of Neptune in a gilded frame, and a small diagram of the planetary alignments with their distances from one another. Pluto's still listed as a planet, so I know they're old.

On another wall is a series of photos of the moon, unsigned and unframed, presumably ones he took himself in a high school photography class. I try to picture him, younger, developing these in a red-tinted darkroom. On another wall, there's a wooden bookcase that starts at the ceiling and ends at a brown desk built into the wall. I imagine him sitting at it, diligently studying mathematics, perusing the newest astronomy magazine.

The bookshelves hold a variety of titles. Well-worn copies of *Catch-22* and *A Brave New World,* tattered paperbacks of *A Clockwork Orange* and *A Handmaid's Tale, Journey to the Center of the Earth.* Below it sits an entire row of Orson Scott Card, J.R.R. Tolkien, Carl Sagan, and Ben Bova. I suddenly spy a pricey little gem, a vintage hardcover first edition of *1984*, and a signed paperback of *Merlin's Tour of the Universe* by Neil deGrasse Tyson sandwiching a worthless thrift store copy of *Fifty Shades of Grey.*

I pull out the Orwell and Tyson books and set them on the desk to log.

In the bookshelf at chest-height sit a series of astronomy magazines and astrophysics journals propped upright by a planetary figurine and a hunk of something that looks like it could be some sort of space rock or comet. I pull it out of the bookcase to do further research. It could be nothing, but knowing the Stones, it's a forty-thousand-dollar rock hidden in plain sight.

I slide out the drawers of the desk to find papers with what appears to be handwritten poetry. I read part of one:

I can't read on. I feel an ache arising in me, one that is not at all professional. Warmth radiates between my thighs, throat so tight I have to force myself to swallow. I imagine myself as *her*, bound at his mercy, mind a clean slate, unable to remember the mess I've made of my life, laser-focused on his next move, his body eclipsing everything else that exists.

I snap a photo of the poem with my phone and force myself to move on. I continue to prowl through cupboards. I tell myself that I'm just doing my job, but that's partly a lie. I'm searching for more.

A stack of board games collects dust in one of the cabinets. Vintage boxes of Monopoly, Risk... games all centered around domination. I'm sensing a pattern, one that is unfortunately becoming an almost problematic turn-on.

While I'm kneeling on the lush carpet, a few decorative boxes stuffed beneath his bed catch my attention, the corner of one juts out a little, as if it's been shoved outward by a diagonal whack of a vacuum. I crawl to it.

What I find inside isn't treasure in a commercial sense. It's nothing that would be worth more than a few bucks on eBay in the best of conditions, but it's like a shiny gold brick to me.

Jackpot.

I pull a stack of dirty magazines out of the box, heavily worn, each with a glossy image of a woman in bondage on the cover. The one on top, a woman kneels, ass presented for the taking, a riding crop against the bare skin, the pink ghosting of the leather punishment tool already stamped on her flesh in several places.

I flip through the top magazine, spreading it wide across the carpet, gawking at the grotesquely pornographic images, each infused with its own flavor of arousing deviancy. My thighs tense at the sight of degraded women in poses of utter submission, worshiping the dominant men above them.

My face burns like a stove coil. These look like my own fantasies, ones I have only pulled out in a masturbatory pinch, perversions I've felt too much shame to explore in depth with others… especially Alan. He couldn't have *been* more vanilla. I doubt he could even name any positions other than missionary and doggy-style.

I flip the page to another woman, ankles and wrists bound by coiled ropes, bare breasts wrapped tightly in knotted lengths. Her reddened face is mashed against the floor, twisted into a look of disgust, pelvis high. Her ass is being penetrated by a glass phallus while three gloved fingers from the anonymous man's other hand are buried deep inside of her, massaging her G-spot. I know that expression, that cathartic pleasure overload, that grimace that looks angry despite the intensity of the pleasure. I can almost hear her growls through the image, the hiss through clenched teeth, the moans begging for more. Faster. Harder. Deeper…

My eyes drift to the box again, where a collection of toys sits eagerly awaiting their time in the spotlight. A hank of rope is wound neatly with the skill of a Boy Scout.

Scout's Honor. That's what he said on the stairs last night before flashing the salute. I thought he was just being funny, but now the thought of it sends a wave of warmth through me. I picture him diligently memorizing the knots for a much more nefarious reason than primitive outdoor survival.

Beside the rope is a stunning collar, one a rich person's large dog might wear, studded with faux gems and gold metal embellishments. There's a five-foot leash plated in a gold metallic sheen attached to the large loop on the collar in the spot where a canine's ID tag would attach. The sound of the metal excites every inch of my body. I look at the mirrored closet door, feeling my body buzz as I try the collar on. I adore the way it looks, the leash drawing a straight gold line through my cleavage, pooling on the carpet near my knees.

21

Orion

I retrieve the empty breakfast plates from the tables in the parlor. Leo and Andromeda don't even look up at me when I do, like I'm just one of the servants they've been so accustomed to their whole lives, people who exist only to make them more comfortable. I set them in the sink and look at the plate I made for Layla. It cools on the kitchen island, untouched next to a mug of coffee that's no longer steaming. It's almost ten. I should see if she's up and let her know it's here if she wants it.

I look at the calendar on my phone. Tomorrow I have a video chat with the guy who runs the FSU astronomy department in the morning and another with an astrophysicist in Big Bear in the afternoon. I should change and hit the gym downstairs before I prep for those, since I can't go for a run with all the new powder last night's storm dumped on the neighborhood.

I make my way through the house thinking about Layla last night, how her face flushed in the foyer when I turned the light on, her flirtation on the stairs, the palpable tension between us as she disappeared into her room.

I open my door, unprepared for what I see. Layla is on her knees wearing a dog collar and gold leash, one I vaguely recognize because I bought it many moons ago. Paid cash. Wore a hat and glasses in the store to disguise myself. The Stones had been in the paper enough already around that time with Leo's legendary yacht fail. I didn't need local media reporting my kinks to the world.

Jesus, I had to be what, twenty-one, twenty-two at the time?

I remember the next day, my then-girlfriend dumped me in a text. She'd started having an affair with some married humanities professor in Concord. While it didn't exactly break my heart, I stashed the brand new leash and collar in with my porn and there it stayed.

Seeing Layla in it now feels like a surreal dream, except that I smell the scent of her vanilla shampoo in the air. The sight of her on the floor on her knees in a collar like this awakens something primal in me and sends a soft, pulsing throb through my cock. It is a deep craving, this desire to dominate, to deliver intense pleasure through sweet pain.

Layla scrambles to put the magazines back, her eyes tearing up with crushing embarrassment, her mouth moving, muttering incoherent apologies, unable to form a complete sentence. She struggles to remove the collar, but my command freezes her in place.

"Stop."

She is still, kneeling before me with a look of sincere apology smeared across her delicate face. I enter, leaving the door ajar, leaning my back against the wall beside it, feeling the cold from the wood leech heat from me. I stare long and hard, feeling myself harden beneath my slacks. I need to choose my next words carefully.

Tears drip down her reddened cheeks, magenta with shame, dripping to the carpet near a pool of gold metal links. I thought she was beautiful before, but the sight of her like *this*, a devoted slave at my feet, steals the air from my lungs.

I study her, committing every curve to memory.

"Please, don't fire—"

"I didn't say you could speak." My voice is low but firm.

She doesn't dare raise her hands to wipe the tears. I lower before her, not a trace of a smile on either of our faces. I slide an index finger through the front loop of the collar, tug her forcefully an inch... *just enough*. She makes a sound, quick and fearful, and I retract the finger and grab the handle of the leash.

I stand and give her a yank, coiling the chain around my fist as she rises like an anchor reluctantly returning to the boat.

Her lips quiver, close enough for me to lean down and taste.

And God, do I want to...

I drag her through the room and twist, releasing the chain with her back to the mirrored closet door. I look at her. She knows what it means, knows to stay, obedient without receiving a verbal order. I can see her heart thrum through her cleavage, pounding beneath smooth flesh.

I return to my bed, lowering onto the edge, scooping up one of the magazines. She trembles there, a prisoner, uncuffed, in chains nonetheless. I let the smut fall open to a two-page spread of a gorgeous woman bound in the air by every limb, legs splayed wide, vulnerable. A man in a leather mask, baby oil, and a chrome cock-ring readies himself to flog her in the three pages that follow.

"Someone's been snooping."

She nods like a chastised child and blinks, fresh tears curling along her features like rain.

"You like what you found?" I ask, tossing the magazine on the bed, leaning back, knees wide like I'm about to get a blowjob.

There is a painfully long silence.

"I don't ask twice," I assert.

"Yes," she says quietly, head lowering.

The slightest bit of a smile tugs at the corner of my lips. My cock stiffens, my girth painfully engorged in the confines of my slacks.

"That's a pretty skirt." I nod at it. The colors suit her, dark tones offsetting the paleness of her legs. "Raise it for me."

Her eyes widen, her trembling fingers toying with the metal links of the leash near her waist.

Her eyes beg me to repeat the question, a confirmation that she heard me correctly.

But I only give orders once.

She releases the leash and reaches to shut the door.

I shake my head. "No. It stays open." I motion to it. "In fact, it's right there if you want to leave."

Her eyes dart to it as the sound of Leo's laugh booms up the stairs, a reminder that others are nearby.

She reaches down, grabs the hem of her skirt, and bunches it in her hands. She lifts, revealing a healing array of bruises. The fabric rises until it's a floral curtain hiding only her sex.

I shake my head. "All the way."

After a moment of hesitation, she hikes it higher, exposing her lace panties to me, ones the same amber hue as Venus.

I catch myself moaning like a starving man might at the window of a buffet. I study her for a moment.

"Lean back against the glass. Spread your legs for me."

All the way across the room, I can see the power she's allowing me to wield over her. Without blinking, she glides her shoulders back against the mirrored door until it is holding her weight. Her heels slide wider through the carpet, one slow inch at a time.

"You are… fucking gorgeous," I say.

She doesn't expect the compliment. It seems to relieve her.

"Anyone can walk in and see you like this right now."

She nods in agreement, but doesn't look at the door. Instead, her eyes stay locked on me.

"Does knowing that turn you on?"

"*Yes*," she whispers. She sniffles, but the tears have stopped.

"Are you wet right now?"

I already know the answer. The skin near her panties glistens. Her hips wriggle almost imperceptibly so that the cold chain caresses her through the thin lace.

"Yes."

"Yes, *what*?"

She stares at me. "Yes, *Sir*."

The two words make me hard as a fucking plank of mahogany. "Turn around."

With her skirt still raised, she spins, rolling from her shoulders to her forehead against the mirrored door, presenting that perfect ass without a single impediment between us beyond the one-inch strip of thong.

"Jesus Christ," I mutter. It's one of the most gorgeous asses I've seen in a long time, cheeks perfect, in dire need of my hand prints on their centers.

"Drop your skirt," I order quietly. "Turn around."

She does, drawing a deep lungful of air in, one so large it pushes her milky cleavage out of the neckline of her blouse. She stands straight, fidgeting with the leash, a dutiful soldier awaiting her next order.

"Take off the leash."

She follows the directive, her expression sad the second the leather leaves her skin.

"Put the chain in your mouth."

This confuses her. I wait, unmoving.

The sound of metal against teeth cuts through the silence. Gold links pour out of either side of her perfect lips like metal drool. I take another mental picture.

"Bring it here. On all fours, like a *good girl*."

After a moment of hesitation, she kneels, then lowers to her hands and crawls until her face is peering up from between my knees.

God damn.

"Drop it," I say softly.

She releases the leash onto the floor.

"That's a very good girl," I coo.

She stares up at me, her attention undivided. For a moment, we linger in this position, her perfect face at the right height for oral. If anyone were to walk in…

Her hair brushes me as I fish the leash off the carpet. I play with the golden links in my hands, the quiet clink of metal resonating between us.

"A collar is not a prop. Not to me." Her eyes bore into mine. She nods in understanding. "It's not a piece of lingerie to be worn for a cheap thrill. *This* means something to me. Do you understand?"

"*Yes, Sir,*" she whispers.

"A collar is a *reward*. For loyalty. For trust. This collar is for someone who is mine and mine only."

She nods.

I breathe deep and take a moment to remind myself that she is an employee here to do a job. What I'm doing right now is highly inappropriate.

"Stand up."

She follows the order, and I rise, too, slipping out from the thin space between her and the bed. I retrieve her laptop and carefully close it. I stack her cell phone on top and place both gently in her arms.

"Now… if you'll excuse me, I'd like some privacy."

She stares at me for a long time, a whole gamut of micro-expressions flashing across her face from confusion to relief to shame to lust. A smile finally graces the soft lips I long to taste.

Without another word, she starts toward the hall.

"Layla?" I lay on the bed, ankles crossed, dress shoes wiggling like windshield wipers.

"Yes?" Hope glimmers in her eyes, as if I just extended an invitation to come back. It pleases me to see.

But the truth is, I don't know the first thing about her. Those bruises could mean someone abusive was recently in the picture, someone who might not take kindly to a sexual overstep.

She's also an employee. My siblings and I are going through enough right now. The last thing we all need is a public scandal. There's no way I'd act on this desire without some serious forethought.

"Please shut the door on your way out," I murmur.

"Yes… Sir." The hope in her eyes is extinguished.

The second she's gone, my fly comes down. I'm plunged into sheer silence with nothing but an elevated pulse, a raging hard-on, and this overwhelming need to put the mental images of Layla and the collar to good use.

22

Layla

I struggle to concentrate as I bury myself in my work, still stunned by the complete ninety-degree turn my day just took into bizarre, unknown waters. I attempt to fixate on something… *anything* else. It shouldn't be that hard. Alexander Stone's mansion is rich in history and full of mementos collected during world travels. Framed familial memories adorn nearly every wall. I study one of young Leo baiting a hook on an aluminum bass boat with the seriousness of a trained professional deactivating a live bomb. Beside it hangs a picture of him celebrating the spoils of those efforts as he struggles to hoist up a stringer full of Northern Pike that looks like it weighs half his body weight.

A few feet away, there's a framed one of young Andromeda getting a piggy-back ride in front of the Eiffel Tower, bored, tired, and wholly disinterested in the amazing sight before her. There's another of her at her graduation from one of the country's most noteworthy cosmetology schools, diploma in hand, makeup elegant, black formless gown perfectly pressed.

Beyond that sit photos of Alexander, presumably. In the largest one, probably from the early nineties, his arm is around Carl Sagan's shoulder as they pose before a large commercial-grade telescope. Next to it hangs a landscape-oriented photo of a wedding. Alexander is the groom. The bride has a Viking-style braid of long red hair beneath a lace veil that goes all the way down to the grass. She looks like Scottish royalty. Her copper locks and green eyes bear a strong resemblance to Orion's. I assume she's his mother. She and Alexander beam, elated and tearful, before an outdoor altar buried beneath an array of flowers. The sky is dusky. In it sits a lowering sun and the ghostly imprint of the moon simultaneously.

Another two feet over, among several plaques boasting academic accomplishments and presidential accolades, there is another bundle of framed photos, one of which is of Orion as a freckle-faced teenager shoving a carrot in the face of a huge snowman, grinning from ear to ear. His hands are in big, puffy mittens, breath visible, cold air biting at his fair cheeks.

There is another of Orion in a suit, on a stage beneath a banner that says Aspect Technologies. He looks as if he's being introduced by… Neil deGrasse Tyson?

I can almost feel Alexander's pride, imagining him waltzing past this office wall regularly, hands clasped behind his back, beaming at his legacy.

I ruminate on the images longer than I should, each a glimpse into the Stone family.

I am envious of Alexander. Now that Danny is half a world away, I can't fathom having the privilege of accumulating such a shrine of parental accomplishments. It's my fault. I should have tried harder with Alan. Maybe I should've begged for marriage counseling or argued less, or pretended to be blind to his extramarital tryst. I vowed to love him the rest of my life, but after a few years of him looking right past me, treating me like a maid instead of a wife, like a nanny instead of a lover, it eventually took a toll.

I'll never forget the day I found out about Kayla, about the affair, about how long they'd been seeing each other, about how he had finally found his alleged soulmate…

And that it wasn't *me*.

That day, a tectonic fissure ripped open in me. I should have tried harder, should have swallowed my pride… not for Alan's sake, but for my relationship with Danny.

Alan asked me to leave. He wanted to enjoy the comforts of our home with my eager understudy shifting gleefully into the leading female role. Danny chose to stay. At first, it was under the guise that I had no decent place to go, that leaving the area wasn't feasible because he was in school. But a year later, he was entrenched. When Alan announced their move to Texas, my life changed forever. I wanted to die. I wanted my heartbeat to cease, wanted my mouth to reject sustenance, my body to waste away so I could blink out of existence.

I tried to curl up inside a bottle of booze so I could drown in a wet cocoon of peace. The night he announced the move, I even swallowed that whole bottle of pills along with it and hoped I'd never wake up. But here I am, still a fuck-up. I can't even die right.

When I woke up in the hospital on that seventy-two-hour hold, I knew I'd tossed my chance at being Danny's mother away for good. Alan's first move would be to weaponize my night of weakness to prove me unfit and gain sole custody. And now I fight this uphill battle just to share him every day.

Danny's a part of me, a human being I created with my own flesh and blood, a child I brought into this world with rose-tinted optimism.

I look at this wall of photos and feel nothing but envy, not for Alexander's vast wealth, or his mansion, or the original Matisse on the adjoining wall. I am envious of his *family* and the decades of memories he made with his children.

Alexander Stone was rich, alright. And it didn't have a damn thing to do with his money.

My phone buzzes, the sound reverberating through an office large enough to house an assembled Tyrannosaurus Rex skeleton. It's Bart Collins. I answer quickly, my heart beating wildly at potential news for my custody case.

"Afternoon, Bart." My heart is in my throat, and it's all I can seem to croak as I stand, paralyzed in fear.

"Hey, Layla. I was looking for you at the office yesterday. Ed said you're out in Rye doing work for a probate case."

"Yes. It's a huge property."

"Wait, you're not working today, are you? It's Christmas."

"I am." My heart thumps harder. I just want him to get to the point.

"Did you clear the holiday pay stuff with HR already?"

"Yeah, I talked to Ed the other day. He said he'd handle it. Clients are extremely wealthy and in a bit of a hurry to get proceedings over with, even if it means throwing more money at it."

"Oh. Gotcha."

"What's going on, Bart?"

"Oh, I just called to wish you a Merry Christmas."

I exhale, disappointed but softening at the sentiment.

"Thank you, Bart. Merry Christmas to you, too."

"Thanks. Kids tore through that paper like rabid wolverines. Bean is in heaven. She's been making cat beds out of all the empty boxes."

I don't smile. In fact, it hurts to hear all of this. I remember what it was like to celebrate Christmas as a family, to hear the shred of wrapping paper, to see the smile of a child who got exactly what they asked Santa for. Suddenly, I feel grateful that, despite everything this manor holds, an ornament-filled conifer isn't one of them.

"Any progress with Danny?" I have to ask. If I don't, I'll be obsessing over it for hours.

He sighs like someone about to deliver bad news. My stomach twists.

"I'm waiting for Alan's legal team to respond after the holidays so we can get a formal video mediation on the books for January. But, I gotta tell ya, Layla, not having a driver's licence isn't going to look great if that comes up during the session."

"You don't have to have a license to be a good parent," I retort, trying not to get defensive.

"No, but they're gonna argue that if Danny's in your care and there's a medical emergency, how are you going to get him to the hospital?"

"An ambulance." My eyes dart across the wood panelling and luxurious wallpaper all around me, finally peering up at the high ceiling as if I could will some higher power to intervene. Instead, it's just molded tiles and upscale lighting fixtures. No God to save my parental rights.

"And what about doctor's visits?"

"Uber. The bus. Bikes. I'll Rollerblade him there if I have to," I growl quietly. "Jesus, I'll probably have my license back by the time a judge makes a ruling at this rate."

"His lawyers are going to try to use the accident and the fact that you didn't comply with the requests to breathalyze as an attack on your character and back up the allegations Alan made about the alcohol abuse."

I want to scream. I ball my free hand into a fist. "I understand."

"I'll keep working on it, Layla. Try not to stress too much. I just called to wish you and yours a happy holiday."

You and yours? What *yours*? I have *no one,* and he knows that. I silently mouth the word *fuck* and manage a phoney smile.

"Yeah. Merry Christmas. Thanks for the update."

"No problem."

The phone clicks, and suddenly I understand this might have been more of a check-in to make sure I wasn't chowing down on a bottle of pain pills after the accident, a prescription I never even filled. He was most likely gauging my sanity during a difficult holiday.

Thankfully, I've been staying rather distracted today, especially while replaying the memory of this morning and my crawling on the floor like a dog, kneeling before a red-headed God like an enthusiastic geisha. I think about how exposed I felt hiking my skirt up, completely at his mercy.

As odd as it seems, I *needed* this morning, this tension, this distraction, this escape from my lonely home and the bitter memories it holds. I needed these mental fantasies in my head, like the one I had earlier about being tugged across this eleven thousand dollar imported office rug on that golden leash, wearing nothing else but a garter belt, thigh highs, and nipple clamps, like the girl in the magazine Orion showed me this morning.

I return to the cushioned chair in front of the desk, one where a guest in this grand office might sit to discuss business with Alexander. I stare at the blinking cursor on the barely touched spreadsheet for this room, but I can't seem to concentrate.

Maybe I just need a little break. Some time to clear my mind.

I pull up Danny's contact in my phone and push the video chat option. Hearing the dull gargle of the ring, I consider what I'll say when he picks up. Should I lead with questions about what presents he got from Alan and Kayla? Should I ask him if he liked the gifts I sent first?

As the sound drones unanswered, I realize it doesn't matter what I say because my son isn't going to pick up. After an embarrassing number of rings, I kill the call and head downstairs in search of a fucking drink. A real one. Something to dull the sting of being ignored by the person who means the most to me in this world. One of the fridges had Baileys Irish Cream in it, if I remember correctly. A healthy splash of that in some coffee and I'll be able to walk around the house with it in plain sight.

The sitting room is loud with simultaneous conversations among four people. I cross through it with a politely apologetic wave. Two strangers are there on the low stools next to Andromeda and

Leo, both men undeniably Semitic from their harsh features, skin tone, wavy black hair, and New York accents. It doesn't hurt that the older of the two is wearing a *yarmulke*, too. Brothers of the deceased, if I had to wager a guess based on their resemblance to the photos of Alexander and their age.

Leo's eyes target me like lasers as I scuttle to the kitchen. I hear him rise and follow me. I feel dismayed. It'll be harder to spike my coffee with him there to bear witness.

I open the cabinet for a mug.

His fingers drum on the island behind me. "Merry Christmas."

I turn and smile. "How do you know I don't celebrate Hanukkah like you?"

"Oh, please, I've been able to finger a *shiksa* in a crowd since before my Bar Mitzvah." He laughs. "Pun *intended*."

I shake my head and pour half a cup of lukewarm coffee, leaving plenty of room at the top.

"I had fun last night." He mindlessly strokes an island tile so softly that I have to combat a shiver.

Dear God, it has been too long since I've been touched like that.

Something in me stirs, a need to be caressed. A desire for human contact. This couldn't come at a more inappropriate time, me a middle-class employee of two unbelievably rich, powerful, attractive men.

"How come you aren't celebrating with your kid?"

"Hmmm?" I'm snapped back to reality by the abrupt question. I was momentarily in an abyss of lust, fantasizing about being used as his gorgeous brother's submissive little play toy.

"I said, Why aren't you celebrating Christmas with your kid?" He cocks an eyebrow at me. "Or is it…. *kids* plural?"

I hesitate, my mind drifting back to the mostly full bottle of Irish cream nearly within arm's reach. "Kid. Singular. He's in Texas."

"Wow. Texas? Is he visiting someone?"

"He lives there." The words kill me a little inside every time I say them.

Leo stares for a long time and then says, "Interesting. Whereabouts in Texas?"

"Austin."

"His dad out there?"

I nod and take a sip of coffee, ready to bolt out of the room and search for a stash of booze elsewhere that I can pilfer like an unsupervised teenager.

Leo looks at my half-filled glass and walks to the cupboard, brushing against my back with his chest even though he has the rest of the huge kitchen. He pours himself half a cup of coffee, too.

As if he were psychic, he reaches into one of the refrigerators and pulls out the Baileys. He unscrews the cap and smiles. He fills the remaining space to the brim with the liqueur and then tops off his own drink before putting it away.

He holds out his mug, and I click against it with my own.

He presses his cheek to mine, stubble against my skin, masculine voice murmuring in my ear, "Shhhh. This can be our little secret."

I sway a little, simmering in his intoxicating cologne.

"Uh oh. Thwarted again," he growls as he pulls away.

Orion enters the kitchen, and I feel the tension between the three of us wind tighter. Orion's green eyes linger on me, blazing with a hot flash of envy as he catches sight of his brother in my personal space. He flexes his jaw, looking like a work of art chiseled out of marble.

"Ms. Whittaker." He nods. It's the first time we've seen each other since I crawled across his floor and spat a gold leash at his feet this morning.

I offer a small wave, unsure if I feel more ashamed about how close Leo just was in his presence, or whether it is because my drink is far more Baileys than coffee while I'm on the clock.

While both men would be considered objectively sexy to just about any hetero woman with a *pulse*, it's Orion I can't stop thinking about.

That quiet, professional demeanor masking such deeply kinky perversions behind closed doors?

That is knee-weakening.

I can sense the juxtaposition of violence and tenderness within him, the darkness and light. He has a fire I long for, a flame that promises both pain and illumination in equal measure.

"Leo, can I borrow you for a bit upstairs?" Orion points to the ceiling.

"Would you rather use the office? I can grab my laptop out of—"

"That's alright." Orion's eyes pierce me with a gaze that could bring a large beast to its knees. He starts toward the door.

Leo follows him out, running a hand through his brown hair and laughing. "Uh oh, new-dad's mad."

23

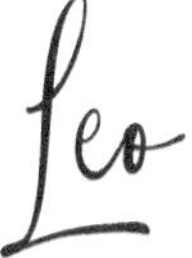

Orion is standing in the room already by the time I reach the door. I'm in no hurry. He can wait if for no other reason than to show that I don't just come the second someone summons me.

I sigh. "What's up? I promised Uncle Bernard I'd play a few games of chess with him before he left."

Orion looks distraught, far too serious for his own good. Fucker's gonna keel over just like Dad if he doesn't learn how to infuse some damn joy into his life.

"I asked Ms. Whittaker not to inventory this room yet." He stares at something on the carpet beside the bed, and I crane my neck to see what it is.

But it's just carpet. What the hell is he staring at?

I point to the drapes. "Open the curtains. It's so fucking dreary in here."

"Our father just *died*."

"And… that affects the curtains… how?"

Orion finally tears his eyes off the spot on the carpet. He looks emotional, all up in his feels. Angrily, he pulls the sheers back and ties them, careful not to step anywhere near where his eyes were just affixed.

"Why'd you tell her not to inventory here? Let's get this fuckin' thing over with so we can all go our separate ways. This house sucks."

"I told her that because I thought you and I should go through it together, see if there was anything we wanted to keep for sentimental reasons."

"Oh, God, you sap." I roll my eyes. "Seriously? Sentimental reasons? Do I seem like the kind of person who hangs onto shit for sentimental reasons?"

"I just… figured there might be something you'd want. Cufflinks or whatever. And to be honest, I really just…" he hesitates, struggling with the words, "didn't want to go through this room alone."

He points to the spot on the carpet that seems to be gobbling up all of his attention, but doesn't say anything.

"Fine. Let's get this over with."

I glance around, waltzing to Dad's bureau and yanking out a drawer. I rifle through some folded clothes, checking the brand tags for anything worthwhile in my size.

Orion searches the side table from the edge of the bed. I watch him through the mirror as he lifts a stack of hardcovers, eyeing each title before putting them back down.

I pull out another drawer and then another, tossing the place like a Gucci-clad burglar. "I'm not really seeing anything my size."

Orion nods listlessly and pulls a small photo album out of a nightstand drawer. "There's more in the closet."

"I'm aware." I roll my eyes and head into the walk-in as he flips through the plastic pages. I click the light. A small portion of the closet is women's clothes, Aria's stupid turtlenecks in cashmere and angora that she always wore during the winter. I make my way to the ties, picking through them like I'm at a rummage sale with a five-minute countdown clock.

"I forgot what shit taste Dad had in clothes," I chuckle.

But Orion doesn't laugh. He seems pissy and defensive. "Just… leave what you don't want."

"So much of his stuff is just so… out of style."

"He was seventy-one. He was hardly worried about keeping up with fads."

"So, we agree then?"

He doesn't answer.

"Being old is not an excuse to stop caring about how you look." I open his jewelry box and try on his high school ring, an ugly gold one with a giant, flat oval of ruby. It looks like a hideous prototype for the first Super Bowl ring. "What're you looking at?"

"Pictures."

"Oh. Wow, I never would have guessed," I mutter sarcastically. "I meant what are they of?"

"Then *say* that."

"I just *did*." We sound like we are young again, bickering over dumb shit just like we always did. "They nudes of your mom? Did the carpet match the drapes on ol' fire-crotch?"

Orion flashes a look of hate at me, a warning. "I swear to God you're on my last fucking nerve."

"Uh oh, I'm scared now." I fidget with a pair of diamond cufflinks, wondering if they'd pair well with any of my high-end shirts. I pocket them and pick up a gold pair for inspection next. "You gonna tell me to go to bed again like you did last night, Dad?"

I laugh. He doesn't.

"You little cock-block."

"Your mouth cock-blocks you more than I ever could."

"Ooooh, burn." I chuck a ring at Orion's head, missing by only a few inches. It pisses him off instantly and I get a rush from the venomous look he shoots me. He wants to tangle for another round, I can tell.

"Stop!" he yells.

"*Stop*," I mimic him in a whiny voice, just like I used to when we were young. "*Cut it out, Leo. I'm telling Dad!*"

Orion looks down at the photo album on his lap. "Do you fucking want any of these?"

"Why the hell *would* I?" I turn back to the jewelry box when I don't get a rise out of him.

"Because you're *in* almost all of them."

"No, I'm not." He's trying to rile me. He knows damn well that Dad was practically obsessed with him when we were growing up. He was an ugly little red-headed copy of the old man.

"You are. Look." He holds the photo book up, but I don't give him a single ounce of attention. I can almost feel his blood pressure rise from here.

"You can have her by the way," I say with a shrug, scrounging through some watches. I stop at a Patek Philippe. I'm definitely taking this one. Could probably pawn it for half a mil.

"Her *who*?"

"The… chick. *Layla*. Bit too much of a *prude* for my liking."

"Oh, so you mean *you tried and failed*."

"Pfft. I didn't fail at shit. You saw me last night. Five, ten more minutes and I'd have been in."

"You struck out. It's fine. It's called rejection. Happens to a lot of men. Now that you're *aging*, you're going to start experiencing an even higher volume of it."

I throw a cufflink. He leans back to dodge, and it narrowly misses his rib, wedging like a bullet in the dent of a down pillow. Orion stares at it and fumes.

I'm really under his skin now.

Problem is, after that last remark about being old, he's fucking under mine, too.

"Didn't see her end up in your *room*," he continues with his petty little jabs. "Looked like it was another swing-and-a-miss in the kitchen a minute ago, too."

He says it so smugly that I have no choice but to chuck Dad's high school ring at him like I'm pitching for the Dodgers. This time it hits him in the skull with a *thump* so painful-sounding even I cringe. I'm surprised it didn't knock his ass out. He's always been thick-headed, but this is ridiculous.

His face flashes with rage, eyes fierce, body tight like a pressurized pipe bomb about to explode.

"You… fucking… asshole!" He stands and tries to calm himself with a deep breath, but I throw another piece of jewelry, something gold. I snicker as he dodges it.

"What the fuck is *wrong* with you?!"

"Dunno," I grin. "I'm a hooligan, I guess. One of those guys who became a monster because *Daddy never loved me*."

Orion holds up the photo album. "I beg to fucking differ!"

That makes me laugh. "Why? Because there are a few pictures of me in a photo album by his bed? Gimme a break."

Orion hurls it hard into the closet. I leap like I'm jumping a hurdle to miss it, amused by how riled I've gotten him.

"*The whole goddamned thing is of you!*" he screams.

"Sure." I throw an emerald tie-clip at him, and he deflects it with his wrist.

"*Goddamn it, stop*," he roars.

"You know what? I take it back." I giggle. "I'mma fuck the shit outta the probate chick. If you want I can record it and send you the audio so you can jerk your tiny little dick off in some dark corner to it."

The comment stills Orion for a moment. Then, he walks around the spot on the floor like it's boiling lava and lumbers toward the door.

"I'll look through whatever's left after your emotionally-bankrupt ass is gone, you spineless fuckin' vulture."

"Awwww, poor baby. Go cry somewhere, you little bitch."

I laugh as he slams the door. If he isn't bawling yet, I'm sure he will be soon. He's been on his fucking period since I got here.

24

Layla

I log some ISBNs into a tab of my spreadsheet and pull up a site to cross-reference the market price for several first-edition astronomy hardcovers. They're so old they feel like they're about to fall apart in my hands. I examine the spine condition on one. Suddenly, something slams against the door, and it bursts open wide. I startle as if a SWAT team just came in, fumbling the book, nerves frayed.

It's Orion, fists balled, muscles rigid beneath the striped button-down clinging to every curve of them. He bolts toward the back wall, swiping a vase off a decorative table, smashing it into irreparable pieces against the nearby wall. He strokes a hand through his hair, then punches a framed picture of Leo on the wall so hard I can feel it rumble beneath my heels.

He whirls around, shaking off the intense pain, glass still tinkling to the ground. The paper version of Leo's face still hangs, lopsided and marred, dangling from what's left of the frame as if out of pure spite.

It is only then that Orion sees me, jolting back like he's just realized he's on the edge of a cliff.

"Jesus *Christ*!"

"I'm sorry," I say, though I'm not sure why I'm apologizing. I suppose it's because I feel I interrupted something private, even though he barged in on *me*.

"No, fuck. *I'm* sorry. I completely forgot anyone might be in here." He turns around, mortified. I could see it on his face before he turned. I can tell in the way he's standing now, hands on his hips.

"My apologies," he says quietly. "That was fucking childish and unprofessional."

"Leo really knows how to push your buttons."

"How'd...?" He cranes his neck around, curious.

I point to the remains of his brother's portrait. Almost as if to punctuate some cosmic joke, the remaining hunk of glass slips out of the frame and crashes onto the floor on cue.

Neither of us moves. I have to fight back the urge to laugh.

"That asshole knows *exactly* how to piss me off, I swear to God." He jabs himself in the chest with his finger. "This isn't *me*, Layla. I don't punch walls like some Monster-guzzling trailer trash little punk named Kyle. I don't *destroy* things. I don't get into fights. I don't know what my fucking *problem* is. He is just bringing the absolute *worst* side out of me."

He plops into his father's chair, a high-backed throne, tufted burgundy leather with brass buttons and embellishments. He looks mayoral, his posture outstanding. There's something about the powerful pose that sends my pulse into overdrive, a primal reaction to his confidence. He's composed despite the blood pooling on the desk beneath his hand. With all the adrenaline and anger, he probably hasn't even realized he injured it.

He follows my eyes down, finally noticing the blood.

"Was the argument about me?"

His eyes meet mine, but his mouth doesn't say a word.

"Was it about the kiss last night? Or him the kitchen a little bit ago?" I feel bold when I ask it. It's quite an assumption considering all that the two of them have dealt with this week, between the death of their father and bitter family rivalries apparently resurfacing.

"I'll take the silence as a yes." I flash a glance at my now-empty coffee mug and then back to him.

"It was about a lot of things. We have a… complicated relationship."

A slight smile creeps onto my face. "There's no competition, you know. Between the two of you."

His gaze becomes more intense. He leans forward as if he can will me to say more with his mind, but I tease him with the silence, in no hurry to clarify.

"Please… elaborate."

I settle back against my chair as if *I'm* the powerful one right now, a complete reversal from this morning… from crawling on my knees. "Leo is… attractive, sure, but personality-wise, he's not exactly my cup of tea. Between you, me, and this Narcissus desk, if I'd have had my pick of the litter last night in the foyer… it wouldn't have been *him*."

He leans one shoulder back in the throne, careful to keep his bloodied hand over the glossed desk as he studies me. "Is that so?"

Then, he chuckles.

"Pick of the litter, huh? You make us sound like a pack of wild dogs."

I grin. "Well, only one of us has had a collar on today, and it wasn't you."

I just stare into his eyes, mesmerizing in the beams of cloudy light oozing in from the second-story windows, ones that can only be accessed by an otherwise-useless balcony with a wooden railing.

"You make it very hard to remain professional, Ms. Whittaker."

My mind flashes to this morning, to his command to lift my skirt, to expose my dampened panties to him with his bedroom door wide open. We both crossed a very unprofessional line.

"I'd like to keep my job… but I am also human. I have desires just like everybody else."

"And what exactly is it that you *desire*, Ms. Whittaker?" His eyes challenge me.

"A man who knows exactly what he wants. If that's me, then he's going to have to *take* me."

There is a painfully long silence as he mulls my words over. He looks down at the abrasions on his knuckles, then back at me.

"If there is one takeaway from death," I motion to the room around me, the one we are both in because of his father's passing, "it's that life is short. We all have to enjoy it while we can."

"I don't typically make hasty decisions, Ms. Whittaker."

"I've gathered as much. It's something I wish I could emulate a little more in my own life, if I'm honest. I've always been just a little too… untamed. Impulsive."

"Wild."

"Yes," I smile and blush a little. "I suppose that word encompasses me best."

We stare for a moment until finally I stand and collect my things.

"Take care of those cuts, Mr. Stone. If you decide you want to try being a little wild, *too*, you know where to find me."

25

Layla

I spent today inventorying Andromeda's room, still distracted by my interactions with Orion a few days ago. The last few nights, I barely slept. The orders he gave me that morning in his bedroom still make my skin tingle at the thought of it. I yearn for more.

In the days since, Orion hasn't sought me out. There was never a soft knock on my door with a desperate man behind it at night. I would have welcomed it. In fact, that afternoon in the office, once he tended to his hand, he disappeared from the second floor altogether.

Still, the thought that he could come up behind me and growl an order into my ear at any second was enough to keep me perpetually turned on, pleasantly sparking every nerve ending between my thighs.

I enter the hall and smell dinner downstairs. I've no idea what it is, but the aroma is divine. I open the door to my room to change into yet another pair of dry panties before I have to look Orion in the eyes again at the dinner table, the buzz of perversion crackling in the air between us.

What I see when I open the door to my spacious bedroom couldn't surprise me more. On the dresser sit two vases, each stuffed with peonies, a luxurious red array from claret to crimson. Between them sits a six-inch box with a gold sheen, tied by hand with a red ribbon. An envelope juts out from beneath it. I touch the ruffles of one of the peonies, so soft, still full of life despite being severed from the root.

I untie the ribbon and pry open the hinged lid. I lift a velvet sheet to reveal a set of three incrementally-sized plugs, each shaped like a golden egg, the blunt ends attaching to stems that flare out. Each has a glittering ruby-like gem seated in the base. I know exactly what these princess plugs are the moment I reveal them. They're unmistakable.

I open the envelope beneath them and pull out the card, which is also elegantly red. I run my fingers over it to revel in the texture.

Inside, in a man's handwriting, it says:

I've given it some thought.
You're right. Life is short.
Consider these a belated Christmas gift.
A good girl would wear the smallest one to dinner.

- O

26

Orion

My dick hardens in my slacks the moment I see Layla enter the dining room in her floral skirt. It reminds me of the one she hiked to her waist in my room on Christmas morning. Since then, I haven't been able to get her out of my mind. The image of her on her knees with that leash in her mouth is one I could almost paint from memory at this point.

She takes a seat near the opposite side of the dinner table, carefully. The slowness with which she sinks into her chair makes my cock throb. I squeeze my fork so hard I feel like it'll bend in half in my palm.

She's wearing it.

I can tell by the heaviness of her lids as she settles against the cushioned seat, a subtle tell that one of the golden gifts is penetrating her.

Leo stabs his salad and smiles at her, speaking through a mouthful of lettuce. He never did have any goddamn manners. "How's it goin' up there?"

Layla seems a mile away when he asks the question.

"Hmmm? Oh... It's going great. I think you'll be *very* pleased."

Her eyes meet mine when she says the last word, and I feel some of the blood in my brain drain south.

"I'm sure I will be," he says flirtatiously.

She sits up a little, a hint of pleasure in her micro-expression. "This place is astounding. Absolutely... *full* of surprises."

The way she bobs an eyebrow at me during the word full makes my dick even harder. The confirmation of her submissively -- and discreetly -- obeying me without hesitation is deeply arousing.

The gift was a test. One that she's passing with flying colors.

"I have bad news, guys. I gotta leave Shiva early," Andromeda announces. "There's a problem with the spring line. The St. Patrick's nails came in. Completely the *wrong* shade of green. We're supposed to be shooting a social media ad spot for it on the first. It's a mess. I have to get back."

Leo and I nod. It's not like she was here to really mourn anyway. She's spent half the time talking about reality shows and playing chess. To be fair, she lasted longer than I thought she would.

Leo, too, *unfortunately*, though I'm sure it's quite possibly out of spite.

"Well, ol' Edmund Fitzgerald and I will miss you." I bob my head to Leo and enjoy watching his expression sour. It's a jab about the famously shipwrecked boat, a nickname I coined when he promptly sank his own. The mention of the Gordon Lightfoot song still sends him into a Pavlovian-conditioned *rage* nearly two decades later.

"Am I ever going to actually hear the story about this?" Layla asks. "I'm so curious."

Leo groans, agitated and sore. The event made him the laughingstock of the Stone family for years. "Just… fucking… Google it."

"I'd rather hear it from the source." The way Layla says it, I feel like someone is on my side for once. It makes me like her more than I already did. Maybe she meant what she said. Maybe there really wasn't much contest between Leo and me.

Andromeda laughs. "Oooh! Can I tell it?"

Perturbed, Leo grumbles, "If you fucking *must*."

"Oh, I *must*." She cackles and turns to Layla.

"*Oy vey*," Leo mutters to himself.

"So, back in the day, God, this had to be what, twenty years ago now?"

"Eighteen," Leo grumbles.

"Wow, okay, so eighteen years ago, Leo buys this super-fancy mega-yacht and decides to christen it. He invites all his friends on it for this big party. Hired a full staff. This thing was nice. From what I was told, it had *all* the bells and whistles. I can't *confirm*, though. I only ever saw it on the news."

Leo glares at Andromeda as he snatches a dinner roll and a wrapped pat of butter from a plate between them.

"So, that first night was... July third... right?"

Leo nods angrily, shoving a ripped piece of bread in his mouth.

"So they're out there off the coast in Mass. Everyone's trashed. The five-star chef this *yokel* hired goes to bed for the night and Leo's bestie at the time, Stephen, wants some *nosh*. So he goes to the galley to make himself a tray of fucking... what was it*? Nachos*?"

Leo nods begrudgingly.

"Too drunk to set a timer, this hammered *klutz* falls asleep with this thing cooking. So... would you know it, the oven catches fire while Stephen's sleepin' one off. This thing spreads through half the kitchen before the dipshit ever even hears an alarm. So, the bosun is scrambling around trying to put this fire out when this fuckin' *shlimazel* wakes up. Stephen panics and throws the rest of his drink on it, thinking it's gonna help put it out... like it's a glass of *water*. So the alcohol, of course, makes matters worse and just fuels it. Crew starts shoving everyone on the lifeboats..."

"Wait," Layla interrupts, "I thought someone said something about fireworks?"

"Oh, don't worry. I'm getting to that," Andromeda manages through a fit of laughter.

Layla shifts in her seat with an extended blink, as if she's relishing the sensation of her new gift. Subtly, she glances at me and I feel another pulse throb in my dick from our filthy, private little secret.

"So they get these guys -- and I do mean *guys*, it was an absolute sausage-fest -- onto the rafts. Fire spreads to the staterooms, one of which has an entire suitcase full of Fourth of July fireworks these doofuses were gonna blow up the following night." She seems tickled by Leo's misfortune. "The fire spreads to that room and… *boom!*"

"Shut… the fuck… up, Andromeda." Leo's so salty.

Without thinking, I rub the spot on my temple, the nearly-healed goose-egg where he beaned me with Dad's ring. I know it's petty, but the second I think about him hurling stuff at me from Dad's closet, any remorse I had over his current humiliation evaporates.

"Insurance didn't pay for any of it."

"Oh, *no*," Layla feigns shock, trying not to smile.

"Oh, yes. This was his *maiden-fucking-voyage*, Layla. Took him longer to *crew* the damn thing than he spent aboard, I'm sure. Dad had to help pay off the rest of the loan because he still had *years* left on the damn thing."

The floor rumbles as Leo's chair slides away from the table. He leaves the remainder of his salad for someone else to clean and disappears into the kitchen.

A few seconds later, as Andromeda's giggles die down, Leo returns to the doorway with a wine glass full of Bordeaux. "I'm hosting a party Friday," he announces.

"*I'll alert the media*," I say snidely, a quote from *Arthur*. It seems fitting considering the film's about another wealthy man-child who doesn't know how to grow the fuck up.

"Aw, of course you'd do something right after I leave." Andromeda rolls her eyes. "Where? Country Club?"

Leo points toward the other side of the house. "No. Here."

I glare at my half-brother, but I'm willing to hear him out. Alexander was his father, too. If he wants to host some kind of memorial or whatever, I suppose that would be a pleasant surprise.

"It's New Year's Eve, and I'm only in town a few more days. Figured it was about time I got the whole gang together."

"Wait... aren't half your friends in jail for cocaine and soliciting prostitutes?" Andromeda scoffs.

"Don didn't even get probation for the coke. And Drew got caught with a prostitute. Singular. Who gives a fuck? Like *your* friends are so much better."

"No parties," I say, quiet but stern. I'm not fucking making Wanda clean up after his scumbag friends.

"Fuck off, Orion. You're not my father, okay? He's fucking *dead*. Don't tell me what I can and can't do. This isn't even *your* house."

"No, but as his executor, I decide what happens *in it* until it's sold."

"Are you gonna be a fucking nerd your *whole* life?"

"Oh, come on, Orion. Let him have his little get-together," Andromeda chimes in. "It's probably the last time he's gonna see the house."

"Oh, now it's two against one?" I look at Leo. "You don't even celebrate New Year's in December. You're fucking Jewish," I protest. "You do that fucking... Rosh Hashana thing, or whatever."

"Yeah, but not all of my *friends* are. So because I'm Jewish, now I can't throw a party that happens to land on a gentile holiday?"

"No! You literally have your *own* New Year's holiday."

"I own a fucking third of this place, you bossy dickhead! You don't get to *tell* me no! I'm being considerate by giving you a heads up. It's happening. Come down and hang out with us or lock yourself in your little room, I don't give a fuck. But I'm having a fucking party Friday and that's final. Suck my dick if you don't like it."

"No, thanks," I growl. He's so crass, it's infuriating.

Leo starts to leave the room and stops right behind me. "Andromeda, make sure you say goodbye before you leave."

She nods and he disappears, leaving behind that stench of the rancid cologne he practically bathes in. Like everything else about him, even his scent offers zero subtlety.

Andromeda groans and pats her stomach, half her salad still on the plate.

"I'm tapping out, too. I gotta pack. Tryin' to get back in time to see my little Bubbaloo before Michael puts him to bed." She stands and squeezes my shoulder as she passes, mumbling into my ear, "Play nice while I'm gone."

"Take him with you. I'm begging you."

"No." She kisses me on the top of my head and leaves me with Layla and the palpable sexual tension between us.

I lean back in my chair and softly slip my tongue along my bottom lip as I stare at her. The silence is long, long enough for me to feel my pulse rise at the thought of being alone with her.

"Layla?"

Her name hangs in the air between us for a dangerously long time.

She rocks forward slowly, lids fluttering again, a gentle reminder she's wearing her princess plug. "Yes, Sir?"

"Would you like some assistance with the inventory in the upstairs office?"

"As a matter of fact, I would," she says, fighting a wicked smile.

27

The second the office door closes behind us, Orion turns to me, close enough to reach out and touch. Aroused, I press back against the door, letting the cold from it seep into me. It soothes my flushed skin, excited by the promise of something deliciously sensual.

His right hand slips to the wall near the light switch, his left onto the jamb, caging me in with his strong arms. I can feel his warmth radiating. He smells like aftershave and mint, a clean mixture that permeates. His eyes paint my skin like a fine brush in long, slow strokes.

"You're wearing it… Aren't you?"

I nod, staring up into his eyes, feeling small, helpless beneath his tall, masculine stature, delighting in the powerlessness of it all.

"Be a good girl and show me."

After a long pause, I swallow hard and nod, tingling with excitement from our bodies finally being this close. He holds my chin between his thumb and index finger, leaning down until he's eye-to-eye with me.

"No," he says firmly. "I don't want a nod. I want a clear 'Yes, Sir.'"

Heat blooms between my thighs at the strict order. Hearing him demand it like that makes me fucking hot.

"Yes, Sir." I don't blink.

His thumb slips between my lips, brushes the tip of my tongue, and presses my lower jaw down as his body slides against mine. There is an intense look, a fascination in his eyes. He studies my tongue like he is imagining how it might taste. My lips close around his thumb and I suck it softly. A broad, handsome smile graces his hardened jaw as he slips it out, glossing my lower lip with my own saliva.

"Naughty girl."

"Yes, Sir."

"Kneel down, Princess."

"Yes… Sir." I can barely get the words out.

He backs away from me, farther than I expect. He takes a seat on the throne and tilts the chair outward so half the massive room is my stage. He motions to the huge swath of floor before him, and I kneel in the middle. The rug prickles my shins as I spread my knees.

He stares at me expectantly in the silence, no trace of a smile left on that gorgeous face now. He motions at my skirt with a finger, ordering me to lift it again, like the other day.

I slowly hike it to my waist.

"All fours," he orders.

I bend forward, sliding my palms across the rug, back arched.

"Put your face on the floor like a good girl."

My heart is racing. "Yes, Sir."

I lower my cheek to the carpet, watching him as he stands. He walks behind me, inspecting my exposed ass like I'm livestock. He *tsks* his tongue.

"Layla, I'm afraid I can't see it yet," he says. My pelvis is hoisted in the air, a degrading position that excites me. I'm turned on at the very real possibility that my body might finally be used for his pleasure.

I hear him crouch behind me. I feel a finger hook through the hip of my panties like an electric shock after so much anticipation. It feels animal, this position. Primal. I feel like a tigress pinned in the teeth of her mate, waiting to be mounted with ferocity.

I feel exposed even though we're both technically still dressed. The gentle snap of my thong against the meat of my hip makes me jump a little, breath hitching. He could do just about anything he wants in this position. My pussy grows wetter at the idea of being penetrated right now by him. A finger, a tongue, a cock... *anything.*

"Take it off. Let me see."

My heart throbs. "Yes, Sir."

I start to rise, but a hand on my lower back presses me back down. "I didn't say to get up. I said to take it off."

"Yes, Sir." I bury my forehead into the carpet, resting the weight of my torso on it. I grip the lace hip straps of my underwear and slide it down over my ass, halfway down my thighs. I grimace at the floor, feeling a moment of humiliation.

I feel fear. Fear of rejection. Fear that he'll see me naked and find me unappealing. Fear that when I turn over, he will see all of me, everything my clothes don't hide. My C-section scar. The yellow bruises still healing from my near-fatal accident. Stretchmarks from where my body once created a tiny human.

To my surprise, there is a quiet groan of satisfaction as his hands softly worship the ass presented to him. It eases a little of my tension.

He likes what he sees.

"Jesus Christ, what a pretty little pussy you have, Layla."

I blush, my cheeks aflame. The carpet feels like a hot stove coil against my face. My body tightens with nerves at the exposure, at the close examination.

"May I?" he asks softly.

I don't know what he's asking permission for, but whatever it is, the answer is:

Dear God, yes.

I nod against the carpet.

In a flash, he fists my hair into a ponytail and pulls me to my knees, body bowing backward, shoulders slamming against his hardened chest as I let out a surprised gasp.

He growls against the shell of my ear. "What did I say, Princess? I'm not looking for a nod. I want a *clear* 'Yes, Sir' or 'No, Sir.'"

"Yes, Sir."

"Do you understand?" He pulls my hair until my back is fully against him, the erection in his slacks marble-hard against my bare ass.

"Yes, Sir. S-sorry, Sir," I stutter.

He relaxes his hold on my hair, but doesn't release it fully. "I won't force you to do *anything* you don't want to do. But I expect crystal-clear communication if you want to proceed. Understand?"

"Yes, Sir."

His hand drifts to the meat of my ass cheek now. He speaks in my ear. "Do you like spankings when you're a bad girl?"

I nearly choke on my own words getting them over the threshold of my trembling lips. "Yes, Sir."

"Good." He presses my back down, and I return my forehead to the ground, eyes pinched, ready to take my lashing for the nod.

There is a long pause, as if he is calculating the *exact* place to publish a print of his palm. I feel myself grow wetter still, thighs squirming uncomfortably in anticipation.

When the sting of it hits, I yip, a flash of blazing white igniting behind my eyelids, a firework, burning bright and beautiful for a few seconds before dissipating.

There is a quiet moment, and I imagine him admiring his handiwork, reveling in the intimacy of the raw skin-on-skin collision.

I hear him stand and walk back to the chair, my gut wrenching in disappointment that he stopped before dishing out another, an even harder one, which I surely deserve.

After a long silence, he says, "Stand up, Layla."

I follow the order, panties bunched into a twisted rope around my thighs. My flowery skirt trickles down my skin like a sheet of rain, covering my glistening privates and the tingling handprint on my ass. My hands clasp behind my back, head lowered in subservience, legs trembling in delight at the thought of being aggressively taken by him, bent over the desk, slammed against the veneer, and stuffed to the brim with his throbbing cock.

"Take off your skirt."

"Yes, Sir."

I pull the elastic band off my waist, drop it down, and step out of it, careful not to catch the points of my heels on it.

"Lose the blouse."

"Yes, Sir," I whisper, stripping my top off, hands shaking with every button. I feel like there is a spotlight shining down on all of my body's flaws, like I'm an imperfect understudy keeping the stage warm until a stunning star arrives to play the part.

"Take off that lacy little thong."

"Yes, Sir."

I peel it down my thighs and calves, kicking it toward the pile of clothes with my shiny peep-toe.

He circles and stops behind me again. "May I touch you?"

"Yes, Sir." My words come out like a desperate pant. I feel light-headed at the thought of it. "*Please*," I add, unsure how I can make my desire for him any clearer.

"Patience, Princess," he says softly into my ear. "I call the shots here. *Not you.*"

There's a long silence where nothing happens beyond the synchronization of our breaths. His fingertips caress my stomach, his touch feather-light. Waves of excitement rip through me as he grazes my flesh. I stand stone-still, captive beneath his touch.

His hands drift up, teasing my skin in a leisurely line up to my breasts. "Mmmm. You've got goosebumps, Princess."

I swallow hard, my body aching for more. The wait is deliciously agonizing.

His palm slides up, cupping one of my breasts through thin lace fabric that matches my wadded panties. My nipples are already at attention when he touches them, excited, straining against the thin material. He pinches one. My body shivers in one embarrassing convulsion against his.

"Did I hurt you, Princess?"

"No, Sir." A smile spreads across my face.

"Do you *like* pain?"

"Yes, Sir." I nod, maybe a little too emphatically.

He moans softly in my ear, pleased by my answer. "Well, Princess, we're gonna need a safe word then, aren't we?"

"Yes, Sir."

"Do you want to pick it?"

"No, Sir." Without thinking, I subtly press back up against his cock, eager to feel the physical embodiment of his desire. "I think I'd like you to pick it."

After a pause, he says, "How about Polaris? The north star, something that can always help you find your way home."

Of course, he'd pick an astronomy term. How fitting. It makes me smile a little. "It's perfect." Then, I add, "Sir."

He caresses my breast again and pinches my nipple a little harder this time. My head lolls back, knees wobbling from the sensation. I hiss a little. *It hurts so fucking good.*

He takes my earlobe between his teeth and slips his hand into my bra, pulling me closer with the rough, masculine grope. I gasp.

Orion unclasps my bra and frees me from the confines of the last of my clothes, save for my heels. I stand before him, naked, pliable, awaiting orders with an eagerness that has me drenched. His fingers skim my other breast, caressing, giving equal-but-different attention to it.

He steps around me to my front, trailing his fingers along my pale flesh adoringly, his eyes lingering on my yellow bruises and healing scrapes, his fingers trailing the faint red burn lines from my seat belt. I debate looking away to avoid the rejection I might see across his face, but all I see is what looks like profound adoration in his green eyes.

"You... are a work of art," he murmurs as he steps back to drink me in. He slides a large hand through his coppery locks. His words draw a genuine smile from me, one vanquished for far too long, squashed by years of constant defeat, of daily battles lost.

He sweeps some blonde hair from my face and presses his clothed body against my bare skin. He cradles my face in his hands, speaking lowly. "I'm going to ask you a question, and I expect you to be very, very honest with me. Can you do that?"

"Yes, Sir." A waft of chilled air hits me, and I shiver.

"Do you like to be tied up?"

I don't want to tell him that I've never been able to get a lover to do that with me, that I've only ever done it in my fantasies, of which there have been many. I fear that if I'm truthful, he'll shy away from it and tell me he's not sure if I'm ready or that he wants to be my first. So, I nod and hurriedly say, "Yes, Sir."

Orion pulls away, leaving me nude and exposed as he returns to the desk. He looks around for a moment and then hoists a green lamp in the air.

"Layla?"

"Yes, Sir?"

"Tell me about this lamp."

"What?"

He flashes me a momentary look of disapproval, a warning. "Layla, I don't give orders twice."

I stutter. "Uh, uh... I-it's just a standard banker's lamp. If I had to guess the brand..."

"I don't need the brand. I need to know if it's valuable."

"Not particularly. Not in the context of this estate. Realistically, it's probably worth... twenty dollars at a tag sale."

"Great." Without another word, he yanks the plug out of the outlet in the floor and violently rips the cord out of the base. I startle. He lobs the lamp onto the swath of rug beneath the massive desk and coils the cable in his hands. He points to the surface. "Come, Layla. Sit. Right here."

"Yes, Sir." Nerve-wracked, I follow the orders, placing my bare ass on the *incredibly* expensive mahogany piece. He steps back to give me more room, eyeing me like furniture he's not certain about the placement of yet.

"Be a good girl and spread your legs for me."

I hesitate for a moment, eventually following the order, placing my pussy on display. It's vulgar. The feeling of humiliation makes my nipples hard, my cheeks red. Mortified, I want to cover my face, but instead I glance away.

"*Wider*, Princess."

Fuck.

The way he demands it makes me even wetter, and I suddenly wonder if my brain is wired wrong, if something is crossed. I feel so fucking aroused and I don't really understand exactly why.

I hear the metal-on-wood of my plug against the desk as I spread myself. My heels glide across the rug as I pry my legs as wide as they'll allow. After a long pause, I glance back at him. The bulge in the front of his slacks assuages some of my fears.

He kneels and drags the tip of his nose across my inner thigh, softly kissing and tonguing the flesh there until he reaches the knee. I bite the side of my bottom lip as I watch.

Orion takes the torn lamp cable and loops it around my ankle, wrapping it around one of the feet of the desk. He repeats the action and tucks it through the center. A clove hitch.

"I keep forgetting you were a Boy Scout," I chuckle.

He gives me an *I'm going to make you cum so hard you need crutches for a day* grin but doesn't say a word.

He strings the cord across and ties my free ankle to the other side of the desk in the same fashion, with only three meager inches of cable left after he completes the job. I feel the dull ache in my hips from the width at which I've been spread.

He loosens his tie, his eyes locked on me. I must admit, the attention, the adoration... It's *intoxicating*.

He steps between my legs, wrapping his tie loosely around my neck, pressing his forehead to mine, and then tugging the fabric until there's pressure on my throat. Not enough to constrict my airway, but enough to make my nipples instantly harden.

"Are you okay?" he asks, this momentary bit of the considerate Orion I've known all week bleeding through the air of dominance.

"Yes, Sir."

He stares into my eyes for a moment and then presses his lips to mine. I kiss him back, grateful to finally feel his tongue against mine. His kiss is full of need, intense with desire. It takes my breath away and sends a ripple of goosebumps over my entire body.

I pull his hands down, knuckles brushing my breasts, cinching the tie around my neck firmly, a green light for more.

He raises them back up, loosening the hold it has on my throat and purrs, "Naughty girl."

He slips the tie off my neck and retreats to the other side of the desk. His hands yank mine above my head with a startling force, and I feel the tie wrap around each, a knot cinching them together at the wrist. There's enough room for circulation, but certainly not enough to wriggle out.

I'm tugged down until my back is flattened against the cold Narcissus. I hear him tie the ends of the fabric to the handle of the center drawer, cinching hard. I thrash a little, just to test the sturdiness of the ties. I'm truly trapped, helpless now. Equal parts panic and arousal rush through me, a lurid blend of conflicting emotions.

He hovers. I stare at his handsome face, upside-down. He strokes my hair away from my neck.

"Are you okay?"

At a crossroads, I can either choose to trust him or test my safe word, and I am *far* too turned on for the latter.

I pant, an instinct grounded in fear and excitement. After a moment, my tension eases a little, my body finally surrendering to its fate, readying itself for him to use as he desires.

"Yes, Sir," I finally say. I wriggle again, body bucking up toward the painted decorative ceiling tiles, a warm, eager toy for his pleasure.

"Good." His hands slide up, thumbs caressing my nipples, which are peaked and vulnerable. He follows my curves down to the jutting bones of my pelvis, forced up by the rigidity of the ten-thousand-dollar executive desk beneath me.

Jesus Christ, what am I doing? Have I lost my fucking mind?

"God, you're perfect," he says in my ear before he walks around to the front to survey his handiwork, still fully dressed save for the tie. His clothes make him feel powerful between my splayed legs.

He leans down, palms caging me. I squirm upward the few inches I can muster in an effort to touch him. One of his hands slips between my legs. His lust-filled eyes study me. I feel pressure inside of me, a reminder that makes me moan softly at the fullness of the gold plug as he presses on it.

His fingers roam higher up, brushing the slick folds of my pussy with a touch so soft it makes me gasp. I grind toward it.

"*Patience*, Princess." His words simmer between us a moment, his retreating hand denying my body the pleasure it craves. "What's the rush?"

The words soothe me like a hot bubble bath. I'm used to the few lovers I've had being in a rush to get off, sprinting toward a finish line. I've never been with a man who seemed like he has all the time in the world. In this exact moment, we feel perfectly suited, each evading deep wounds and outside problems for one carnal evening.

"Mmmm. You're *so* wet." Orion glides a finger up my slit, removing it just before it brushes my throbbing clit, teasing me without a shred of mercy. I dig my head back into the desk as if I can reshape the wood with my skull.

"You have such a pretty little pussy." He smiles down at me. "It looks good enough to eat."

He slowly pinches one of my nipples. My eyes flutter. I want to beg him to do it again, to use his teeth…

His fingers drag down. This time one slips deep inside of me, nice and easy. I groan like some ancient newly-awakened demon.

"Quiet, Princess. We aren't alone," he coos, plunging it back into me with an agonizing slowness twice more before adding a second.

I wish I could cover my own mouth, but my hands are tied, tingling as his own curl upward hard, pressuring my G-spot.

"Jesus Christ, Layla, you make me so fucking hard."

I want to beg him to fuck me, but all I can do is mewl at the pleasure.

"You like being fucked by my fingers?"

I nod wildly and draw in a deep breath as heat rips across my cheeks. "Yes, Sir."

"You're so fucking tight. Especially with the plug in." He thrusts his fingers again, and I writhe against my restraints. "Have you ever been fucked in the ass?"

My muscles tense around his fingers at the question.

"No… Sir," I say with a fearful hesitation.

"Relax." He slows the pace of his hand, dragging his fingers softly over the skin of my belly with the other. "Don't tense. It was just a question."

"I… that…"

"It was just a question. Not a request or a demand. Don't tense up." He thrusts his fingers deeper in me, and I gasp.

"Have… *you*?" I can barely open my eyes. His hand feels so good.

"Mmm-hmmm. It's my favorite." He nods. "But we aren't doing that. Don't worry." He slips his fingers out of me, and I feel loss and need, a burning desire for his touch. I feel excited. Maybe it will be his cock next. "In fact," he rubs my clit with the pad of his thumb and my pussy pulses, "we aren't fucking at all tonight."

My body turns cold, and my eyes widen. It was the last thing I wanted to hear. I suddenly want to backtrack. Maybe anal might not be so bad. This can't be the end…

He circles my clit softly exacting another moan from my lips. I twist and tug against my restraints, cord taut, completely and utterly at his mercy. "Tonight, you are going to take a nice long shower…"

My eyes roll back in my head as the slippery circles slow.

"You're going to take out the plug and wash every inch of this beautiful body. You're going to snuggle into your bed, and you *will not* touch yourself. Do you understand me?"

As he utters the last part, his middle and ring finger slip inside me again, plunging deep and hooking skillfully upward. I whimper, the back of the desk driving its ninety-degree angle against my skull as I reluctantly nod. "Yes… Sir."

"You will fucking come *if and when* I *say* you come, Princess. Are we clear?"

"Yes… Sir." It comes out as more of a breathy plea to reconsider. I don't want him to stop. I don't want him to leave me wet, dangling on the edge of an orgasm.

"If I find out that you touched that pretty little pussy for any reason other than to wash it, all of *this*…" he thrusts his fingers deep into me so skillfully that I squirm, ready to cum right now, ready to defy his order and beg forgiveness instead of permission, "is done for good."

My eyes bolt open, and my body slows to a standstill. The thought that he has enough self-control to deny my orgasms, to deny fucking me, sends a shock-wave through my being.

"Do I make myself clear?"

I swallow hard. *Twice*. "Yes… Sir."

He slips his fingers in again. The way his hand moves makes my breath hitch. I wish it was his cock filling me, stretching me, plunging into my depths. "If my Princess follows orders, I'll make it worth her while. I'll make her cum harder than she ever has in her life."

The threat of that makes my taut legs flex. His hand slips out. He steps closer, his erection touching me through a barrier of fabric. He grips my hips so hard that it sends a delightful shock of pain through my sides. His hands slip down between my ass and the desk, grasping both my cheeks so hard I inadvertently moan. I wish I could cry out or scream, but my mouth stays silent.

"You cum when I say you can cum."

"Yes, Sir." I feel tears prick my eyes, and I work hard to stave them off.

Orion steps back, and I want to beg for his return, but he doesn't go far. He lowers to his knees and strokes his tongue languidly up and down my pussy, taking his time with every inch, fluttering against my clit with the tip of it. I thrash backward against the desk, feet sparking with numbness, tingling from my pull against the cord. The drawer rattles against its rails as my body tightens again.

"Sir… Sir… *please*… I'm going to cum," I warn him, my voice pathetic in this vast room.

His tongue retracts, and I feel him blow a stream of cool air as I work to calm myself with deep breaths like some drowning woman mercifully yanked to the surface of the water for a lungful of air.

After one more long upward stroke of his tongue, I feel the restraint on my left ankle loosen and fall, then the right. I feel his hands softly caressing my outer thighs, sliding them together with care, as though he knows my muscles and tendons need patience after being stretched.

He unties my hands with deft precision, kissing each wrist softly before carrying them to my heaving chest. An act of humanity. An offering of thanks. I try to rise.

"Go slow." He strokes my hair softly.

I stay down for a moment. Tears roll from the corners of my eyes, and out of nowhere, I sob, flooded with a variety of emotions.

Shame. Elation. Arousal. Gratitude…

Without missing a beat, he wipes my face dry with slow, soothing movements. He helps me to my feet with patience, like a caregiver with someone feeble. He kneels before me, a position of worship, his red-orange hair at the height of my belly, beckoning me to touch it. I run my fingers through as he slips off my heels.

He rises, takes a seat on the throne again, and pats his lap. "Come here."

I approach, tears subsiding. As I stand in front of him, he runs a finger along the scar on my lower abdomen, then places a soft kiss on my belly.

"Thank you for your trust, Layla," he mutters sincerely, staring up at me. My name sounds so sweet on his lips right now.

He pulls me onto his lap and cradles me in his arms, my legs draped across his knees, unbothered by my arousal soaking into his expensive slacks. It is at this moment, in his comforting clutches, that I realize I haven't been held -- *truly held* -- since I was a child.

I wrap my arm around his neck and cry, shuddering against him. "I'm sorry."

"Shhhh. Don't be." He wipes my hair from my face and stares into my eyes. Seeing me. *Really* seeing me. He kisses me, sensual, unhurried. I faintly taste myself on his lips.

28

Orion

The days since my father died have been a blur, a chaotic scramble of probate paperwork, a whirlwind of company headaches, random outbursts from Leo, and devastating grief.

I miss my father. The reality of his death settles in more each day. It crushes me every time I awaken and remember he's gone. I feel fear when I think about where he is now, if there's a Heaven or an Eden, or simply nothingness. Memories evaporated.

Or maybe Dad has reverted back into energy, an invisible force reappearing as a brilliant star in the furthest reaches of the galaxy.

My only reprieve from the heartache and aggravation have been the moments I've stolen with Layla the last few days. Times like yesterday, when I cornered her in the living room while she was researching the chandelier. I stripped her panties, hooked her leg over my shoulder, and licked until she trembled like a leaf, while Leo droned on about something trivial on the phone in the next room, able to walk in at any moment and catch me tongue-deep in her.

Then, there was last night when I ordered her to shower with the curtain open while I watched from the doorway. I commanded her to masturbate while I slowly spun the faucet knob toward cold. Her tits tightened and her stomach flexed as she massaged her clit, softly begging permission to cum. I denied her release, edging her further into a frenzy, informing her I'll only permit her orgasm when I fuck her. I want to feel that sweet release of hers with my cock.

Then there was this morning when I had her on my lap, pussy bare, legs spread, knees dangling over the far edges of my own, the unzipped back of her dress against my chest. My hands were beneath the fabric rolling her hardened nipples, my eager prick alive, throbbing more with every slow grind of her pelvis.

I bent her forward, commanded her to bunch the bottom of the dress up so I could watch that perfect ass grind against my designer slacks. As her legs began to shake, I grabbed her throat, tightening my grasp just enough to make that beautiful face pink, using it to pull her harder against my lap for more friction.

I masturbated her with the other hand, fingers soaked, whispering orders into her ear as she danced on the precipice of an orgasm, lost in my touch.

The way she dutifully obeys my orders awakens something animal in me. The sound of her sweet voice begging, whispering my name, gets me so hard I can't fucking think straight. And the thought of being the first man inside her gorgeous ass one day is almost enough to send me over the edge myself.

During every encounter, I remain patient, despite the incessant, silent pleas of my raging erection. I haven't jacked off this much since I was a goddamned teenager. Every time I think about burying myself to the hilt inside her, feeling the erotic pulse of her orgasm rip through us both, milking my cock to its own mind-blowing finale.

I can't hold out much longer. The need to fuck that gorgeous angel grows by the second.

Though we have succeeded in desecrating my childhood home with these stimulating perversions, afterward, I hold her for a few minutes, relishing the intimacy of our encounter. While she seems to revel in my embrace, melting into me, I must admit my motives with this are somewhat selfish. With wounds raw, the devastating loss and grief teetering on intolerable, the affection and comfort are often for *me*.

Over the last few days, she has blossomed as a submissive, finding pleasure in the catharsis, in the silencing of intrusive thoughts, in the abandonment of worldly problems as she has embraced her willing, kinky nature.

I adore the power that I have over her.

And, fucking hell do I love the power she yields over me.

God *damn*, the hold Layla has on my mind burns like the heat of the fucking sun.

29

Leo

I snort a line of ketamine off D-cup cleavage. The rush of it hits me, the nasal burn, the crackle of synapses firing off in my brain like small explosions. As the chemicals flood my body, I can't for the life of me remember this bitch's name.

Tara? Teresa? Tawny?

I honestly don't care. All I know is I'll try my damnedest to get a blowjob from her before the Times Square ball drops. With lips that full of collagen, I imagine she's got to at least be *mediocre* at it.

I try to kiss her, but she plays coy and pulls away, wiping the remnants of Special K off my nose before muttering, "I'm hungry."

"Then go eat. I'm not paying a team of caterers just to stare at your fat ass."

"Hey!"

I smack her sequin-covered behind. "It's a compliment, babe. I heard you had those butt injections."

She smirks. "Don't believe everything you read in the tabloids."

Tia Maria.

That's her fuckin' name. She's that nobody actress from that Christmas series on Lifetime, shooting down in Boston. It's all coming back to me now.

Someone knocks on the door, and I sigh, irritated.

"Yo, Leo, are you takin' a piss or you fucking in there? I need to know if I should go upstairs and use one of the other bathrooms or not."

It's Stephen, my friend since Hebrew school, the only other non-Stone Jewish person here tonight. To this day, he's still my best friend despite turning my Trinity superyacht into a twenty-nine-million-dollar aquarium decoration. Stephen Silverman, Guinness record holder for the *world's most expensive plate of nachos.*

Tia and I suck face for a second before we leave to mingle. Stephen bolts in as I exit, and I shiver at the thought of the state he's going to leave it in when he's done. He's a frat-trained animal, never sober a day since he dropped out of Yale.

Don and Drew are chatting near the Saturday Night Fever-style illuminated dance floor I had my party planner acquire. Without even realizing she's gone, it occurs to me that I abandoned Tia immediately for them.

Don is wearing a sequin suit top, boxer shorts, and a top hat. At this point, I think he's more vodka than man. I can almost see his blackout approaching as his tongue waggles. He pounds his bare chest beneath the suit top to the beat of whatever shit the DJ I flew in from Vegas is playing.

Drew, however, came dressed for some kind of gala, but has since removed his tie and looks somehow more disheveled than Don does, and he's wasted. Drew has a drink in one hand and stares at the graph of his evaporating crypto portfolio on his cell in the other. I have the urge to knock it out of his hand, but I don't feel like replacing that or the glowing squares underfoot.

"Droopy-Dawg," I shout. Drew looks up at me, stuffing the phone in his suit pocket. He comes in for a hug.

"Oh, man, it's good to see you." He squeezes me too long and too tightly for the festive occasion. Just when I think it's an appropriate time to pull away, he stills me. He shouts with as much reverence as he can muster with a belly full of booze and amps blasting. "I'm so sorry to hear about your dad, Leo. He was a good dude."

I shrug it off. "Eh, what can you do?"

"I really liked him," Drew drawls. I can smell the cloying scent of the booze on his breath. A caterer brushes past with a tray of drinks, and he snatches up two of them, handing one to me. "Here. Cheers. To Papa Stone."

I clink glasses with him.

"*L'Cheim!*" he yells.

"That doesn't make any sense," I holler back.

"What?"

I yell louder. "I said, that doesn't make any sense! That means 'To Life' but the motherfucker's dead."

Don interjects, "Hey man, you shouldn't call your dad a motherfucker. Have a little respect for the de-deceased." He hiccups.

"But he *is* a motherfucker, technically. He fucked *my* mother. He fucked *Orion's* mother. So... you know... technically he *is* a motherfucker."

"*Was*," Don nearly drools on his shimmering jacket. "Was a motherfucker."

"You look like a *clown* in that blazer," I say, flicking his lapel.

"Where's Orion?" Drew asks.

"Probably up in his room. Little pussy's been bawling like a little bitch all week."

Don and Drew stare at me for a moment, as if I'm somehow out of line.

Don finally speaks, "Dude, his dad just *died*."

"Boo-fuckin'-hoo. Same here. You don't see *me* bawling my eyes out." I scoff.

"Yeah, but... you're kind of a sociopath," Drew says, smacking me with his elbow playfully.

"I really liked your dad," Don yells. "I remember that one time when we were kids and there was that, like, blood-red lunar eclipse and he threw a bunch of us kids from the neighborhood that giant party on the lawn down by the woods and let us stay up all night so we could watch it."

"He got me my first telescope, remember that? Real expensive one," Drew adds wistfully.

Suddenly, I remember Dad's wedding day to Aria. He'd calculated with precision and planned it for the next Selenelion, the horizontal eclipse, when you can observe the sun and moon simultaneously. I recall them reciting their vows, the setting sun in the sky to our right, the rising moon to our left, captured with the fervent click of shutters by several of New England's most experienced wedding photographers. I can see his face in my mind, his broad smile at the altar, the utter disregard of his vows to my dead mother a decade before.

"When's the wake?" Don asks.

I laugh and back up toward the throng of drunk, affluent people on the dance floor. I spread my arms out wide. "Donny-boy, you're lookin' at it."

30

Layla

The quiet knock at my door sends a bolt of excitement between my legs to the spot dully throbbing from all the delightfully maddening edging lately. I know exactly who it is. I know his knock well already.

"I'm sorry. I need just another minute."

"Of course. Take your time."

I imagine him standing outside my door like a sentry, a true gentleman to the untrained eye.

I glance at my body through the giant mirror above the dresser and do a spin to inspect my lingerie. Dark navy thigh-highs with scalloped lace edging. Navy garter belt. Matching lace thong on the outside -- I have already learned my lesson about denying him access to every inch of me. My ass is still tender where I received a bare-handed punishment for it. Three whacks on each cheek, hard enough to see stars.

My God, that man knows how to spank.

My earrings dangle to my collarbones, faux sapphire with cubic zirconias around the edge. My breasts are squeezed into a soft navy bra, microfiber to match the thin panties, scalloped just like the garter. Orion ordered the ensemble for me and asked me to wear it tonight, along with the largest of the princess plugs. How could I possibly refuse? The man has been edging me right up to the point of no return every day since I found the leash. I got turned on just sliding the hosiery up my thighs. Surrendering to him is addictive, a sensual drug I wouldn't dream of quitting.

I slip the only dress he hasn't yet seen me in over my head, tug the black fabric down, and tie the collar. I let the strings dangle down the slit in it exposing a spicy little slice of cleavage. I smooth the front and check it in the mirror. I slip into my heels and sweep the freshly blow-dried hair from my face. I grab my laptop and phone and finally open the door.

As expected, Orion is waiting there, looking devilishly handsome in a tailored suit, dark blue with gold cuff-links. He runs a hand through his red hair, hair so soft that the feel of it in my fingers drives me wild. He does a full scan of my body.

"This okay?" I ask, feeling a dozen butterflies flutter in my belly at the sight of his warm smile.

"Everything is… wow."

The response makes me blush.

"You're gonna make it impossible to get any work done up there." He motions toward the stairs that lead up to the third floor. "After you, gorgeous."

Loud bass vibrates the wood beneath my feet from the party on the first floor. I try to picture how many people Leo has crammed in to warrant the DJ I hear announcing something into a microphone.

I start up the steps, glancing down at Orion. "You have to promise to catch me if I lose my balance on these heels."

"I'm afraid you'll have to just use me to break your fall. I'll be far too distracted by the view to help either of us."

I grin, knowing he intentionally stayed a few steps behind to commit my ass to memory. "I wasn't expecting you to be in a suit."

"I did my obligatory round at the party to say hello to some old acquaintances."

"What's the vibe down there?"

"Mostly everyone's fucking high or hammered. No one could walk a straight goddamn line right now if they tried."

"It's New Year's. People always over-indulge."

We reach the landing, and Orion takes the lead, fishing a key out of his jacket and finally unlocking the mysterious door at the end of the hall.

"I can't believe I get to finally see what's in here."

"Sorry that I haven't gotten you in sooner."

"Don't worry. There's been more than enough to inventory in the interim, trust me."

"Took me forever to find the key."

"Where was it?"

"His jewelry box, of all places. I hadn't even bothered to go into his room after Leo... never mind. It's here now, and that's all that matters."

He feels around for the light switch.

"Jesus, I haven't been in here in a few years at least. Not since they put all the new lighting in. Aha..."

Suddenly, the cavernous space illuminates as if on a dimmer. Some of the bulbs dangle from ceiling beams, some glow from LED strips mounted beneath the second-story balcony, some bloom out of marbled glass wall sconces between massive bookcases, each chock-full of hardcovers.

My jaw hangs agape, the only possible reaction I can imagine to the sheer size of this room. The high ceiling is domed like a cathedral. A rounded wall at the far end feels like it has some thirty feet of windows from floor to ceiling. The moon is round and full beyond them, the night sky bathing everything outside in a muted hue of pale indigo.

The carpet is grape purple, the wood dark, accents all black or chrome.

Orion motions to something huge near the windowed wall on a heavy-duty tripod. It's a telescope. But not the kind you'd use to watch your neighbors fight from a block away.

The kind you could see God with.

"The observatory." Orion motions to the room.

"Ho-ly shit." It spills out of my mouth before I can think of something elegant.

"I know." He soaks the place in with a nostalgic twinkle in his sage-flecked eyes. "Some guys have a man-cave. Dad had… this."

"This blows any man cave I've ever seen out of the water. Love the purple, too. If Prince saw this before he died, he would've shot a music video here."

"Actually, there's a picture around here somewhere…"

"Stop," I playfully put a hand on his bicep, always stunned by how incredibly hard it is. The man is all dense muscle behind that flattering suit.

His eyes fixate on mine with a look of lust, of desire. I want to pounce on him right here, already distracted from the task at hand.

"If you don't stop looking at me like that…" I force myself to turn away. "Work first. Play later."

"You're right. We need to focus."

I take a seat in one of the plush purple chairs and awaken my laptop from sleep mode. "How do you want to do this?"

"Maybe I could do a walk-through and give you the specs of everything I know. That should give you a good springboard for the appraisal and coordinating with the Realtor."

"Perfect." I poise my gel-tipped nails over the keys, long overdue for a manicure.

"You sure you want to do this now?" He asks, running a hand through his red hair and cupping the back of his neck. "It's New Year's Eve. You could be partying."

"Pfft. Downstairs? Please."

"Down there, in town… there's a whole world beyond this place, you know."

I fight the urge to frown, stuffing my thoughts down deep. He doesn't know that I have to save money for my bitter custody battle over Danny. Or that my license was revoked because I launched into a tree and couldn't breathalyze without ending up with a DUI. Or that if I got an Uber to a bar tonight, I'd drink myself into oblivion.

"I'm good," I say, staring at the blinking cursor.

"Okay, well…" His attention turns to the rest of the room. He takes off his suit jacket and drapes it over the back of the large, purple desk chair. He puts his hands on his hips and sighs. "Where to start… where to start…"

"You said your father had some kind of specialty lighting installed. How about we start there? The furniture I can handle on my own. I'm just hazy on the tech."

"Yeah, good call." He sits on the desk, another bulky executive one that I'm sure had to be brought up to the third story with a crane. I can't imagine it coming *out* of the house via the stairs unless it was in pieces.

"This room was outfitted with a hundred-and-sixty Ketra architectural lights. There are, I think, ten Crestron brand control panels located throughout the forest-facing rooms of the house so everything can be fully automated."

My fingers fly across the keyboard, clacking at the speed of a courtroom stenographer to keep up with the dictated information.

"You'll want to double-check when you do the listing, but I think when the cable guys came out, they calculated this room to be sixteen thousand square feet."

"Jesus."

"What?"

"I think my old house was like eleven *hundred*. And I felt rich when we bought it."

There's a silence between us. Something hanging there, demanding attention.

Finally, he says, "We?"

I feel embarrassed at the slip-up, the glimpse into my personal life that I've been careful to shroud from him. "My ex-husband and I."

Fuck. Maybe I should have just lied, said it was a roommate or something…

He nods and looks away, but I could swear the look on his face seemed like mild jealousy.

Or maybe that's just wishful thinking. I take a moment to remind myself that this stuff we've done behind closed -- or open -- doors is just *fun*, a sizzling-hot distraction from the problems awaiting us beyond the walls of this manor.

"So, the second-floor balcony up there has floor panels that unlock and lift up to hide all the cabling beneath. The video switchers are on the lower level, along with all the touch-screen controls. Dad always loved fiddling with all the options. I'm sure he's probably got a custom setting named *New Years* if I scroll through the presets long enough." He smiles at the thought of it.

"I wish I could've met him," I say softly.

"Yeah?"

"Of course. I've been rooting through his stuff, learning about his tastes, picking up little tidbits about him along the way. He seemed like a fascinating man. Passionate."

"He really was."

"I can sense the resemblance." I point to Orion.

"No way, if you see photos of him in his forties, you'd realize Leo could almost be his doppelganger."

"No, I meant his personality. The part that matters. At least, to me." I shrug. "I've seen photos of all of you kids and your mothers. I can tell Andromeda looks just like... was it... Bambi?"

"Yes, Bambi. Like the deer."

"I don't know your mother's name. I just know she had that same gorgeous red hair like you."

"Her name was Aria." He snickers a little. "Apollo Range Instrumentation Aircraft."

I stare at him, confused.

"Sorry, little stupid inside joke. Something Dad used to call her. Used to say Aria was just an acronym for her full name. Never mind, it's a dumb joke." He stares toward the moon for a moment, presumably longing for a time when they were both alive. "Anyway, like I was saying, there are six or seven video switchers in here and downstairs."

He produces a remote from one of the desk drawers and points it at a bare wall to my right. A white motorized screen comes down. He motions with the remote up to a projector on the left wall. "Over there is a fully-equipped home theater."

It flashes on, casting a logo on the giant screen that says Sony 4K. In front of the screen sits a comfy-looking L-shaped sofa that I've only just noticed.

"Premium projector. Hundred-and-twenty-inch Black Diamond screen. Dolby Cinema speakers."

I click away on the keyboard, trying not to imagine how fun that thing would be to watch a *schlocky* Mystery Science Theater 3000 movie on, cuddled beneath a warm blanket on that cushy couch.

"When they were installing all this, they also put in nine touch panels throughout the rest of the house for climate control, lighting adjustments, security, yada-yada-yada…"

"Copy that. 'Yada-yada-yada.'" I pretend to type it verbatim.

He laughs. "Anyway, this place was originally just for Dad to observe stars and study planets, but the tech guys were somehow able to sync the telescope imagery to the projectors all around the house."

"That's got to be amazing during a blood moon or something."

"Yeah, or meteor showers and the northern lights. He used to throw eclipse parties for us kids and our friends. Used to let us stay up all night eating junk food and shit while we watched."

In this moment, I wonder if Danny will ever have such fond memories of his childhood with me. Or will I simply cease to exist in his adult stories, like I went extinct?

I train my eyes on my screen in hopes Orion won't see the tears forming in them.

"There's a function on each touchpad where you can turn the lighting red throughout the house, which is supposedly optimal for stargazing. I don't know. I never really saw Dad use it. There's also a day-mode that's supposed to rotate a spectrum of cold-to-warm light in the house as the day passes to mimic the circadian rhythm, but as you can see, we don't use that function much. It's always just been kind of dreary in here. The *real* asset is the telescope. Are you ready for the specs? I don't want to overload you."

"One sec…" I click keys for a few more seconds and then nod at him, ready for more.

"Okay. It's a Lunt double-stack H-Alpha. Two hundred and thirty millimeters."

"…Any idea what he paid for it? That could help me with the depreciated value."

"Forty grand. Thirty-five to forty. Somewhere in there."

"*Jesus*," I mutter quietly to myself. "*That's a brand new car.*"

"Yeah, maybe," he says, wiping some dust off the telescope.

I didn't realize he heard me, but then again, I *am* basically in a giant damn echo chamber.

"It's a sweet one. Double etalons, narrow bandpass. The B3400 blocking filter makes for some insane shots of the sun. It's got the Doppler True Pressure Tuning system, Starlight focuser, custom stabilization base, the whole nine."

"Is this an item I should put on the list for Ed to try to mediate for you and your siblings instead of liquidating?"

Orion shakes his head, melancholy in his expression. "No. I have my own. Leo and Andromeda barely look up from their phones, much less at the stars. Plus, this one is seventy pounds without the base, so it's not really portable. Can't take it out into the woods to view anything."

"Yeah, I guess with this many windows, your father didn't need to take it anywhere."

He shakes his head and presses a button that slowly dims the bulbs and strips in the room until the huge, full moon is the only light. He tosses the lens of the telescope to the carpet and peers into the eyepiece, swiveling it to survey the night sky.

"Dad had another one for a while, a portable scope he used to take everywhere. But after the first heart attack, he sold it." He pulls away and points to the acres of snow-dusted trees in the distance. "He said he didn't want to be out there, huffing and puffing in the frozen woods and risking another event. He was worried about dying alone."

A profound expression of gloom befalls his face, lips twisting into a morose frown. He stares out the window, and a few moments later, I hear the quiet hitch of his breath. He's crying, losing the battle against the dual wells of tears. He covers his face with a hand, embarrassed, but still his shoulders shudder. Wet hisses cut through the quiet like slices from a sharp knife. He can't reel it in, no longer able to keep all the pain hidden.

I go to him, press my chest to his, and hold him. He clutches me tight in his arms, like he may never let me go. I stroke his hair and pull his face down against my neck. His breaths turn ragged like he can't get enough air. His muscles tighten beneath my grasp. He clings tight and moans into my shoulder, a guttural sound of pure pain like he's trying to turn itself inside out.

Despite all of the things we've done this week in private, this is the most intimate of them all.

I press my lips to his ear, wondering what I can possibly whisper to ease the suffering, to soothe his ache. But what happens after we die is above my metaphorical pay grade. I have no clue what happens or where we go. Do we get a chance to do it all again, subconsciously wiser and more evolved? Do we blink out like a bad bulb and cease to exist? Do we frolic through some long, cloud-laden vacation with those who have gone before us?

I don't say a word. I just stroke his hair and embrace him tighter, hoping that he can feel my compassion.

After a minute or two in my arms, his breathing slows, our noses brushing sweetly for a moment before his lips melt against mine. I kiss him back, savoring the skillful slip of his tongue as his pain bleeds into passion.

I know I'm just an exciting distraction. A Band-Aid on a stab wound. But in this moment... I *want* him. I'd do *anything* to make the way I feel when he kisses me last forever.

Orion cups my jaw in one palm, the fingers of his other hand clenching my updo to draw me closer. He pulls back, lips lingering an inch away, forehead pressed hard against mine. He rubs my bottom lip with a thumb, raw need glimmering in his eyes behind the moon's reflection.

"You've been a very good girl this week."

The words make me weak, a bullseye shot for the praise kink I didn't even know I had until I met him.

"It's time for a reward." His thumb slips over the threshold, diving deeper into my mouth, pulling down my bottom jaw to peer inside its warm depths. It is a damp cocoon eagerly awaiting his cock, one I've only felt through fabric despite his exploration of nearly every inch of me.

"Don't *you*, Princess?"

As soon as he utters it, I'm wet, aching for pleasure, conditioned like one of Pavlov's dogs.

The tease has been delightfully agonizing, but I long to feel him inside of me. I crave the permission to cum, needing that sweet release after all this frenzied edging.

"*Yes, Sir,*" I pant, trained that a nod, on its own, doesn't yield results. "Please, Sir."

His warm mouth claims mine, an act of passion that excites my whole body. He scoops me off the ground with an ease I don't anticipate. He presses me against the desk, lips peeling from mine with the reluctance of duct tape.

"You taste so *fucking* good," he growls, unfurling his Windsor in a flustered flurry, ripping the tie from his collar like a whip. It whacks the desk and I jolt at the violent noise. He unbuttons his shirt sleeves and rolls them up. Heat rips through me at the sight of his masculine silhouette cutting through the moonlight. He blindfolds me with the tie, my remaining senses heightening the moment he cinches the strip of fabric.

I shiver with anticipation in the sixty or so seconds that follow, seconds where I can feel the thump of my heart, hear the rustle of fabric, smell his cologne. This is a thing he likes to do, tease me with the daunting silence.

Out of nowhere, I feel his lips graze my neck. It rattles me, this intimate contact. I feel the collar of my dress untie and open. His warm tongue slips against my neck, and I blush. It slides across my collarbone, dips down through my cleavage, and stops at my bra. I feel the tug of fabric before his hands spin me in place until I'm facing away. The slow pull of my zipper cuts through the silence. I feel the vibrations of its tiny metal teeth chatter in my skin.

His nose grazes the base of my neck, lips dragging my shoulders, firm hands slipping the dress down my arms and over my hips. I hear it rumple on the floor.

"*Jesus Christ*," he breathes in my ear, my long earrings pinned between the goosebumps on my neck and his flexed jaw. "You have no idea how much you turn me on."

I smile, mouth open. I hope he can feel how hard he makes my heart pound through his own chest.

"*You drive me crazy, Layla.*" He moans it in my ear, uttering my name like I'm his darkest fantasy in the flesh. It arouses me. It suddenly feels *real*, this raging hunger for one another. In this moment, I'm not just a fun fling, a random set of holes to violate.

No. I'm… *Layla.*

A hand slides around my chest, up through the valley between my breasts, until it is around my throat. My mouth closes, toes clenching. The hand tightens, and my whole body tingles at the danger, the trust, the absolute pleasure. He pulls me back against him, squeezing with a force that restricts my airway just enough to send a fleeting bolt of fight-or-flight panic through me.

"Remember the safe word?"

"Yes, Sir."

"What is it, Princess?"

I exhale slowly to still my body, feeling the slight wheeze of air escape through his grasp, a vocal reminder that I can still breathe if I expend more effort. My nipples are so hard they could pierce the fabric of my bra and jab into his flexed forearm.

"Polaris." The north star to guide me back home.

I smile, warmth radiating from my face like a space heater.

He rests his head against my temple. "Don't be afraid to use it."

"I wouldn't *dare*," I joke, my strained tone defiant.

The comment elicits a chuckle from him before he fishes in his pocket for something. Soon, I feel something as it unravel. Maybe shoelaces or a length of paracord. My hands are jerked together against my ass. The cord is wound several times around each wrist, binding them without a second's hesitation. After I'm cinched, he slips a finger in along the skin of my forearm to ensure the circulation isn't being cut off.

"Struggle," he orders. I follow instructions, writhing hard against the ropes. I truly cannot escape.

"Too tight?"

"No, Sir," I say, feeling a delightful tingle in my palms already.

After another twenty seconds of suspense, I feel a slow shower of kisses along my shoulders. He embraces me hard in his arms from behind, and his hand shoves roughly inside my bra, cupping my left breast as he bites the spot where my neck meets my shoulder. The pressure is hard, riding the line of pleasure and pain as my moan echoes off the cavernous walls. His teeth sink hard enough to leave a mark, surely.

One that says: *Orion was here.*

His jaws unlock, and his hands are greedier now, pinching and tweaking, grabbing my pliable curves like we are entrenched in battle, my body is under fire, barraged by an assault of delightfully erotic sensations.

My bra is taken off. Not neatly by the clasp, but by the violent shred of fabric, the rip of masculine hands. The straps pull, the stitched material clawing at my skin until the weakest part gives out. The gruff hands yank me by the garter until I once again face him, the elastic snapping my skin with a stinging *thwack* as he releases. A hooked finger plucks one of the straps so hard the clasp tears through the hosiery.

The aggressive war waged against my lingerie is followed by a languid pause for tenderness, a switch in gears, an interlude of adoration. In my ear, he utters soft words of appreciation. For my body. For my trust. He French kisses me so deeply and slowly and patiently that my toes curl, the knuckles cracking inside my pumps.

With his mouth still entangled with mine, his hand eases beneath the elastic of my panties, a finger encircling my clit before slipping inside of me with ease. I tremble against his skilled hands.

A moment later, he rubs the wet finger against my aroused nipples. At first, it's slippery and hot, soon cold from the stream of cool air he blows on them. My areolas warm again as his tongue swirls each, sucking them clean with a satisfied moan. He draws one between his teeth, the slight pressure making me squirm against my restraints.

He dips his finger in me again and drags it across my bottom lip, slipping it inside. I suck it clean, my mouth extending a silent invitation to replace his finger with something thicker. He groans as if he can read my mind, as if he can hear my brain's plea.

His other hand burrows into my hair, gripping tight. The finger on my tongue slides deeper, toward the back of my throat. I fight the urge to gag as his knuckles brush my lips.

"Uh-uh. Keep that beautiful mouth open, Princess," he orders, lifting me a little by my hair as he slips his fingers back out to the tip of my tongue. He smudges my own saliva across my lips. His other hand clenches, and I feel my scalp light up, sending exhilarating chemicals through me.

"I have something else I want to put in that pretty little mouth of yours," he growls into my ear, pulling me by my blonde locks.

"Yes, Sir." My voice is breathy, heart slamming against the walls of my chest. I feel my pussy pulse at the thought of finally getting to taste him.

"I want you to choke on my cock, Princess."

"Yes, Sir," I say with a smile. I've been waiting *days* for this.

"Snap your fingers."

The order confuses me. I tilt my head like a dog hearing a strange noise.

"I don't give orders *twice*," he growls sternly, clenching my hair harder. I feel wetter every single time he does it.

I snap my fingers behind my back.

"Good," Orion says softly and releases my hair. He drags the hand along my skin until it cups one of my breasts. His lips brush the shell of my ear as he thumbs the excited nipple. "You can't very well use your safe word with your mouth full, can you?"

31

Orion

I pull the chair away from the desk. I will not have my view obstructed by a single fucking thing. I tug Layla by the sexy little garter belt a few feet and make her stand there in her blindfold.

I don't think I've ever been this hard in my entire fucking life. Thank God I jerked off twice this afternoon, otherwise seeing her like this would throw me over the edge. She's so vulnerable right now, desperate for release after days of torturous edging.

I strip off my shirt, draping it across the back of the chair. I kick the shoes off next, setting them out of the way. I slide off my belt, fold it in half, and snap it near her ear. She jumps, surprised, perfect breasts bouncing at the crack of the leather.

"No belt today, Princess," I growl in her ear as I toss it on the floor. "Only rewards for this good girl."

I reach behind and give her gemstone plug a firm push in, a gentle reminder of its existence. She moans at the pressure, melting against me from the fullness. I can't even fathom how amazing she is going to feel around my cock with that occupying so much space inside of her. I want her tight and warm and wet, stuffed to the hilt from each direction.

I leave her standing there while I remove my slacks and fold them next to my shoes, tossing my boxers atop them. It feels so bizarre to have made her so wet, made her moan and squirm, brought her so close to so many orgasms, and yet this is the first time I've been naked in front of her. I feel oddly exposed, but it doesn't seem to dampen my erection. I've been waiting for this moment since I saw her in the collar on Christmas morning.

I sit in the chair and drink her in for a long time, allowing my nerves to calm while heightening her anticipation.

"Get on your knees."

She lowers slowly to the purple carpet beneath her, the moon bathing her curves in a way that makes her look like a marble sculpture, something beautiful on display for the whole world to see.

"Come suck this cock like a good girl."

"Yes, Sir." She crawls closer toward my voice until her nipples brush my knee, and she lets out a little excited gasp at the contact.

My cock is painfully engorged, a battering ram with orders to pound. As she licks her lips, my fingers thread through her once-elegant updo and guide them to the throbbing head. I press her down slowly, stuffing my girth into the small, hot tunnel of her mouth, not letting go until I have bottomed out at the edge of her throat. I groan watching her body squirm, the slight panic that comes from a restricted airway, the body's natural instinct for survival. I draw her head completely off it, watching the lines of drool drape from her mouth like wet streamers across my thighs.

"God damn, Layla," I growl, louder now, zero fucks given about the houseful of people below. "You okay?"

The emphatic nod and smile flashing beneath my tie says it before her mouth can. "Yes, Sir."

I smile even though she can't see it. I pinch a nipple until she gasps and slap the side of her tit and she yips at the gruff sensation. She blindly seeks her way back to my cock again. When I finally allow her within reach, she draws the angry-looking head into her mouth greedily. I slide her head back down on it, feeling the resistance of the back of her throat and pushing just past the barrier with a growl. Her ass rises, fingers flailing behind her back like frantic sign language. I watch closely, but a snap doesn't come.

I roar loud and guttural as I pull her head off my saliva-drenched cock. She smirks with pride, pleased to elicit such an animal noise from me.

Jesus Christ, she is so fucking hot.

I can't take it anymore. Goddammit, I *need* to be inside her. Like, fucking… *yesterday*.

My hand slips around her throat gently, and I lift. "Oooh, you're gonna fuckin' get it now."

The look on her grinning face is priceless. Like I just promised her a gift.

I grab the waistband of her panties and shred the torturous fabric barrier from her, granting myself full access to that inviting little pussy, one wetter than I've ever seen before. My dick pulses at the thought of how it'll feel buried inside.

I leave her there, breaths heaving as I dig through my folded slacks and pull out a foil square, ripping it open with my teeth, and eagerly rolling it on my rigid dick.

I press her ass against the edge of the desk, just enough for her to balance. I tug the blindfold off her eyes, down to her neck. She swallows hard, and I wrench the looped tie toward me as leverage so I can taste her tongue.

After the kiss, she studies me with a steely gaze, lips open and pouty, irritated from friction. My fingers pulse against the flared end of her gemstone plug, a gentle simulation of what it would be like if that perfect ass were being fucked. She studies me, naked and virile, her eyes following the hard cuts and deep valleys between my muscles to the girthy cock awaiting her.

"Spread your legs for me, Princess," I order with a nod.

She obeys, sliding them wide. I hold the looped tie around her neck like horse reigns with one hand and lean back for a better look at that wet, gorgeous cunt. I guide the head of myself against the tight slit I so desperately desire to be inside. I try to press inward, increasing the pressure, changing the angle, but her pussy's tight and the plug is large. My width feels like too much for such a little thing. I feel like I'm going to break her.

She watches intently for a moment before her eyes flit up to mine. I feel her pelvis rock, her back arch, her muscles struggling to relax enough to accommodate my size.

I release the tie and grab her ass, using it to drive her angled pelvis onto it. She leans back against her tied hands and gasps as the crown reluctantly slips past the threshold of her pussy. I groan, unable to be delicate about the task any longer. I can't help myself. I want *more*. I want *all* of her.

I plunge deep and we moan together, in unison, as I fill her with my cock, unable to stop until I've slid as deep as I can go.

"*Jesus Christ, Layla, you feel so fucking good,*" I whisper, buried to the hilt.

I kiss her deeply while I thrust again, only noticing the sheen of sweat on her once I bottom out.

Every nerve in my body feels awakened as I still myself. Being inside her is like standing in a raging fire, her body scorching Earth wherever she touches. I'll carry the ashes from tonight with me for the rest of my life.

I massage her clit as I pump again, her body starting to relax and allow me in. Her stifled moans escape more with every thrust of my hips until she is full-blown groaning into the night air.

I don't know how much longer I can last. Her pleasure-ridden expression, the divine grip of her pussy, the bounce of her tits, and the friction of the plug through her walls are a combo teetering me on the brink.

I pull out, needing a moment to reel myself back, wanting to satisfy her first. After all the edging, she's earned it.

I pull her with the tie around her neck through the room, over to the sofa. I sit on the very edge of it and admire her body as she stands before me in nothing but those fuck-me pumps, thigh highs, and my tie.

"Come, Princess." I stroke my bare thighs, an invitation to resume.

"I thought I'd never hear those words." She grins.

I chuckle, a moment of levity cutting through the darkness.

She traipses toward me, and I grab the backs of her thighs roughly. She lowers onto me, legs flexed as I guide her down until she is impaled on my dick. As our bodies meld, she gasps again. Trembling in my hands, she raises and grinds. I massage her clit to give her the friction she needs as she rides me.

"Sir," she pants, sounding like she is about to cry.

"Yes, Princess?" I hold her waist, grinding small circles up against her with my pelvis, waiting for the question.

"Please, Sir. May I cum?"

The question turns me on. I can hear how close she is in the shake of her voice. I feel my cock flex inside of her at the thought of it.

I caress the sides of her face, her bottom lip. Despite the disheveled hair and my tie draped across her sweaty skin like a lopsided necklace, she looks so goddamned beautiful.

I kiss her gently, caress an aroused nipple, and then coo into her ear, "Yes, Princess. You may."

A relieved smile graces her delicate face, eyes glimmering with gratitude. She grinds again, tightening around me, gripping my cock like a fist. I thrust up into her with a steady rhythm.

Even the brilliant display of fireworks exploding on the back lawn isn't enough to pull my focus off the stunning image of her body, desperate to achieve its long-awaited climax.

Drunk men cackle with laughter several stories below the observatory windows, the commotion occasionally cutting dully through the glass. Her eyes are lost, rolled back, bouncing breasts painted by the vibrant array of colors outside. My hand finds her throat, squeezing just enough to heighten everything. I grit my teeth, struggling to stave off my own orgasm.

Her scream rips through the air, rivaling the violence of the explosions in the velvet night sky. It's followed by a seizure, one that takes over her entire body. I smile and release her throat. Her legs soften around my thighs, torso heaving with every breath. I roll one of her pebbled nipples between my fingers and her pussy pulses, a feeling that nearly tips me over the edge into my own abyss.

With her body relaxing, so pliable in my grasp, I grab her hips and pound myself up into her, my need for her depths consuming me.

"Orion…"

The way she utters my name in this moment makes me feel alive. She feels so goddamn good that it takes mere seconds to meet her in oblivion. I bellow, a wail that sounds like mourning. I cling to Layla, my arms pulling her close, my sheathed, spurting cock enveloped.

I cradle her shaking, malleable body against my chest until our breathing slows. I reach around and untie the hank of paracord around her wrists, slipping the fibrous loops over her hands to free them. I caress the rings on her wrists, encouraging a feeling of normalcy to return. She wraps her arms around my neck, her face nestling into the crook. The only sounds she's capable of are deep breaths and loud swallows. I stroke her back softly, my spent cock still crowded by the plug. I pull out and discard the condom, drawing her body back against mine. Her heart thuds against my chest, our sweat blending.

I cup her face lovingly in my hands, both of us slowly descending from our intense orbit in outer space. "Are you okay?"

Tears pour from her beautiful eyes as she finds the will to focus on me, lip quivering as much as her voice. "*Yes.*"

I clutch her to my chest as another barrage of fireworks pops. Her fingers rediscover their need to stroke my hair. She judders, sobbing from the massive dump of chemicals in her body, *The Drop* as some people call it.

Through the tears, I kiss her, softly, deeply, with a tenderness I didn't know I was capable of.

32

Layla

Orion spent the night taking care of me, covering every inch of my aggravated skin with affection, whispering tender words of gratitude, each a reminder that, for once, I am appreciated. Valued. Desired.

After I watched the fireworks in his arms, he brought me water, begged me to drink, fed me fresh grapes as a peasant would a queen. After, he showered me, shampooed my scalp, and scrubbed fluids from our bodies. The sweat, the spit, the tears…

He toweled my hair with reverence, wrapped me in a silk robe, and carried me to his room. He draped me on the center of his lush comforter and lay by my side in the moonlight.

This is perhaps my favorite part of our intimate sessions, the care I receive after we partake in these deviant pleasures.

He touches my collarbones softly and asks, "Would you like to sleep with me tonight?"

"I… don't think that's wise. Leo might catch me sneaking out in the morning. I'm here to do a job, after all. Probably wouldn't look right. If that got back to the guys at the firm, I could lose my job."

"Fucking *Leo*." He says his brother's name with a level of anger I can tell spans decades.

He unties my robe and rubs my skin beneath, brushing my breasts, my ribs, my thighs. In the din of the moonlight, his hand lingers on the scar just above my pubic hair, one that goes nearly from hip to hip straight across, the only visible proof that I once brought a life into this world.

Orion's finger traces the long trough. His quiet voice cuts through the silence of the night. "Boy or a girl?"

Tears fill my eyes, and I press my head back into his down pillow as they roll toward my ears.

"*Polaris*," I whisper before tying the robe closed. Without another word, I retreat across the hall to my own room and cry myself to sleep in the darkness.

33

"Yes. Whittaker. Two Ts. First name L-A-Y-L-A. Mmm-hmmm. Okay. Thank you. You can email your findings to the… oh, a *mailing* address? A courier? Yes… Sure… that makes sense. I'll email you all the info I have. Good. Yes, absolutely, I'll take what you can get."

I bid the voice on the other end of the line a farewell, hanging up my cell and tossing it onto the desk. A piece of furniture on which I have done filthy things to Layla's body.

This morning, as my coffee grew cold, my curiosity succeeded in besting me. I charged headfirst into an unsuccessful internet search in an effort to learn more about the Goddess in my employ. After all her body's endured at my hands, the utterance of her safe word over a simple question left me confused, stirring in the dark for hours. The second she left, I felt rejected. As if the rest of our night might've meant nothing other than clearing some pipes for her. Routine maintenance. A fun fuck.

To me, it was intimate.

To me, it *meant* something.

She has allowed me enough trust to bind her, to restrict her air, to dominate her while we're apart, to inflict real pain...

But not enough trust to *know* her.

I felt awash with shame as I found myself typing her name into my browser first thing this morning, searching for her social media, plundering the internet for news articles or related obituaries to explain her reaction. Her digital footprint is enviably small, her Facebook set to private. No Insta, Bluesky, or Truth Social. The only things I could find were public records. Her on the New Hampshire Board of Appraisers, divorce filings to a one Alan Whittaker, her two-line bio on the Collins, Collins, and Collins site, and a brief mention in the Concord Monitor about her car accident paired with a picture of the wreckage that made my blood nearly freeze in my veins.

That drop... the severe curve in the road... the skid marks of rubber forever on the blacktop...

She shouldn't have survived.

Her car was suspended in a tree over a perilous ravine. If she had swerved a second earlier or later, she'd be dead.

The photo is a reminder of life's fragility, a realization that tomorrow isn't promised to a single fucking one of us.

That was why I had to make the call. I care about her. I don't know when it started, all I know is that I do. I need to know more, need to know what I'm getting into. I knew it could be seen as a violation, but she refuses to speak.

The door bursts open and Leo waltzes in, looking around Dad's office like he's touring some free museum he doesn't give a fuck about.

"Happy New Year, Annie," he says.

I ignore the nickname. I won't let it get a rise out of me. Not today. Not in the wake of one of the hottest nights of my life.

"Nice fireworks," I say, with sarcasm. Then, I remember Layla, tied and shaking on my lap, bathed by their colors, and I guess there's a part of me that said it truthfully. Then, to deny Leo any compliment, I add, "Glad Stephen didn't do to Dad's house what he did to your motor yacht."

"Shut up." Leo's face sours. He plops into the seat across the desk from me like he owns it. "Shiva's over, thank God. You can pull all the sheets and shit off the mirrors."

"Yeah, I'll get right on that." More sarcasm. "Have Wanda do it. I'm busy."

I really am, but mostly because I spent half the morning on Google with my stupid deep dive.

"Oh, she's back?"

"Should be," I glare at him, wondering if he's interrupting for a reason or if he's just bored.

"I think I'm probably gonna head home on Monday. Stephen and I are gonna hang out a little more before I go."

"I'll make sure our hired messenger gets on a horse and yells it through Rye like Paul Revere."

"Don't be a dick." He rolls his eyes.

"Oh, I'm sorry, I forgot you had the market cornered on that."

"I just came to see if you needed any help with any of the fundraisers he had coming up."

"Who? Dad?"

"Wow, you're *bright*. I see that Ivy League education was really a *worthwhile* endeavor."

"No," I say tersely. "I'm fine."

"You sure? He has events scheduled that overlap with some of the ones you're already committed to."

"I had planned to cancel some."

"Well, now you don't have to do that. I can go in your stead if you want to divvy them up."

"Now why on *earth* would Leo Stone do one single goddamn *nice* thing for me?"

I lean back, trying to figure him out. He's *always* got an angle.

He shrugs. "You can't be in two places at once. I could do the one in Concord that's on the same night as the one way up in Bumfuck, Maine. You could take your little fuckin' Birdie up there, or whatever, and I could do the other. My place is a forty-minute drive from that venue."

"You know a bunch of celebrities are supposed to be at the Concord one," I say it to inform him, and then I realize *that's* been his angle all along. He wants to rub elbows with socially relevant people, to be photographed alongside them, back in the media for yet another fifteen-minute burst of fame.

Once I realize it, I don't hesitate. In fact, it's a bit of a relief. "Yeah, fine. That works."

"I'm sure you're gonna wanna do the one in Texas next week now that you're fucking the help," he announces, staring at his manicured fingernails.

"What?"

"Don't deny it, Annie. I came to get you both for the fireworks show last night, and I heard you laying pipe in the fuckin' observatory."

I don't say anything. I just stare.

"Didn't think you had it in you, little brother. Haven't seen you with a bitch since high school. Honestly thought you were a fuckin' queer the last few years."

"I'm not. I'm just… *private*."

"Yeah. Sure." He shrugs. "So, that's why I figured you'd be taking her to the Austin one, since her kid's there."

I feel a rush of anger, livid that Leo of all people is somehow privy to this personal information, spouting it off like it's common knowledge, when I can't pry any answers out of her.

Truthfully, from her reaction last night, I feared she had a child who was no longer alive.

I play it off as if I'd known this information, too. "So… that means you want the one in Portsmouth?"

"Bingo."

I sigh, resigned. "Wear a nice suit, don't get drunk, and *don't* embarrass Dad, that's all I gotta say."

He rises and leans over the desk, clutching his tie against his chest. "I don't know if you've heard the news, Annie, but the guy is fuckin' dead."

He leaves the office, and I stay still in the chair, reeling.

34

Layla

"No, it's The Torah Shrine, The Passover, and Lady in the Bath," I say into the phone, my contact from the auction house on the other end, failing to listen. I notice one on another shelf of the glass curio case. "Oh shit, here's another. It's… hold on… I'm putting you on speaker."

I scramble to hit the speakerphone button. "Did I lose you, Ms. White?"

"No, I'm still here."

"Good. One sec. I have the site pulled up on my phone."

I click on the browser, scrolling through a site full of pricey metal designs until I find the right sculpture.

"This one is… uh… The Simchat Torah plaque."

I notice another figure on the shelf below and groan. The art in this place is never-ending. "Lord, here's another. Hold please." After a brief search, I mutter, "A Jerusalem Ketubah."

"Wow. Okay. So five total Frank Meislers?"

"Yes, ma'am. The website says they're metal alloy with gold-plated elements. The decedent's son said they're all limited edition, numbered and signed, and they'll be shipped with the COAs."

Out of the corner, I see the glint of Orion's red-orange tresses before I notice how perfect the suit he's wearing looks on him. He knocks on the open door, and I wave him in.

"Okay, Ms. Whittaker, I'll start getting everything ready on this end so that when we receive the items, we'll have everything all set to add these to the next auction."

"Great. Thank you." I smile, but it's at Orion, who looks dreamy, face resting softly against the door jamb.

"You got it. Talk soon," Ms. White says, ending our call.

I set my phone atop the cabinet and stroll toward him, trying to hide the big, dumb smile on my face. He slips inside, leans his back against the wall, arms folded across a chest I can't get out of my mind. Hard muscles and sweat, bathed in moonlight…

Focus, Layla.

"Well… good afternoon, Mr. Stone."

"*Orion*. Mr. Stone is my father." His smile fades. "Was."

In an attempt to cheer him up, I press my breasts against his crossed forearms and fidget with his belt buckle. "I actually thought you preferred 'Sir.'"

"Mmm. Only when you're in a state of undress."

We stand in silence for a moment until my hand snakes beneath the waistband of his boxers and wraps around the girth of his cock. His eyes drift shut, and he stiffens in my hand.

His green eyes open and peer down into mine. "As amazing as that feels, I've sought you out for a different reason."

I reluctantly remove my hand and flash a pout. I re-buckle his belt and take a step back. My arousal starts to replace itself with the fear that he will say playtime's officially over, that my hasty exit last night pissed him off, that my inability to open up about Danny is a deal-breaker. I feel like he's about to fire me.

"I'm leaving," he says.

My stomach twists as it registers, my heart turning to stone mid-beat like I just stared at Medusa.

"I'm going back to Bethlehem."

I suddenly want to weep. *What have I done?* "Was this because of…?"

He laughs, and I'm confused by the reaction.

"What? No. I'm going up there for the weekend. I need to grab some fresh clothes and, frankly, I could use a little change of scenery. This dark house is so depressing."

"Oh. But you're… coming *back*?"

"Yes, of course." He laughs again and caresses the side of my face adoringly. "I came here to ask if you'd like to join me for a couple of days."

"Really?" My smitten heart flutters with joy.

"Yeah, I'd love to take you to dinner. I know a great little place there. Elegant atmosphere, amazing food. You in?"

I nod, the one instance between us when it suffices as a satisfactory answer.

"Great." He smiles. He seems relieved. "I'd like to leave in two hours. Will that work for you?"

"Yes." I blush. "There's a little bit of a problem, though."

"Okay."

"If this restaurant is fancy, I'm kinda… out of clothes. You've seen every dress I brought already."

He checks his watch and considers something for a moment. Then, he takes my hand and leads me out. "Come with me."

I follow him without question. He leads me through the kitchen, through a huge walk-in pantry, to the basement door. Down the concrete steps, past the door to the gym, he opens a room marked STORAGE. It's full of floor-to-ceiling wooden shelves, probably used for canning decades ago, an old root cellar converted into something more modern. In the back are a series of portable closets. He opens the doors to each, revealing rack upon rack of expensive vintage clothing.

"These were Bambi's. When she died, Dad kept them in hopes one day Andromeda would want some, but I don't even think she remembers they're here."

I touch them. Silks, sequins, smooth sheers… everything from casual summer dresses to sweaters to blouses, to Oscar-worthy ball gowns.

"I'm sure some of these'll fit."

"These are *gorgeous*."

"Some of them are super dated. Legend has it, she lived for a good shoulder pad back in the day. Super materialistic, from what I've heard. Explains a lot about Leo and Andromeda."

"I can't believe this. Some of these are stunning!"

"You can have any of them. I'm sure you'll look better than she ever did." He smiles, "Then again, you look best in nothing but a smile."

I look away to keep him from seeing how much the compliment made me blush again.

"There's more down here, too." He pulls out some drawers beneath, revealing mounds of accessories. Belts, scarves, you name it.

"Find stuff for both nights." He wraps his arms around me and fondles my breasts through the fabric as I melt in his arms. "Something nice."

In an instant, I'm turned on, putty in his rough hands. He bites my earlobe and growls, "An enviable queen for dinner, a slutty peasant for dessert."

35

Layla

"Ready to go?" Orion asks from the foyer as I descend the stairs toward him.

"Yes."

At the bottom, he takes my suitcase, most of it Bambi's garments. He locks the door behind us, and I look around the long drive for a car. Orion breezes past a row of frozen bushes and places my suitcase and his duffel in the golf cart parked near the walkway that leads to the back of the property. He slides into the driver's side and pats the seat next to him.

"Hop in."

I laugh. "Is this… a joke?"

"No." He looks serious. "Why?"

"Bethlehem is a two-hour drive in a regular car. I hate to break it to you, but we aren't getting there any time soon on that thing."

He laughs harder than I expect him to, the first truly joyous one he's let out since I've known him. "Oh, we aren't driving."

"Then, wait… I'm confused."

"Just get in, Layla," he hollers up into the air playfully.

I slip in beside him.

"Hang on tight."

Before I can find something to grab, he floors the gas, and I shriek. Laughing, he zips us down the driveway, whips a donut, and shoots us through a small snow drift so hard that our luggage nearly flies out.

"Jesus, this is a golf cart, not a four-wheeler!"

"Ha! I love this thing," he yells, slowing slightly. It's a long drive across the property, snaking down the snowy trails, blistering winter air in our faces.

Minutes later, we pull up near a square helipad several acres from the mansion.

"Wait-wait-wait-wait-wait," I stammer. "Is this some kind of practical joke?"

Orion parks the cart, stuffs the key in his coat, and grabs our luggage. He leans under the vehicle's awning and grins. "Please don't tell me you have a fear of flying."

"Orion, that's a helicopter." I point to the black metal aircraft in front of us.

"Correct." He nods, his touchable red hair tousling with the movement, more vibrant than ever against the gleaming pure-white powder all around.

"W-why have I never seen this? You didn't show me this on the tour for the inventory."

"Because it isn't *Dad's*." He holds a gloved hand out to help me to my feet. "It's mine."

I'm suddenly too nervous to take his hand. "What do you mean it's *yours*?"

"I mean… um… I used money to buy it. And then… it… became… mine."

I sit for a moment, stunned.

"Bought it back in… 2015? 2016? Somewhere around there."

"*You're* qualified to fly this thing?"

"That's what my Private Pilot Certificate says." He raises an eyebrow. "Do you… need to see it? I'll show it to you."

"No." I laugh. This is insane. "I just, I thought we were driving."

"Driving's for *schmucks*, as my Dad always used to say." He points to the chopper. "I used to fly him around all the time in this thing. He nicknamed it The Birdie."

He extends his hand again. This time, I take it.

***

Winter in New Hampshire looks so different from the rattling belly of a helicopter, like something out of a fairy tale.

Orion works the controls with such ease. It's a whole new side of him I've never seen before. He looks so relaxed, as if he's flown it a million times. It feels like his entire demeanor changed when we walked out the front door of that mansion. Like he's free. Free from grief, from the tension between his brother, from the suffocating darkness of that place. He's lighter now. Playful even. It is such a pleasant surprise. A part of him I wasn't sure existed until now.

I find myself lost in my thoughts as we cruise over the snow-covered coniferous forest below. I can't get the way I felt earlier out of my head. My heart sank when he said he was leaving. My stomach lurched at the thought of our time together ending. I know that we're just supposed to be having some kinky fun, a release valve from life's crushing pressures, something to pass the time until our pains lessened… but I'm starting to feel like this all has backfired. I'm starting to realize that I'll be far more devastated when we inevitably part ways than I'd even been before I met him. I'm torn between wanting to milk every moment of joy out of our remaining time… or back away so I don't end up any deeper in this.

There's no way a relationship between us would work. We are from wildly different worlds. Orion is a man so wealthy he doesn't even brag that he owns a fucking *helicopter.* I'm a woman who couldn't have her shit together less, a failure in so many aspects of my life.

He points to a raised swath of woods and speaks into the mic on his flight helmet, his voice oozing in through my earphones. "That's the start of the White Mountain National Forest." He points to our right. "In a bit, you'll be able to see Mount Washington and Mount Adams out that way."

I stare at the world beneath us, a view unlike any I've ever seen.

"This is so beautiful," I say into my microphone.

He smiles at me, warm and genuine, returns his eyes to the world beyond, and slips his hand into mine.

***

"Welcome to *mi casa*," Orion says after he unlocks his front door. He motions for me to enter and follows with the bags.

"Dear God, I feel like my whole house is the same square footage as your living room."

He shakes his head and smiles.

"What time is the reservation for?"

He shrugs. "Whenever we get there."

"Oh, man." I feel nervous. "I thought this place was going to be really fancy. I'm afraid I may have gone a little overboard with what I brought."

"No. It's fancy. I just have a standing reservation. Private table." He pops his keys in a wicker bowl. "So bring your best. I'm wearing a suit."

"Okay." I blush.

"Make yourself at home." He takes my coat, hangs it on a rack by the front door.

I am in awe of his place. It's large, but in every other way, it's the antithesis of his father's mansion. It is bright and open, with huge picture windows overlooking miles of snow-covered forest and mountains in the dusky distance. With all this glass, I feel like I'm in an aquarium.

The walls are cream, the furniture cozy. The surfaces are all quartz, glass, and chrome,

269

seamlessly blending for a clean overall look that feels simultaneously simple and sophisticated.

The lower level is open concept with luxurious appliances glistening in the kitchen. Towering fiddle-leaf fig trees bookend each side of the windowed wall in the living room. In one corner, there's a treadmill, a few sets of weights, an exercise bench, and a taupe yoga mat. On the other side sits a huge couch and ottoman facing a massive flat-screen.

"Feel free to look around. I'll give you a proper tour later. There are a bunch of rooms upstairs. You're welcome to claim any of the empty ones if you want your own space, but the master suite is on the left if you want to stay with me." His smile is soft as he fills a tan watering can at the sink. "No pressure. I know that didn't exactly seem to be your… *thing*… last night."

My shoulders slump a little. I touch the leaves of a neon pothos, long tendrils draping down from a pot on a shelf with cookbooks. The plant is real, which likely means all the others are alive and not just plastic decorations.

"Yeah, I'm sorry about that," I finally say.

"Don't be," he says, taking the canister over to a tall dracaena by the stone fireplace and watering it, heading to the fig trees next. "I shouldn't have asked what I did. It was none of my business."

"It's not that. It's not really fair that I'm all up in your childhood home with your baby pictures, learning about your family every day, and I can't even…" I don't know how to finish what I'm saying.

"It's fine. Really."

I point up the stairs. "I'm going to go get dressed."

"Perfect. I'm right behind you as soon as I water all these bad boys."

***

We roll down a recently plowed street in Orion's Mercedes Electrified GV70, a sleek and curvaceous beast. Last year's model. So clean, it looks like it just drove off the showroom floor.

Who knows. Maybe it did.

"I can't help but notice the Stone name is on a *lot* of the buildings around here," I say, watching the Alexander Stone Building of Arts and Sciences whizz by us.

He smirks. "Dad and I both like to spread our good fortune around, especially for higher education. We've been fortunate enough to be in positions to help out, especially if it relates to astrophysics or astronomy." He manages a sad smile. "Mom used to say, 'Dad didn't have his head in the clouds, he had it in outer space.' It was true. I caught the bug from him."

I lean against the headrest and find myself smiling at him, smitten.

He pulls into the parking lot of a restaurant. Evergreen holly bushes edge the stone walls. He raises a finger for me to wait. He opens my door and helps me out, keeping my hand clasped in his. I feel a bit shocked that he'd be seen like this in the town where he lives. We travel down the shoveled path, and he opens the front door, allowing me to enter first. I try to hide my grin, one of delight. Here I thought chivalry was dead.

We approach the hostess podium. The waitstaff bustle around in pressed all-black uniforms through the establishment. Dimmed pendant lights bloom soft amber over each luxurious booth.

"Ah, Mr. Stone. Good to see you," the young woman says. "*Oooh. Two* tonight?"

I swear he blushes. "Yes, ma'am."

"Fantastic. Follow me." She brings two leather-bound menus into a room past a stone bar with a gold-marbled mirror behind it. We pass beneath a whimsical archway lined with an assortment of faux hanging flowers. She places the elegant booklets down at a four-top, dark wood with an almost-black gloss finish.

A waitress enters just as she exits.

"Good evening, Mr. Stone. Can I get you both started with a drink?"

My need for one is *strong*. I'm so out of place, an impostor in someone else's designer dress and cheap Claire's earrings, seated in a restaurant I definitely can't afford with a wealthy man I don't deserve to be in the presence of.

36

Orion

Once the cocktails came, the conversation started flowing. Our waitress, Amanda, sets down the Wagyu steak and Maine lobster surf-and-turf we agreed to share in the spot where our goat cheese balls and bacon-wrapped jalapeno poppers once sat.

"...So...Dad always told me she was pretty materialistic. Kinda shallow, focused on fashion and makeup above all."

Layla plucks the strap of the satin gown she's wearing, one that fits her like it was tailored to her body. "Well, I'm not going to lie, from what I've seen, she had impeccable taste. I wanted half the stuff I saw in the closet downstairs."

"Take it. Seriously. Anything in those closets that you want. The rest is just getting donated or tossed." I fork some lobster into a small ceramic bowl suspended in a chrome contraption above a lit candle that keeps it hot. "But, with Bambi the way she was, I think that's why Andromeda ended up like she did, building an empire around makeup and fake nails."

"Nothing wrong with that, though."

"I mean, no, but… when she's gone, what kind of mark did she leave on this earth?"

"Not everyone is fortunate enough to leave behind a legacy."

"Everyone *can*. Every day, with every decision, we choose what kind of world we leave in our wake."

"Well, some of us try to make our mark and still fail. Even bearing children isn't a guarantee that you're going to be remembered anymore."

I want to ask her forty questions about that proclamation. But, after last night, I hesitate to speak about the matter.

"His name is Danny," she says after a long silence, allowing me in at her own pace. Her fork shoves a medium-rare piece of meat around on her plate. Her eyes meet mine, sad and glassy. "The answer to your question last night. He'll be thirteen in May."

I stew on this for a moment. I have so many follow-up questions to ask, but I fear they'll only spook her. Maybe I can convince myself that this is enough. It's a start.

She takes a long final sip of her cocktail as the waitress arrives with a fresh one. The moment she leaves with the empty glass, Layla says something else. "He lives with his father… if you were wondering."

"If I'm honest, I was." I nod softly.

I want to ask her why any court in America would allow a boy to be taken from such a nurturing woman during such formative years. I want to ask her what she thinks of this, but I can see from the tears she's fighting that even thinking about it at all is devastating her.

"I'm probably going to lose him for good soon." She puts her fork down. I presume she's no longer hungry after the mention of this sore subject.

"Does he live in New Hampshire?" I ask, already knowing the answer thanks to Leo doing what he does best... running his mouth.

She shakes her head. "He did. He's in Austin now with his dad."

"I'm sorry."

She nods, sullen. "I've been fighting for shared custody for a while. Thought I'd at least get him for summers and Christmases. But, a couple of weeks ago... my ex... I was furious about what he was saying on the phone. It was icy. This animal darts onto the road..."

She stares at the ice in her half-downed refill as if she can will it to replenish with her mind.

"I almost died. Flew off a cliff. Crashed my car into a tree, which... saved my life, unfortunately."

It crushes me to hear her say such a thing, as if the permanence of death would somehow be an upgrade to her reality.

"Now my lawyer says his father is trying to weaponize all that against me."

She rattles the ice nervously, and I gently take the glass to my half of the table and slide my wine glass full of ice water into her hands.

Normally, I wouldn't tell her what to do with her clothes on, but she's knocking them back and I feel compelled to intervene.

"I want you with all of your faculties tonight. I have some… *things*… at home that might get your mind off all of this, but sobriety is an absolute requirement," I say. "Understood?"

"*Yes, Sir*," she says, two words that instantly make my dick harden.

"As far as Danny goes, I appreciate you trusting me enough to tell me. I don't take that lightly."

"I'm sorry I recoiled when you asked about him last night. It just… hurts. I feel like he's been poisoned against me." A tear rolls from one of her eyes, taking a streak of powder makeup with it.

"I understand completely. I shouldn't have asked. It wasn't my business." I lean back, deciding we'll take the rest to go. Almost as if she's psychic, the waitress holds a box in the air with an expression that asks if I want one. I nod, and she brings it. I shovel the remaining food into the container.

"I feel like I should offer something in return since we're being raw and honest with each other. Would that make you feel better?"

She nods, the ghost of a smile on her lips. "I strangely think it might, yes."

I pretend to think for a moment, even though I already have something on my mind. Finally, I close the box and say it. "My mother drowned when I was a teenager."

"Oh my God. Orion..."

"She and Dad were in Saint Lucia with a bunch of other married couples from their old country club. I wasn't there. I heard all this from the people who were. I guess, one night, the men all went to see some show, some of those fire dancers on the island. The wives all got drunk and went for a swim at the beach. I guess the current pulled Mom under. Took search and rescue six days to find her. Dad... never forgave himself. It's also why, as big as his property is, it doesn't have a pool. He had it cemented over and put that shallow reflecting pond that you saw in."

"I'm so sorry." Her hand reaches out, rubs mine softly, eyes outpouring empathy and compassion. It's something I have noticed a lot, a trait I find intoxicating, especially in this time of grief.

"You shared something deeply personal with me, so it's only fair. I'm also telling you because, as a teenage boy, I didn't have my own mother around. Same with Leo. Bambi got cancer when he was, I think, eleven. We both grew up without mothers. Say the word, Layla, and I'll do anything in my power to help with your son."

It is clear the comment took her off guard. The look on her face is indecipherable, cycling from surprise to gratitude to disbelief.

"Wow. Thank you," she finally says, stunned. "But... I'd never ask that of you. I made my bed."

She takes a long, slow chug of the water and dabs her lips with her cloth napkin.

I want to ask what Danny is like, what personality traits he got from his mother… but I don't. Instead, I admit something private to her. Something I've never told a soul, including my father during our long talks about life, love, and the cosmos. "I think I'd love to have a child one day."

I feel instantly exposed when I say it, unsure why I just bared it aloud. It is something that usually stays tucked in the back of my mind, a splinter of hope that the best parts of me might live on.

"Yeah?" Her eyes glisten beneath the lights, and I can't help but melt a little at how beautiful she is.

I nod. "Although I'd be devastated if he turned out like Leo."

We both chuckle at that.

"Fatherhood would suit you," she says.

That makes me smile. "Why?"

She shrugs. "You're infectiously passionate. Patient. Attentive. Caring. Considerate."

I feel bashful. "That's… funny."

"Why?"

"Because I'd describe you the same way. Within twenty-four hours of meeting you, you were pulling pieces of glass out of my bleeding arm and gluing me up."

"I was a few semesters into nursing school when I found out I was pregnant," she says with a smile.

"You never went back?"

She shakes her head. "I was a stay-at-home mom until he was in school. His dad wasn't around much back in those days, and Danny got involved in a lot of after-school stuff. Peewee football, chess club, Mandarin lessons, et cetera. When I went back to work, I needed a career with a little more flex in the scheduling."

I think about the morning in my room, when I couldn't breathe, a complete stranger stroking my hair so soothingly. "Is that where you learned the trick for my panic attack? Nursing school?"

"No. My son used to get them a couple times a year, especially whenever he'd hear Alan and me bickering."

"Oh. Well, I was shocked at how well you took charge with my shoulder. I must say, it's already healing nicely."

"I know. I *saw*." She winks. I remember us last night, naked and writhing, her arms bound behind her, the deafening fireworks barely masking the sound of her orgasm...

"You're the sexiest nurse *I've* ever seen. And you did all that triage in nothing but a *towel,* no less."

I have to look away to keep my smile at bay from the memory of it.

"Orion *Stone*."

"What?"

"You're *blushing*." She leans toward me and smirks.

"Yeah, well…" I look around, willing my cheeks to return to their pale, lightly freckled state. "You seem to have that effect on me."

I finish off my drink and rise with the leftovers before this conversation can turn any more risque, and offer a hand to help her up. "Come on. Let's get outta here."

"But… we haven't gotten the check yet."

I laugh. She cocks her head to look at me strangely.

"Why are you laughing?"

"I don't get a check here."

"Why not?"

I hesitate for a moment and then look her in the eyes. "Because I own the restaurant."

Her expression is priceless. I wonder how she'd react if she knew I own four more in town.

37

Layla

Orion's house fascinates me. For someone as wealthy as he, the place contains surprisingly little flash. It feels modest, functional, and comforting, a clean canvas in which his passions and priorities sit at the forefront. Unlike his father's house perched at the edge of a main thoroughfare in Rye, Orion's house is tucked away, a hidden gem on tranquil acres of forested land with a spectacular view of the distant mountain range. For someone so scientific, a man who only seems to utter numbers and polite formalities during work calls, his place feels so rooted in the earth, cradled by the arms of Mother Nature herself.

"Okay, come here." He pulls away from the viewfinder on his telescope, one that looks every bit as expensive as his father's. It's perched next to a wall of glass in his bedroom, aimed high into the black night sky.

I swap him places, feeling his warm hands grip my waist, my back nestled against his chest.

He pulls my hair to the side and kisses my neck as I peer into the viewfinder. I smile, even though he can't see it, a smile that's just for me. Despite the filthy things we do to *and for* each other, he still manages to make me feel safe, a delicate balancing act for a Dom, I'm sure. I'm addicted to this intimacy.

"What am I looking at?"

I squint at a white circle with an azure aura around it, ghostly magenta fog blooms outward into an oblong oval tapered on each end. It looks like I'm staring into the bloodshot eye of God himself, and I suddenly feel so small and insignificant looking through this lens. I shiver at how minuscule we are as humans, mere specks in the unfathomable grandeur of the universe.

"That is a nebula, and the white thing in the middle is a star."

"It's beautiful." I twist the knob to adjust the focus, feeling my zipper slide down my bare spine, the material curling like the petals of a rose. He lays warm kisses in a trail down my vertebrae.

"It's part of a larger constellation," he says when he reaches my lower back where the zipper ends. "Want to take a guess at which one?"

The dress slips down to my waist. My bra unclasps, patters against the tan carpet, cups replaced by strong, kneading hands as I stare into the sapphire iris in outer space.

"The… Big Dipper?"

The hands slip away, leaving my breasts exposed in front of all this glass. The dress slinks over the breadth of my hips and falls. He softly bites my ass like he's testing the strength of the skin on a juicy peach.

"*Nope*," he whispers afterward, against my skin.

"I'm afraid I might need a hint."

I hear him stand, sensing a grin when he mutters, "I was hoping you'd say that."

I hear the metal click of his belt buckle opening, the *whoosh* of leather through the loops of his slacks. I feel it slip around my throat so softly, the hole-punched end weaving back through the buckle. It tightens gently around my throat, and my body buzzes at the very thought of it.

The danger.

The domination.

He pulls me back against his chest using it like a leash, the familiar and exciting tug of it lighting my nerve endings on fire.

I hear the distortion of my voice through the gentle squeeze of the leather. "*Orion's belt was going to be my next guess.*"

His free hand cups one of my naked breasts, thumbing the peak of its pebbled nipple as I melt into him.

"*Technically*," he whispers in my ear, "*that's the Orion nebula. The belt is a little higher up.*"

"*Nerd*," I jest, my laughter strained.

He snickers, and the belt tightens. I rise to my toes, completely at his mercy for air. A moment later, it loosens and unclasps. He tosses it on the bed behind us.

"Come. There's something I want to show you." Our hands interlace, and he drags me across the bedroom to a wall with two doors. One is a closet hanging halfway open, button-down shirts and pressed slacks peeking through the darkened crack.

The second is closed.

He reaches into the nearby nightstand drawer and produces a key, unlocking it and swinging it open wide.

"The place came with his-and-hers closets, and since there's never been a *her*, I converted this…"

He trails off, sliding the dimmer switch up. Light bathes the walls of a modest sex dungeon. Peg-boards are mounted to the back wall, neatly holding a small variety of paddles, ticklers, crops, and floggers. Shelves on the right hold an array of lubricants and toys ranging from large wands to small vibrators. Sleek silicone ones in their original packaging, sit on another shelf, each resembling abstract art far more than a human penis.

Shelves on the right hold canvas bins, each labeled with things like "Glass wands," "Cuffs," and "Nipple clamps."

From a beam in the ceiling behind him hangs a black sex-sling from a heavy-duty chain, the bowed top spinning freely, the stirrups lined in fur. There is a small table against one side with a heart-shaped Liberator wedge sitting on it.

"I'm a little ashamed to admit that, while I've put a lot of work into this, you're actually the first person who's ever seen it." I could swear I see him blush a little when he admits it. "Well, other than my cleaning lady. *Once*. We weren't intimate. She just got a hell of a shock when she came in to vacuum. Hence the lock."

"Wow." I smile. "You are *full* of surprises."

"I used to dabble and play in a dungeon in Massachusetts a while back. They shut down two years ago, and I decided to build a little mini version of my own."

"A room like this," I wander around, spinning the swing, "it'd be a *shame* not to christen it."

"I agree." He leans against the far wall, allowing me space to explore, to experiment without his influence. I can feel his eyes studying me, burning with fascination.

I study the wall of punishment toys, feeling the textures from the soft flogger tassels to the comical tire-tread design on a rubber-coated paddle. There's an unspoken thing between us right now, a freedom to choose the direction of the evening, the chance to decide my own sexual fate. Since we became intimate, he's respected my needs, slowed at the presence of my pained whimpers, allowed my body the chance to adjust to new things, and listened for any utterance of a safe word. Because of this, I'm excited for the night ahead.

I slip the braid of a whip through my fist and tickle the feathers of a duster, finally lifting the riding crop off its pegs. I slap the end in my palm, enjoying the sharp, satisfying *crack* it makes as it assaults flesh.

I approach him and kneel, my face level with the bulge in his beltless slacks. I raise my hands, and he takes the offering.

I want *pain*. A physical kind. Enough to forget the emotional kind we spoke of earlier. I desire to lose myself in the burn, my mind forced into the present, unable to travel to the past.

Tonight, I don't want to be a discarded mother. An impossible ex-wife. A warm sack of meat dangling in a fucking tree. Tonight, there will be no thoughts of smashed glass or revoked licenses. Death and mistresses. Leo. Lawyers. Mediators. Phone calls sent to voicemail…

None of it.

For tonight, I need the catharsis, my slate wiped temporarily clean, my sinful soul absolved.

Orion walks past me. He eyes the back wall for a few moments, finally plucking a steel bar off a hook that has two sets of cuffs attached to each end. They clink against the metal as he returns to me.

"Stand. Panties off."

"Yes, Sir." The minute I say it, I am flooded with a rush of serotonin, nipples tightening at the promise of a filthy night ahead.

Once my underwear is wadded on the floor, he cuffs each wrist in its own leather handcuff and then yanks it toward the floor until I double over, a lazy marionette, hair dragging limply across the carpet as I dangle.

"Spread your legs." They feel like magic words.

"Yes, Sir."

I slide until my feet are shoulder-width apart. He cuffs the steel rod to my ankles and stands, leaving me there, my wrists pinned, legs splayed open indefinitely from the rigid spreader bar.

The moment I hear the first vicious *crack* of the crop, feel its almost electric sting across my naked ass, I feel a tear of joy fall from my eye, burrowing in the fibers of the carpet.

/ # 38

Orion

The once-pale skin of her cheeks is now a blotchy magenta, starting to purple from all the strikes. The air hangs heavy with her pained yips, her guttural growls of fury and rage, and the controlled, "Yes, Sirs." Her cunt is drenched, glistening, an inviting shade of pink that matches the stripes from the stick of the crop. I'm desperate to feel her around my cock, eager to taste the salt of her tears as our tongues meld.

Her spread legs tremble, hands threaded through the carpet to keep her from toppling on those spiked heels. I release her wrists and ankles, toss the bar aside, and scoop her in my arms.

She stares up at me, eyes red and glassy, blonde hair disheveled. She clings to me, fingers clenched into muscle. I have the urge to fuck her right here like a dog in heat, carpet rubbing her knees raw as I force myself inside.

But the sounds of her sobs soften me, and I think she needs a break. I lay her on my bed, hurl her heels at the floor, and caress her reddened skin as she cries. I cover her with a sheet and rise, killing the lights before returning. I strip, slow and careful, so as not to disturb her emotional trance. I flick the globe projector on my nightstand on, one that turns the ceiling into a night sky freckled with burning, fairly accurate constellations. I slip beneath the sheets next to her and stroke her hair as she sobs beneath starlight.

Minutes later, Layla moves close, our bodies entwining, emotions ebbing, leaving zen-like calmness in its wake. She pulls my hand down to the slick, heavenly opening between her thighs. The pain in her eyes is gone, replaced with desire. There's a similar look in my own.

My fingers penetrate her, and she gasps, head twisting back into the pillow for a blissful moan before she kisses me, thighs widening invitingly, her tongue soft and willing.

In seconds, I am slipping inside her, sinking my cock into her depths. My ears are a receptacle for her pleasured moans. My teeth clamp onto one of her lobes like a stubborn clip-on earring, and she pants, soft and sexy. She's tight, walls slick, pulsing around my shaft, her feet scrambling for a foothold on the backs of my calves.

She commands the attention of every single one of my senses. The taste of her sweat excites me. Her fingernails dig into my shoulders. The breathy sound of my name fills the room, symphonic and dreamy. I fuck her slow and long with no sense of worldly time, savoring her in every possible way. There is nowhere in the world I'd rather be right now than right here inside of her.

Layla

I adjust in the car seat, a delightful ache beneath my jeans as signs for Franconia State Park whizz by.

"That was one of my favorite places to hang out when I was a teenager." I point up the side of one of the mountains a few miles away. "That little overlook right there. I used to pack a lunch and just sit until the sun set."

Orion's smile is gentle as he looks out over the snowy vista. "That's funny," he finally says, shaking his head.

"Why?"

"I used to do the same thing out there at Basin Falls all the time."

"Wouldn't that be crazy if we were out there on the same days, both just... being alone?" I laugh at the ridiculousness of the image, two lonesome teenagers eating sandwiches in silence on opposite sides of the park.

"I don't think it would be *that* crazy." He clicks on his blinker and shifts lanes before glancing back at me. "We seem to like a lot of the same things. I just hope you're not already tired of the place I'm taking you."

"You *could* just *tell* me." I laugh.

"Not a chance. It's a surprise."

***

"The Ice Castles of North Woodstock?" My brows knit into a confused expression as we park. "What *is* this?"

"Woah, you've been to Franconia a million times, but you've never been to Ice Castles?!" His voice rises an octave. "Well, I'll be dipped."

I laugh at the expression and the faux southern accent in which he says it. I love being around him like this. He's so… relaxed.

He opens the car door for me and holds my hand as we walk the snowy path into a village of structures made completely out of ice. Every wall and building has the texture of an instantly frozen waterfall.

"This is insane," I exclaim like an excited child.

He just smiles. Dusk settles overhead, and we explore this wonderland, the frozen walls glowing neon, lights illuminating them from the inside. This place is the most magical place I've ever been, a stone's throw from the tiny town I grew up in.

How the hell have I never heard of this?!

We wind around every new bend, dodging excited down-jacket-clad tourists and giddy children at every turn. We weave through, admiring the huge ice archways and tunnels. We enter a new section beneath an ice bridge with the texture of a thousand icicles gently melded. The entire structure is illuminated a shade of bright violet from within. We enter a clearing of snow with a raised bowl of indigo-tinted ice. Running water spews up through the middle.

"An ice fountain? How is that even possible?"

"I don't know," he says with a chuckle, taking a seat on a frozen bench so he can take it all in.

"This place is *fascinating*."

"Glad you like it." He waves me over. "Come on."

He holds my hand through a frozen maze that ends near a row of glowing ice slides, family members taking turns sliding down the huge, human-sized ice luges.

Nearby, a boy who could be Danny's doppelganger takes off a mitten and touches a neon green glowing wall of ice. The resemblance is like a punch to my stomach.

Danny would love this place.

"You okay?" Orion sweeps a tuft of my blonde hair behind my ear with a chilled finger and examines my expression with concern.

I fake a smile. "Yeah. It's… nothing."

He's not buying it. Not even a little bit. He puts the pieces together the second he sees the kid. Those gorgeous green eyes return to mine. "Do you want to go?"

"No." I crack a little bit of a smile. A *real* one. "Not until we go down that ice luge."

I point and he laughs.

His eyes return again, this time full of something unspoken, something that makes my heart flutter. He doesn't say a word. He just kisses me so tenderly that I feel my brokenness begin to mend.

40

Orion

"We're taking The Birdie back to Rye in the morning, right?" Layla asks.

"Yes." I set the grocery bag on the counter and plop the plastic gallon jug of two percent on the tile beside it.

"You're gonna drink all that *tonight*?"

"No. I never said that."

"It's gonna go bad if you leave it here," she says, hanging her coat on the rack by the door and then returning for mine. As she turns away with it, I get a glimpse of what a real future might look like with her. The warmth and humanity, the small acts of care. I thought pulling glass out of my shoulder was a one-off, but after spending time with her, I see it's who she *is*.

I think forward, imagining the day her inventory of Dad's house is over. I imagine her walking out of his front door, never to return, the job done. I feel a pang of something awful when I think of never seeing her again, never tasting those lips, no longer feeling her hot skin beneath my stinging hand, never getting to watch her come down from that sexual high…

I shake it off, trying not to let it ruin the mood of the evening. We had such a fun day pretending to be normal people, people who aren't grieving trauma, people who don't participate in perverse behavior in private.

We are here. Now. In the moment. And I refuse to let it pass by. I'll soak up every memory I can before she's out of my life.

"Want any?" I ask, holding up the jug. "Last call."

She looks at me, confused, brows scrunched. "I'm… good."

"Okay."

"You gonna tell me what's in the bag?" She motions to the paper sack with the folded top.

"Nope," I say, snatching it up and starting upstairs with my spoils. "Relax and unwind for a few. Meet me upstairs in ten."

Up in the master bath, I put the stopper in and draw water, watching the claw-foot tub fill. I adjust the temp and pour the milk in. The steam looks like fog rolling off the surface of a white, opaque lake. From the bag, I pull out a single rose, massaging the red head of it until it comes apart in my hand. I kill the faucet and sprinkle the velvety petals atop the surface.

I hear a *creak* behind me, feet on wood at the bathroom's threshold. I rise and turn to see Layla standing there with a soft smile, head leaning against the doorway.

"Madame, your milk bath awaits." I motion to it before unbuttoning my cuffs and rolling my sleeves up.

"For me?"

I nod. "The lactic acid in the milk helps soothe irritated skin."

"And the rose petals?"

"Flair."

She laughs. "You certainly get points for that."

I reach beneath the sink and pull out a three-pack of bath poufs, the ones that look like a rumpled wad of mesh on a string.

By the time I turn around, she is slipping that gorgeous body out of her damp, mud-muddled clothes. She blushes and attempts to cover her nudity, a reminder that dirty sex and BDSM are not always synonymous with being exposed and vulnerable.

I offer a hand, and she takes it, using it to steady herself as she slips into the hot water. As she pivots away from me, I see bruises and welts from last night, beautiful proof that I left my mark.

"Stay… right… there." I fold a towel on the floor and kneel. I submerge the pouf in the cloudy water and caress the gorgeous curves of her ass with it.

"Looks like a galaxy," I say, my voice faraway, like I'm recalling a fairy tale.

There's nothing between us but the patter of water as I softly sponge every aggravated, raw inch of her skin with gratitude. She spins in place, and I'm right at the glorious triangle where everything meets, where creation begins.

Her fingers stroke my hair, and she smiles down at me before sinking to her knees in the water until her nose brushes mine. Her lips are open, teasing.

"Careful, Orion," she coos it like a lullaby. "A girl could get used to this."

***

"Strawberry me, please." Her tongue extends, and I want desperately to take it in my mouth. Instead, I take another chocolate-dipped delicacy from the plastic bakery container and rub the tip against her lips until she playfully sinks her teeth in like an animal. I trail the rest of the exposed fruit across one of the rosy nipples peeking out of the tepid water. I lean in and suck every last smudge of its juice off.

"I don't want to go back tomorrow." She juts her lip out in a pout. "I want to stay another day and pretend I deserve to live like this."

"No can do, Princess. I have to go back." I lay my arms on the side of the tub, chin resting on my folded hands. "This week I have to go out of town. On Tuesday."

"For what?" She dances the pouf on the surface of the water like a toy.

"Charity fundraiser for a university's science program."

She whines and pretends she's going to slip in the tub and drown herself in protest. Then, she frowns. "I'm going to be all alone in that place with your blowhard brother?"

"About that…" But for a long time, I don't say anything. I don't know if I should.

"Go on." She tosses the mesh ball by her feet with a milky splash.

"Would you like to go with me? It's an overnight trip."

"Go with you… like, as in your naughty little concubine who stays tied up at the hotel?" Her smile is devious.

I snicker. "As my date."

The minute I utter it, I feel a certain hesitation about asking just now. This all suddenly just got more real. Like she's more than a fling. Maybe she is.

She smiles and mulls it over. "What would my boss think about me traipsing about at charity functions instead of doing my job?"

"I hired you. I think I kind of *am* your boss."

"Fair enough. Obviously, the answer is yes." She giggles and bobbles her head. "Are we taking Birdie?"

"No. Too far for Birdie. Private jet."

She whispers behind the back of her hand like she's telling me a secret, even though we're alone. *"I've never been on a private jet before."*

I mimic her hand movement and whisper, *"It's quite luxurious if you're used to flying coach."*

She sinks deeper into the water, a descending submarine in the white murk. "I'm in, obviously."

I smile, strangely relieved.

"Where will we be jet-setting to?"

I study her closely as I say it. "Austin."

Her eyes widen and then fixate on the ceiling for a long time. Finally, she bobs back up and her eyes lock on mine.

"That's… where Danny lives."

I nod and stroke a damp hunk of blonde hair from her forehead. "It's kismet."

She leans over the tub's edge and kisses me. It is filled with gratitude and passion. As she pulls away, her tear-filled eyes glimmer with hope.

41

Orion

I awaken bathed in the light of dawn with Layla snuggled in the crook of my arm, body soft and naked against mine. She fits perfectly there, like she was tailor-made for the spot. I watch the rise and fall of her gentle breaths, my lush comforter, for once, pulsing with life. I want to wake her with a kiss, with the cup of her breast in my hand, one of my knees nudging its way between her warm thighs…

Instead, I let her sleep, her features so relaxed that waking her would feel like a crime. I slip out of bed and throw on some shorts, cranking the thermostat up a few degrees as I pass it on the way out to the living room couch. I pull my laptop out of its case, set it on the cushioned arm, and power it on.

As the operating system belches out its obnoxious chime, I fish through the pocket of the laptop bag until I find the small bit of plastic I seek. I hold the tiny USB flash drive in my palm as if it holds nuclear launch codes or something of equally vital importance. I found it in a drawer in Dad's desk, one I had tied Layla to with a lamp cord last week. The flash drive was the only thing in the entire drawer, stored in a velveteen pouch like a bag of diamonds in someone's safety deposit box.

The decision of whether or not to plug it in, to prowl around through its contents, has been weighing heavily ever since I found it three days ago. Part of me wonders if it'll be a letdown, some Excel spreadsheets, photos of a random nebula, or *worse*... intimate, private media involving my mother... or Bambi... or a mistress... or a man.

Since its discovery, my mind has raced to imagine what might be on it. For some inexplicable reason, this morning I just can't wait any longer to see what it holds.

I plug it into a free port, and a tan folder displays automatically. I take a deep breath and double-click.

The contents appear to be a series of videos, all named with seemingly random numbers. No going back now...

I see one containing a lot of snow and hope that my father's clothed in it. I double-click, wincing, hoping I don't soon learn of some paternal secret that should've been rightfully taken to the grave.

The video player opens, and the frozen thumbnail springs to life. The camera stares down at a moving hill of snow. Boots dangle into view, and it seems Dad is in a ski lift, heading to the top of a mountain. The camera whips, and I realize the recording device is strapped to his face, a

GoPro with the elastic headband for sports. My mother's face comes into view, and she smiles.

"I'm so nervous!" she exclaims, giddy.

"Don't be. You'll do great!" he says and rubs the thigh of her snow pants.

"What if I pull a Sonny Bono?"

He laughs, and the sound fills me with equal parts joy and pain. It's a relief to hear it, this noise I never thought I'd hear again.

Dad helps her off the lift at the summit. His camera follows her as she shuffles to the edge of the hill, poles poised, trying to psych herself up.

"You got this, Love," he hollers.

She counts down quietly, urging herself to take the plunge even though it's just a beginner bunny slope. Finally, she shoves with the poles and thrusts down the hill, slowly at first, then picking up speed. She makes it to the bottom, clomping her skis in the soft powder to turn around. Her arms raise in the air in celebration, and Dad hoots in support before following her down on his own skis.

The smile on Mom's pale face, made pink by the cold, is the last thing I see before the flurry of activity where Dad is trying to figure out where the button is to end the clip. The video cuts out, and I find myself smiling, my nose bristling with the itch of welling emotions.

I play a few more similarly named files. They're all clips from a Canadian vacation with Mom, possibly around the time in my youth when handheld cameras were just getting extremely accessible for everyday consumers.

There are more videos with a different type of file name and extension. Judging by the age of Andromeda in one of the thumbnails, they look much older. It is only when I see it that I recall Dad walking around with a little handheld camera once in a while when we were kids, an insignificant memory I must've blocked.

There are other file types too. One is a video of Andromeda playing one of the rats in the Pied Piper at her private elementary school, the camera whipping to Bambi, healthy and mildly amused. It looks like it was shot with one of those cumbersome camcorders, the shoulder-mounted ones shaped like half a cinder block, the kind newscasters carry in the movies.

There is a clip of Leo sulking at his Bar Mitzvah, a younger Aunt Kay with enough hairspray to be a flammable danger to others, trying to goad the bored teen to dance with her. Dad encourages him. Begrudgingly, Leo limply drags his clown-sized dress shoes across the laminate as he and Kay stumble their way through a simple box step.

There is another one of Leo spinning a *dreidel* at Hanukkah, probably fourteen or so. Andromeda leans against the dining room table next to him, a different one back then, one not nearly as posh. In the clip, a curious four-year-old me reaches atop the table and grabs at the toy. Leo knocks my hand away viciously, followed by a loud, "Stop it, Orion!"

He spins the *dreidel* again as he and Andromeda sing. I tiptoe and clip the edge of the whirling toy with a finger, halting the wooden top.

Leo shoves me. "I said 'stop it,' you little ginger freak!"

Ah, some things never change.

Young me topples backward against the buffet table, the same one with the same lit *menorah* on it last week.

"Leo!" Dad's voice booms. It takes me by surprise. I honestly cannot remember hearing my dad ever yell now that I think about it.

The camera plops on the table, and Dad races over, much younger than I ever remember him being.

But then again, this clip is probably thirty years old.

Dad grabs Leo by the arm as young me sobs uncontrollably. I have no memory of this.

"Leo Nova Stone!" Dad growls. "Orion is your *brother*."

The sight of Dad standing up for me warms my body like a full glass of single-malt whiskey.

"You and Orion are *family*, Leo. Family *protects* one another. Brothers should fight *for* each other, not *with* each other. Family is what matters the most in this world." Dad's eyes are steely. "I want you to apologize."

Even through the grain of the video, I see the roll of Leo's eyes before the reluctant utterance of '*Sorry.*'

"No, Leo. *Genuine*. That's your brother."

"*Half*-brother," Leo growls.

That enrages Dad. "Don't *ever* let me hear you call him that again."

"But it's true! He is!"

"He is your *brother*!"

"You always take his side!" Leo yells, arms crossed. Even in his forties, he's the same emotionally-stunted dickhead he was back then.

"He's four, Leo! You're fourteen. *Act* like it."

Young Orion stops sobbing and teeters over to Leo to hug his distressed older sibling.

Dad points at young me. "He loves you to death, Leo."

After a long silence, Dad plants a kiss on Leo's head and scoops young Orion inward, holding both sons in a loose hug.

"Can *I* spin it now, Daddy?" Andromeda pipes up. Dad picks the *dreidel* up and hands it to her before returning to the spot behind the camera. The video cuts.

I stare at my computer, overwhelmed by it all. I feel something twist in me, a rope of anxiety with too much weight on it, fraying quickly. Dad's words echo in my head:

Family is what matters the most in this world.

But the best parts of my family are gone now. In the ground. Buried in six feet of soil.

I click another video, one where Leo is led onto the lawn by my mother, Aria, her slight hands over his eyes. She opens the front door and walks him out onto the porch to face a brand new Camaro with a giant bow on top. She pulls her hands away, and Leo looks disappointed, muttering something about a Dodge Charger before the camera jostles and the clip ends.

There is one of Andromeda collecting a high school diploma in a cap and gown, an honor roll sash draped across her chest. She shakes hands with all of the staff on the stage as Dad hollers with pride from behind the camera.

The last video is longer. It's of Dad and me, camera propped behind the wheel of his fishing boat, one we spent so many afternoons on. I'm older, nearing twenty, and I remember it like it was yesterday. Lake Winnipesaukee. We came back with a livewell full of rainbow trout and grilled them up for dinner.

"This is nice," Dad says in the video, looking around, squinting into the sun. Not a cloud in sight.

"It is," I squint, too, even beneath the brim of a New England Patriots hat. It's a team I abhor, a loaner from Dad so my fair face wouldn't scorch. I used to fry like bacon out there on the water.

In the clip, I stitch a hook through a worm and cast it far, eyes little green slivers peering off into the distance. Dad does the same, casting his off the other side and propping his tennis shoes on the chrome side rail, kicking back in his captain's chair. For the rest of the video, we sit in silence, enjoying each other's presence, offering the occasional ice-cold beer from an integrated cooler built into the floor.

These are the times I miss the most with my father, times when we were content simply being in each other's company.

Feet pad down the stairs, and I catch a glimpse of Layla in my button-down shirt -- and nothing else -- from the corner of my eye.

"Good morning," she says, sweet as a songbird.

"Morning," I barely manage, emotions swelling from the last video. I close my laptop, already feeling my mood darkening, a black storm cloud rolling in, choking out any sun.

I'm wrecked. I'm grateful these exist, priceless gems I couldn't buy retail for all the money in the world, these revered artifacts of Dad's past.

Of *our* pasts.

"Want some coffee?" she asks, opening cupboards in search of a mug.

I nod, fearing that if I speak, I might break down. I set the computer down and join her in the kitchen, pressing up against her ass as I grab two mugs from the cabinet above her head. She purrs, backing up against my groin. I press my face against her neck, my hands slipping to her breasts as I whisper in her ear. "Grounds are in the cabinet below you."

She nods, and I pull away, shuffling through the pile of mail on the kitchen island behind her. I sift the bills out and chuck the junk mail in the recycling bin. That's when I see them, in the cabinet with the trash. Two presents, wrapped and forgotten in the chaos of the last few weeks. Gifts I bought for Dad for the holidays. I remember now... I didn't want them taking up counter space, and I knew that when I took the bin out on Thursday night, it would remind me to bring them on my weekend visit.

The problem was, I wasn't *here* on Thursday. I got the call that he died on a Wednesday night, and flew straight down. And now here they are, just sitting. Still wrapped.

The gifts were nothing special. Just two sets of etched constellation-themed pint glasses, one for the Northern Hemisphere's winter sky, the other set of four for the summer sky. There isn't much you can get for a billionaire that he doesn't already have. But I knew the astronomy geek in him would've liked these.

I pull them out and set the bulky cubes swathed in Star of David wrapping paper on the island. It all suddenly feels too real, too heavy. I can't find air to breathe. My chest feels caved-in. I gasp, but nothing feels like it's going in. Dread overwhelms me. I feel dizzy.

"Are you okay?" Layla's voice cuts through my hysteria, full of concern, tinged with alarm. I don't know if it is a second later, or a minute, or much, much longer...

All I know is I'm on the floor, back against the island, chest heaving at far too fast a pace to sustain. Her hands squeeze mine, but I'm unable to focus on anything but the struggle for air.

"Orion, that's it. Knees up, head between them. You're gonna be okay."

She strokes my hair softly, the way my mother used to. The soothing ease battles the bottomless fear, both entrenched in a violent war in my body.

"Watch me, Orion. Watch how I'm breathing." She demonstrates some slow breaths, but I can't see her through my rainstorm of tears. She's unbothered by my pitifully emasculating display, seemingly only concerned about the pace at which I'm breathing.

"You're alright, Orion. It's a panic attack. Just a panic attack. You'll get through this. Watch my breathing."

She presses hard on my chest, forcing my back against the cabinets, constricting my air a little, and then releasing it so I can sync with her movements.

"There you go. Just like that. Nice and easy."

As I force my chest to slow, it's like I feel the languid return of sanity. I slide my head down into her lap, drawing my limbs in tight as I cry. She strokes my hair with her feather-light touch.

All I can seem to chant is, "He's gone, Layla. He's gone." Over and over.

To which she simply keeps replying with a soft, *I know. I'm sorry.*

42

Leo

A frantic knock at the door summons Wanda, who, in turn, summons me. The young man on the icy porch smiles. Now that I can tell from his attire he isn't some Mormon here to convert me, my curiosity's piqued.

"Mr. Stone?" He ruffles his hair, parted off to the side in a boyish manner.

"Please make it quick. I'm busy."

Yeah, busy playing the dusty copy of Dead or Alive: Beach Volleyball on the PlayStation 2 I found in my bedroom closet, a relic from my teens that's proven just as addictive now as it was in my youth. Time is ticking. Those busty bikini-clad Asian broads aren't going to win their own challenges, now *are* they?

"My employer asked me to bring this in person."

He hands me a manila envelope, and ice rushes through me, killing the half-chub in my pants faster than a taser shock. What does that goddamn bitch of an ex-wife want from me now? She already took well over half my shit.

"Did I just… get *served*? Don't you have to say 'You've been served' by, like, law?"

The kid laughs, turning away, starting back toward his car. "No, Sir. He just said to deliver it as soon as possible."

With that, he slides into his beat-up, three-colored Corolla and cruises down the long driveway and back onto the ice-covered streets of Rye.

I shred the envelope, bumping the door closed with my ass, wishing Wanda was within earshot so I could yell at her for not screening guests better. Heading upstairs, I pull out the contents, my face stupefied.

At first, I think that this packet is something legal involving Dad's estate or Aspect company holdings. It isn't until I see the racy eight-by-tens in all their glossy glory that I realize how wrong I am. I eye the apparent threesome in the series of photos, blurred bodies writhing in a tawdry mass through a gap in what appears to be hotel drapery.

I look at the envelope.

Orion Stone.

Whoops. Wrong *Mr. Stone*, I see.

What the fuck *are* these? They look like something out of a blackmail scene in a political conspiracy thriller. One man in his early forties, two decent chicks, maybe mid-thirties, tits out, lingerie twisted, makeup smeared.

That's one lucky bastard, whoever he is.

There are papers, too. Financial stuff. Dictated notes about a Mr. Alan Whittaker.

Custody petitions for a one Daniel Whittaker, along with some copies of other court documents bearing headings like:

IN THE FIRST JUDICIAL COURT IN THE STATE OF NEW HAMPSHIRE IN AND FOR THE COUNTY OF MERRIMACK.

ROGER R. LANSING,
Attorney for Plaintiff,

ALAN TRENT WHITTAKER,
Plaintiff,

VS

BARTHOLEMEW L. COLLINS,
Attorney for Defendant,

LAYLA ANNE WHITTAKER,
Defendant

DECREE OF DIVORCE

Oh *my*, whatever have I stumbled upon? Maybe these busty beach-volleyball babes will have to linger in limbo a while longer.

43

Leo's knock on my old bedroom door is incessant. I recognize the annoying pattern from when we were kids, although back in those days, he loved to barge in, hoping to catch me masturbating or in some other embarrassing state.

Just like old times, he wafts in without a formal invitation. Some things really *don't* ever change.

"Welcome home, Annie."

Leo plops down on my bed and I flash back to this morning's video of him knocking four-year-old me into a buffet table over a fucking *dreidel*. Then, I think about the subsequent mortifying meltdown I had in my kitchen, whimpering like a wounded animal on the floor.

I notice something in his hand, a torn envelope… one bearing *my* name. He tosses it on the comforter in the spot where I'm trying to unpack.

"Opened your mail today. Honest mistake. Guy said he was looking for Mr. Stone, and well," he points to himself with a grin. No need to finish the thought.

I pick it up and look for a return address. There isn't one.

"You know, if you wanted some amateur jerk-off material, I could've loaned you a few nudie mags. Would've been a lot cheaper." He lies down on the bed and kicks my folded pile of clothes over. He folds his hands behind his head and stares at the glow-in-the-dark plastic stars still clinging to the ceiling tiles in my room, each carefully arranged into existing constellations.

"...But I'm guessing getting your rocks off wasn't the point of all this, was it? I'm guessing you paid Dad's old PI to gather intel on ol' Layla and the ex-hubby."

I don't deny it. I'm as transparent as a fucking window. He's got me dead to rights.

"This makes you look like a stalker. You know that, right?" He laughs, louder this time.

I don't move. If I don't give him the reaction he's seeking, maybe he'll leave.

"What were you hoping to accomplish by having her spied on, *hmmm*? Or did you just wanna read the instructions on your little Real Doll?"

Rage coils tightly within my chest. I feel like I'm ticking, my fuse dangerously short, ready to explode.

"Call her a that again... and I'll break every bone in your goddamned face," I threaten quietly.

He cranes his neck to look at me, in shock. "Well, well, well. Did somebody suddenly grow a pair of fucking *balls* all of the sudden?"

He stands quickly. I'm unsure if this is to better taunt me or to be in a better position in case I swing.

"Word of advice, little brother," he pats my chest aggressively and it takes every shred of strength I have not to knock him the fuck out. "Don't be like our father, Orion. You can *screw* the help. Just don't *marry* them like *he* did."

I stare at him long and hard. "What's *that* supposed to mean?"

His body judders with laughter. He's enjoying every nerve-wracking second of this exchange.

"You never asked how he met your mom?"

I wrack my brain to recall the story, but I come up blank. It occurs to me that in all these years, I may have never asked.

Leo whispers in my ear, just like when he was a teenager getting the last word in, "Your mom was *my* mom's fucking *maid*, you twat."

Like a puff of smoke, he is gone, breezing out of the room, leaving me with the grenade he's just thrown.

44

Layla

I crack open a sparkling water and look up through the window above the breakfast nook at the threatening storm clouds, ones promising another foot of snow tonight. I'm nervous about its presence, praying it doesn't ground our flight to Austin. I finally have a chance to see my son without destroying the pittance remaining in my savings account, and I'm eager to take it. I can't wait to see how much he's grown since I saw him last.

Leo enters the kitchen. "Jesus, not *you*, too."

"Hmm?" I turn, cold can still to my lips.

"It's the curse of this damn house." He rolls his eyes, opens an imported beer from one of the fridges, and tosses the cap on the counter. It bounces onto the floor. He makes no attempt to retrieve it. "Everyone who stays in this place ends up with their necks twisted up toward that fucking sky, staring at the stars or the clouds or the goddamned nebulae."

I offer a humorless noise to acknowledge that he said something, a small effort to appease. He usually leaves the room pretty quickly when he can't elicit the attention he so desperately seeks.

I see Orion in the dining room behind him, briskly walking with a terse expression like he's on the warpath. I wish I could teleport myself to another room in the house. I wanted a quick break and a cold drink because the central heat is cranked up in the room I've been working in.

Leo glances at me, and I get the feeling that even though I was in the kitchen before them, I'm intruding on something private.

"What the *fuck* are you talking about?" Anger burns in Orion's eyes, glaring at Leo.

Feigning innocence with his hands up, Leo laughs, ever the bully. "Hey, don't blame the messenger, Dickhead. Honestly, I don't know how you went thirty-four years without putting it together."

"Putting it together? They were married when I was born. What was there to put together?"

"Rumor has it... there was some... *overlap*." Leo shrugs.

Orion growls, pacing like he's about to lose it. "What the fuck are you talking about?"

"Ask Aunt Kay if you don't believe me."

"I'm not asking Kay shit. I'm asking *you*."

"When mom was going through chemo, Aria was... comforting. Like... *real* comforting, if you catch my drift."

Orion looks like he wants to say three different things, but they're all jammed tight in his mouth. "You're lying," he finally manages.

"Aria worked for us for, like, two years before mom died. Few months after mom gave up the ghost, Aria moved from the servant's quarters downstairs right into dear-old-Dad's bed."

"Fuck… you." Orion is losing it. I fear he may send himself whirling into another panic attack over this family drama I shouldn't even be listening to.

But where the hell can I go? The pantry? They're right in the doorway.

"What was it, some fourteen months later, they were married?" Leo scoffs. "They kept it real hush-hush for a bit, but eventually Dad caved, told sis and me that they were engaged. Andromeda didn't talk to him for a fucking week."

"How *dare* you?"

"How dare *I*? I wasn't the one who dared, Orion. That was Dad."

"Leo, these are people that are fucking *dead*!"

"You figure that out all by yourself?" Leo retorts with sarcasm.

A flame flickers behind Orion's green eyes. "I meant: They're dead and can't defend themselves. I swear to God if I find out you're lying, if this is like the time you said I was adopted, I swear I'm going to—"

"Is that…" Leo's looking at me now, ignoring his brother, "my mother's fucking sweater?"

He points to the vintage Saint Laurent lavender mohair sweater I'm donning, one that looks like it cost thirty bucks but went for fourteen hundred dollars back in the nineties.

"Yes," I say, alarmed, like I just got caught with a handful of cash mid-robbery.

Leo's pissed. "Who the *fuck* said you could wear my mom's sweater?!"

"Well…" I don't want to throw Orion under the bus, but I also don't want Leo to assume I pilfered it from storage and had the balls to parade it in front of him.

"*I* said she could have it. All your mom's shit is going to the thrift store soon."

"What gives you the right to just give her shit away like that?"

Now it's Orion's turn to laugh. "Jesus Christ, Leo, she's been dead for three-and-a-half decades! Do *you* want the clothes?"

"No! But I also don't want someone wearing that shit right in *front* of me." He points to me. "Go upstairs and take it off."

I start toward the door, mortified.

"No." Orion stands firm, his hand out to halt me.

Leo turns to Orion, toe-to-toe, not one to shy from confrontation, seemingly incapable of de-escalation.

"Annie, I swear to God—"

Before I can assure Orion the sweater isn't worth an altercation, Orion smashes a fist into Leo's face, knocking him backward into the stove. Blood dribbles down his expression of utter shock, nose gushing. Orion pounces again in a flash, his fist exploding into Leo's jawbone this time, mussing the rivulets. Leo thrusts forward, thrashing wildly.

I yelp like I'm watching Rottweilers fight, unsure how to separate them without getting bitten myself. Neither halts at the sound of my scream, both entwined. Orion lands another forceful shot, and I hear something *crack*. I don't know if it was Leo's face, Orion's knuckles, or something on the counter, but the sound is awful.

After two more hits, Leo slips to the floor out of his younger half-brother's reach, hands raised in defense.

"Stop!" Leo manages, a waterfall of burgundy liquid pooling on his trousers from the split in his swelling lip.

Orion looks unscathed, save for the crimson smeared on his knuckles. His fist stays reared to punch again, unconvinced Leo has actually surrendered.

"Just… stop," Leo begs, sounding sincere.

"Apologize to Layla," Orion growls.

"That's not necessary," I say, hands trembling.

"Fuck, I'm sorry!" Leo spits it spitefully, not at all genuine.

Orion grabs his sibling by the hair and forces Leo to pay attention. "If you *ever* talk to Layla like that again, I'll beat you until you're unrecognizable."

He releases Leo's hair and stands straight. He wipes his fist with a kitchen towel on a nearby hook, hurls it roughly down to Leo, and starts to walk out to the dining room. He stops in the doorway and looks back at his brother. He speaks with an eerie calmness.

"Pack your shit and get the fuck out. We'll handle all the probate shit through the lawyer. I'm fucking done with you."

45

"We have been cleared to land at Austin-Bergstrom International. We should be taxiing on the runway in about… fifteen minutes," our pilot says quietly over the intercom. "The weather is a sunny, seventy-two degrees. Clear skies."

Our flight attendant takes a seat in the back with a smile affixed on his face.

I point to the brown-and-green grid of land parcels circling below as Austin comes into view through the small windows. "Almost there."

There's a dull ache in my knuckles as I return my hand to the armrest, the pain a reminder of my altercation yesterday with my brother.

Layla leans across me to get a better view, rubbing my sore hand softly. "It's crazy to know there's snow all over Rye right now and it's summer-dress weather here."

I feel awful for the way I reacted yesterday in front of her. That's not me. That's not who I am. I'm normally composed. But to hear him so carelessly besmirch my parents -- two people who can't defend themselves -- and then being so aggressive toward Layla… it set me off. I saw red. It wasn't until Leo was on the floor drooling blood like a battered invalid that I felt the true gravity of what I'd done. I regret it. I feel ashamed. I destroyed our family further.

Dad's words in that old video echo in my head: *Family is what truly matters in this world.*

I should have been the bigger person and walked away or ignored the fucking clown like I usually do.

Mom. Dad. Layla…

It was just the perfect storm.

I'm angry Dad isn't here to give me guidance, furious he can't mediate a truce, livid that he can't confirm or deny Leo's allegations about my mother and the origin of their relationship.

I can't stop thinking about the look on Layla's face after it happened, that expression of horror, that scream. I can only hope my plan for this trip, the one regarding her ex, will make her see me in a better light. I would go to great lengths for her happiness.

I just hope this doesn't blow up in my face.

***

"Whoa, this place is *gorgeous*. Easily the nicest hotel I've *ever* stayed in." She looks around, all smiles. "Glass walls. Penthouse suite in a high-rise? Swimming pool one story up. And did you see the size of that *tub*? You could fit three people in that thing!"

"That thing could hold a lot of milk," I say. A little joke, a small reminder that I'm not the monster she witnessed yesterday.

As she examines the suite, I realize I'm less enamored by the place. With the kind of wealth my family's accumulated, I've stayed in nicer accommodations. That said, I'm thrilled she seems so delighted.

The view is undeniably stellar. The Austin skyline is visible from every inch of our living room and glass-railed balcony, from the bridges over Lady Bird Lake, to the sleek curve of the Google building, to the row of middle-class homes converted into pulsing bars on Rainey Street.

"I wish we were here when the bats all shoot out from under the bat bridge," Layla says, unzipping her carry-on.

"I've been here a few times and never gotten to see that," I say. "Just videos on the internet."

"I saw it last year when I came to visit Danny. It's incredible. They form an almost solid black line through the air. It moves and morphs so fluidly. It's awesome to watch."

She pulls a wrapped present out of her case, a long rectangular one. A consumer-level telescope. The kind Aspect made back in the nineties before Dad started pivoting the company to more serious endeavors. He had forty of them in the planetarium closet for gifting to the kids that came over to watch the show. I figured one would make a nice icebreaker gift for Danny when she sees him.

"You think he's going to like this?" she asks.

I peer down at the gentrified city below, people ant-like from up here, walking in neat rows on the sidewalks. I watch one kid fly through an intersection on an orange scooter. They're more popular here every time I visit.

"I don't know him, so I can't say for certain. But I will say, if Dad were here, he'd have insisted Danny have one. He used to give those out like Halloween candy."

"I wish I could've met him."

I turn away from Austin to a sight far more beautiful.

Her.

"I wish you could have, too."

She hoists up a pile of clothes and smiles nervously. "I'll be ready to go in five."

46

Layla

I feel like I'm going to vomit as we approach the door to Alan's house. I've never been this nervous for anything in my life. I don't think I said a single word to Orion in the ride-share.

What if they aren't home?

What if Alan turns me away at the door?

What if Alan's new wife tries to intervene?

What if I say the wrong thing? Or do something that fucks up my dwindling chance at shared custody?

I hear Alan's voice through the Ring doorbell. "Layla? I… wasn't expecting you."

"I know." I swallow hard, trying my best to quell the nausea. I hate having to face him after all the vile things we've said to each other. If I remember correctly, his last words to me were that he wished I were dead right before I careened off a curve. Since then, they've not answered my calls.

The door peels open, fresh paint unsticking loudly with every inch. Alan stands before us, T-shirt clinging to his chest. He's been working out. Apparently, the honeymoon isn't over for him and Kayla yet.

"What're you doing here, Lay?"

Alan's eyes lock on Orion like a target.

"You bring him for backup?"

"No." I breathe deep and point to Orion, my hands shaking. "Alan, this is Orion Stone. My… friend."

I panic. I didn't know *what* to call him. Plus, who he is isn't really Alan's business.

"Okayyyy. Why are you *here*?"

"Well," My lips try to form words and fail horribly. I feel like I should have rehearsed something, but I didn't anticipate clamming up like this.

Wrapping paper crinkles in Orion's left hand. His right slips to the small of my back, a gentlemanly gesture that Alan's eyes seem to linger on.

"Mr. Whittaker, if I may, I'm in town for an event. I asked Layla to join me since she has family here. I was wondering if you'd be so kind as to allow her a little time with your son."

"*Our* son," I mutter softly, though I know it's not helping to remind him.

"I… don't think that's a good idea."

"Sir, I've hired a car to take them to the zoo, and I thought while they were doing that, I could, perhaps, treat you and the missus to a nice lunch. There's a little Brazilian chiaroscuro place downtown that I simply have to go to every time I'm here. Best cuts of beef and lamb I've ever had in my life."

The look on Alan's face changes. "Is it Fogo?"

Orion smiles, nods. "Yes. You've been?"

"Oh, hell yeah. I love that place."

"My treat," Orion says with a slight smile.

"I don't know." Alan's words sicken me again. I feel like my chance to see my son is slipping away.

"Alan," I step forward, "No one has been taking my calls. I didn't get to talk to Danny at all during the holidays. *Please* let me have this. I'm talking a couple of hours. Max."

"Kayla's at work today. Danny and I were going to go to the park. Throw the ball around."

"Blow it off," Orion says with a wave. "Let him go look at monkeys with his mom while I treat you to bottomless Picanha and a pineapple Old Fashioned as a thank you."

My ex-husband glances back and forth between the two of us. Orion was already briefed about Alan's weakness for food. He didn't pack on forty pounds during our marriage for no reason. When Orion asked what he could do to sweeten the deal, this was my plan A.

There was no plan B.

"Are you... *dry*?" Alan asks me.

I feel mortified that he would ask such a thing, especially in front of Orion.

"*Alan...*"

"I asked a legitimate question. Are you off the sauce right now? Because I'm not letting him go with you if you're..."

He doesn't say it, and I feel blessed to not have to hear the word *drunk* come out of his mouth.

"Dry as the Arizona desert," I lie. I chugged two nips of Jack Daniels in the hotel's bathroom before we left to preemptively take the edge off this awkward fucking encounter.

"Fine." He says with a nod. "Danny!"

My heart skips a beat, my face warming at the thought of seeing my son again. I hear the clomp of feet on the stairs.

"Yeah, Dad?"

I hear him before I see him, and I look back at Orion, hope percolating

"Your mom's here."

Danny's head pokes out of the space between Alan and the door frame, higher than I was expecting. I swear he's grown five inches since I saw him a few months ago.

"Get dressed. She's taking you to the zoo."

"But... I thought you were taking me to the park."

"I was. Then Mom showed up."

"Can I do it tomorrow?" Danny argues, looking away as if I am not right in front of them. It's such a simple thing, but it cuts me like a knife.

Orion speaks up. "Unfortunately, it has to be today. We fly back tomorrow. Only in town until breakfast, I'm afraid."

"Can I get a hug?" I ask.

Danny trudges out, begrudgingly embracing me with an annoyed sigh. I shatter inside.

"Go get changed. *Quickly*."

Danny pulls away and heads back up the steps toward his father. "I want you to put some tennis shoes on. And bring your hat and some sunscreen."

"*Dad…*"

Alan just flashes him a look of frustration.

"Oh, and Danny…" I take the wrapped telescope from Orion's hands and offer it as an olive branch. "This is for you."

"You already *got* me presents." Danny has a sour look on his face, like I'm some stranger trying to lure him into my van.

"I know."

Although I have no idea if he liked any of them since he hasn't answered my calls…

"It's just a little something to show you that I love you and that I was thinking about you."

Danny stares at the box for a moment before taking it.

"Go get cleaned up." Alan gives him a playful shove. Then, he looks at Orion. "Mind if I change real quick?"

"Not at all." Orion fakes a smile, the same kind I see him give to Leo, one full of disdain. "I'll order up a second car so they can take this one." He points to the man idling beside the mailbox in a sleek Toyota.

"No need. Save your money. Let them take that one. You and I can take my truck."

Orion nods, no doubt trying to keep from laughing at the save your money bit. "Sounds good."

Alan points to him. "You can repay me with a piece of their Tres Leches cake. Ever had it?"

"Afraid not."

"You're gonna love it." Alan points behind him. "Be out in a minute."

"Great." Orion and I say in unison.

The second the door closes, I turn to Orion. I want to kiss him, deep enough so he can sense my gratitude, but it wouldn't be appropriate. Not here in front of a recording doorbell.

"I don't know how to thank you. This might be the nicest thing anyone's ever done for me."

"Hey," the smile on his face isn't as bright as it usually is when he looks at me. "What are friends for?"

I know this is a comment about how I referred to him in front of Alan, but what was I supposed to say? This is my… *wealthy employer*? My *Dom*?

I don't even know what we *are*. I just know that I shouldn't be broadcasting… whatever it is that might be.

47

Layla

The thirty-minute drive to the zoo outside of town was filled with painful silence. Once there, we walked in through a rickety gift shop and I bought our admission tickets along with a cup of goat feed for Danny while he looked at stuffed snakes, sneering when I asked if he'd like one.

"What do you want to see first?" We enter the park, and I motion to a sign, a map of what appears to be the smallest animal sanctuary I've ever paid to enter. "There are monkeys and wolves on the left, or the Reptile Pavilion on the right."

"It says there are bears." He points to a paw icon in the center.

"Alright. Bears it is." I tousle his blond hair, hair he inherited from me, not his brunette father. He yanks his head away.

Great. Not quite thirteen and already at odds with my very existence…

We start down the left path, trodding past a row of empty cages that all have signs tacked up apologizing for having nothing inside. I am starting to wonder if this zoo even has any animals. So far, they seem to be just a myth.

"How was your Christmas?" I ask, trying to break the ice again.

He shrugs, eyeing the wolf enclosure where a single white wolf is passed out on its side in the heat atop a large dog house, dappled by the sparse shade of one of the few trees around. The ground is dry, arid, and inhospitable to any growth not heavily drought-resistant.

"What'd you get?"

"Presents."

"No-*dur*," I say, sticking my tongue out, making silly eyes at him, trying to lighten the mood. He used to giggle like crazy when I did that when he was little.

He sighs as if he's talking about paying taxes. "Scooter. Helmet. Rollerblades. These." He points to his Jordans.

"Did you like any of the stuff I got you?"

"Yeah, sure. Thanks."

His indifference is suffocating the flame from my soul. If he keeps it up, all that will be left of me is a heap of cold ash.

"How's school?"

We eye the saddest-looking monkey in existence, one that looks like it's suffering from a *deep* depression.

Same, monkey. Same.

"We're on winter break right now." He shakes the cup of feed in his hand, bored.

"I just meant, like, you know, before the break, how was it?"

"It was fine." He kicks a rock in the direction of a tiger cage. The large feline is nowhere to be seen, probably sleeping this heat off somewhere. Even in January, it's sweltering even without a pelt of fur.

"You got a crush on anyone?"

"Mom!"

Even though he's disgusted, it feels good to hear him use the moniker. It's a title I *earned*. I paid my dues. The nine months of carrying him. The rough labor. The permanent bladder weakening. The long scar. My bouquet of stretch marks.

…Not to mention every bit of work, stress, and sacrifice in the years that followed.

"I'm just *asking*," I say, nudging him with an elbow as we approach the bear enclosure down the dirt path edged with scraggly berry bushes. This place is so much smaller than I anticipated. After a couple of minutes of walking, we're already halfway through the circuit.

He stands at the railing, watching one of the black bears itch its back on the enclosed bridge that extends over the path from one habitat to another. Another bear lazily bobs in the swimming pool beneath a faux waterfall.

"Do we really need to do this?" Danny asks, and my heart sinks a little. "You know, this whole thing where you pretend you care now that you and Dad are done?"

What the fuck?

I try to remain calm, but I'm appalled, taken aback by the question. "I am not *pretending* to care, Danny. I love you. More than anything in this world, I love you."

He scoffs, refusing eye contact. He doesn't look twelve-and-a-half right now. He looks thirty-one, bearing the heavy load of life.

"I don't know what your dad has been telling you, Danny, but I need you to know that I would… I would do literally *anything* to have you back in my life."

"Anything but get back with Dad," he growls.

"I hate to break it to you, baby, but I didn't leave Dad. Dad left me. And he's married again. So, no, I can't do that."

He scoffs, like I'm weaving some tall tale.

"I *loved* your father. I would've made him happy if he'd have just told me how. But he didn't do that. He thought other people were the answers to his problems. He didn't give me a chance to fix anything."

"You didn't even fight for me."

"That is *not* true, Danny." I realize my voice is loud enough that I've drawn the attention of both black bears. I'm shaking, I'm so frustrated. "I have been fighting for you every *moment* since Dad left."

"That night. He told you to get out, and you just… walked out. You just… laid there and took it. You walked out and you didn't come back."

"You think I wanted to leave my own house? I picked that house out. Your dad didn't even want it. Then, to add insult to injury, he sold it and left town with you a year later. What good would it have done to stay that night, Danny? I had nothing left when your dad dropped that bomb on me. I had to leave so I could still salvage a *shred* of dignity. I hired a lawyer the next morning and started fighting for you right then and there. I never stopped. I'm *still* fighting for you. Every day."

"Dad says you're a drunk."

The single sentence eviscerates me, lays my insides bare on the dry soil in front of these caged animals.

I *knew* Alan had been poisoning my son. I could feel it.

How the fuck am I supposed to explain that I hardly touched a drop of booze my whole adult life before Alan discarded me like a bag of trash?

How can I explain that it was the *only thing* I found that could numb the pain, to quiet the thoughts that I was being replaced?

How can I tell him that there were months where I crawled into a bottle because the alternative was a fucking coffin? That it soothed my suicidal thoughts and gave me so much comfort that I went flying off a goddamn *cliff* because of it?

"I'm not a drunk," I say flatly, trying not to let anger for my toxic ex bleed out onto my son.

"Dad said you got a DUI before Christmas." He finally looks me in the eye, the first time in an hour.

"Your father lied to you then. I got in a *car accident*. I nearly died. I was in the hospital for days, Danny. An animal darted into the road. I swerved and went off a friggin' cliff. I tried calling you while I was there, but you didn't answer."

"Are you done with your lecture?"

I feel like I've been smacked in the face by a plank of wood. I am staring right at him, but I can't recognize my own son anymore.

After a long silence, he sighs. "Can I go feed this to the goats so we can leave?"

I stare blankly, feeling the stab of his rejection. Finally, I nod.

He turns away, leading us through the loop toward the billy goat enclosure. As I watch him walk ahead, indifferent to my existence, a deluge of tears unleashes from my eyes.

48

Alan sits down at our booth with yet another plate of food from the upscale buffet of sides and salads in the next room. The amount of food the man has been able to put away is *astounding*. He has a belly, but a smaller one than I'd have imagined after seeing how much he eats.

I slice up a chunk of fresh lamb, glistening on my fork, freshly cut off a skewer that arrived while Alan was gone. A man comes our way with beef. Before he arrives at our table, the waitress sets down a whiskey with a brick of ice that barely fits in the glass for me and a cocktail for Alan.

"Thanks again, man. This place is like a blowjob. I only seem to get it on special occasions."

Charming.

He pops a marinated olive into his mouth and waits for me to agree, as if my life must be similarly droll.

"My pleasure. Thank you for allowing Layla some time with her son."

He shrugs. "Might as well. Probably gonna be one of the last times." Then, he shovels *caprese* in his mouth.

This news stuns me. "Wait, what do you mean?"

"Well, I've been fighting for full custody so Danny can have some stability and won't have to travel all over the goddamn place all the time. It was looking hairy there for a while but then, you know, before Christmas, she fucked up. Basically handed him over on a platter."

I stare at him as if I can will him to continue with my mind. He does.

"You know, with the DUI thing."

"What DUI?"

There was no mention of any DUI in the packet the investigator provided. Only an accident report and the bit from the papers about her driving off the road.

Wait, was she… driving drunk?

I start to think back to the times at the dinner table that she turned down expensive Bordeaux or Chablis, only to be goaded into drinking by Leo. I've barely seen her drink.

Although there have been times when I could have sworn I could taste it behind a veil of mint gum or Listerine. At my restaurant, she was really putting them away…

"I didn't know about a DUI," I finally say.

"Well, I think they dropped the charge because she didn't blow. She works for those *scheister* lawyers, so I'm sure they helped her out, too. But, you know, my lawyer said her getting her license revoked was a big win for us."

Her license revoked? What the fuck am I hearing? I thought she was just using ride-shares because her car was totaled.

"Plus, it's gonna be pretty open-and-shut now that we have his letter to the Judge."

"Letter to the Judge?" I almost feel dizzy hearing all of this shit.

A swarthy man offers us a skewer of meat, and we both nod. He slices off a piece like butter. Alan takes his tongs and peels the hunk away as he slides the knife through the last bit. I do the same. My body is on autopilot, nerves jangled from what I'm about to do.

"Alan, you seem like a smart, level-headed guy," I say as the man with the meat leaves, trying to butter Layla's ex more than the roll he's stuffing in his face.

"You seem cool, too. No idea what you're doing with a *dud* like Layla. You seem like you've got your shit together. Even your suit… that Men's Warehouse?"

I resist the urge to laugh. This suit cost eleven thousand dollars. "No, local place in New Hampshire."

"Damn. It's nice," he says while chewing. "You look like you got money."

I look around, uncomfortable with the alleged compliment.

"You could do a lot better than her. The woman's a train wreck," Alan adds candidly.

"It isn't like that," I lie, positive Layla wouldn't want him privy to her private matters.

"She's working for me. She's inventorying an estate I'm executor for."

"What brings you to Austin?"

"I'm attending a fundraiser for a building for UT. Department of Astronomy. The government cut contracts in the middle of the construction. Normally, my father attends this kind of stuff, but…"

I shove some food in my mouth so I don't have to continue that thought. Finally, I compose myself enough to change the subject.

"Mr. Whittaker…"

"Oh, please," he points his fork at his plate, "you take me to Fogo, you can call me whatever you want."

"Alan, if I were to hand you a blank check right now and ask you to write a number on it to let Layla share custody, hypothetically, what number would you jot down?"

"Excuse me?"

"How many *zeros* is essentially what I'm asking."

Alan laughs with a mouth full of food and sits back against the dark brown, slick material in the booth. In this moment, I'm having trouble believing that this pile of human mush was ever Layla's type. She's stunning and delicate.

Did she just… not realize her worth? Or did Alan Whittaker look like John Stamos fifteen years ago? What is the deal?

"Look, I admire your balls, I do." He stabs another hunk of meat and stares at it on the end of his fork before looking back at me. "I *knew* there was some sort of ulterior motive to this proposition." He shakes his head. "It's not happening. I don't care how much money you came down here to Austin with. You're here in your fancy little suit, offering me your chump change. Sorry to burst your bubble, but Danny isn't for sale."

"I'm not trying to *buy* your son, just to be clear. I'm trying to—"

"Oh, trust me. I get it. I'm not an idiot." He shakes the meat on his fork, and a dab of juice flecks onto the breast of his shirt. He doesn't notice, but since it's a solid orange Longhorns polo, the *au jus* is *all* I notice. "You think you can come wave a little bit of money around and this custody case'll just go away? Nah. Not happening."

I sigh and dig a folded envelope out of my jacket's inner pocket. "I was afraid that you'd say that."

Fuck. I didn't want to have to resort to blackmail.

A million dollars would've been a small price to pay to give Layla a gift that would change her life, but Alan's forced my hand.

"What's that?" Alan nods at the photocopies of the vulgar glossies the investigator sent over.

"I didn't want to have to even take these out of my pocket, Alan. Before I show them to you, I should note that… they also never have to see the light of day. Your new wife, Kayla, never has to know about these."

Alan places his fork on his mounded plate and reaches for what I'm presenting.

"I'm sorry," I say as I hand them over.

He unfurls the folded papers and barks out a laugh when he sees the first one. He flips to the second, giggling joyfully. It's such a bizarre reaction, one I never expected.

"What's so funny?"

He holds them up. "This? *This* is what you were trying to blackmail me with?"

I just stare. I hate the sound of it. I'm fairly certain it's illegal, too, so I don't respond for fear of digging a deeper hole.

"You thought you were just going to show me these and I was gonna crumble and sob and say 'Please, Mister, if you promise not to show these to my wife, my cunt-of-an-ex can have summers with her kid?'"

I don't want to admit it, to him *or* to myself, but that's *exactly* what I hoped would happen.

"Hate to break it to you, pal, but you see her?" He points to the blurred woman in the photo on his left awkwardly craning her neck in a stained king bed to gobble his dick. "Her name is Kayla Whittaker."

Oh, God.

"Kayla Whittaker… as in… the woman who took my last name when we married." He points to the other woman, one he's fingering. Her face is scrunched in a violent scowl, naked body on display. "That's Kayla's hairdresser. As you can see, we're all good friends."

He cackles loudly and slams his fist on the table so hard that it draws attention from patrons all around us.

"We've got an open relationship. We do this kinda shit a couple times a year. Kayla loves it. Hell, sometimes, you know, if it's like *Shark Week* or somethin', she just sits in a corner with a glass of wine and watches me with these chicks. She gets off on it." He hoists the folded photos again and stuffs them in his jeans pocket. "I'm taking these. She's gonna love 'em."

Fuck. Fuck. Fuuuuuuck.

Well, goddammit, that failed *miserably*. The grenade went off in my face the second I pulled the pin.

"You know, part of that is why Lay and I didn't work. I fuckin' hate monogamy. Being trapped with one person my whole life makes me feel claustrophobic. Layla don't *share*. She was rigid. Kayla, though… she's open-minded. She understands humans weren't designed for that, especially *men*. We're biologically programmed at the genetic level to procreate with as many females as possible for the expansion of our species. Layla didn't wanna hear any of that. She's like dead-set on the one-woman-one-man bullshit. Drove me fuckin' nuts."

I nod, although this revelation about Layla makes me like her more, not less. I feel the same, always desiring to belong to someone, to fiercely protect that person like it's us against the world.

This guy talking about genetics and biology like he has ever cracked a science textbook makes me want to self-lobotomize.

"Look, I know you're probably tryin' to do what you think is the right thing here, but it isn't. Danny doesn't want to live with his mom. These last couple of years… they drifted apart. He doesn't want anything to do with her. He's happy here. That's why he wrote the thing to the judge."

He's said it twice now, and I'm dying to know what the hell he's talking about.

"Lay didn't tell you about that?" He chuckles. "I'm sorry. I shouldn't laugh. Maybe those dickhead lawyers haven't even showed it to *her* yet. Hang on, I'll let you read it if you want."

He whips his phone off the table and starts clicking around through his apps, finally producing a photo of a handwritten letter.

He offers it to me, and I read it, my stomach sinking with every word. Afterward, I give it back, gutted.

"The original was submitted around Christmas. Lawyers say it'll hold a lotta weight in court." He shrugs. "Sorry you ended up on this wild goose chase, my man."

Another man comes up to the table with a skewer of chicken. Alan takes some greedily.

I decline. Suddenly, I'm no longer hungry.

49

Orion

"Almost ready," Layla says at the open door of the bathroom while putting a dangly earring in.

"You look incredible," I say, drinking her in, black sequin gown nearly touching the floor, a slit up one thigh that ends just shy of the lace band of her thigh-highs. Her spiky heels raise her damn-near three inches and make her ass look spectacular.

"Thank you," she murmurs. I know she'd be smiling now if she hadn't spent the last hour crying. Her lids are puffy, scleras irritated, but her shadow and liner are camera-ready. I'm in awe of her ability to rally after the day she's had. It seems like every time something knocks her to the floor, she is able to rise again and take more punishment. Her spirit is wounded and indomitable in equal measure, a beautifully stubborn trait I rarely see anymore.

I admire her. She's tough as hell, but also nurturing, ready to comfort at a moment's notice. I think about how she must've been as a mom. I can't imagine how ungrateful Danny would have to be to shun that kind of affection.

I'd *kill* to have my mother back.

I stare at her gorgeous profile from the suite's couch and I feel my cock harden at the sight of her. So vulnerable and elegant, full of pain and hope…

I rise, checking my watch. Ten minutes until the limo is set to arrive downstairs.

Just enough time to have a little fun.

I approach as she presses a powder puff to her face. I slide my hand up into her hair, fisting a handful roughly. The look on her face changes from one of serious concentration to arousal the second she feels the hard tug of her scalp. Her breath hitches as I pull slowly. She stares in the mirror, head back like she's on a Gravitron, the G-force taking over.

I slip my other hand into the low neckline of her strappy dress, cupping her breast, massaging its perky nipple as it hardens beneath my fingers. Her breaths morph into ragged pants as I trace the shell of her ear with my tongue, all the while staring through the mirror into her eyes.

"*Are you wearing your plug like a good girl?*"

"*Yes, Sir,*" she pants as my roaming hand slips the other breast out.

"*Good girl.*" I snake around her and take that beautiful, rosy areola in my mouth, nibbling the tip of it harder and harder until she mewls. Her hand slips up into my hair. Stroking it seems to be a fetish of hers, one I am happy to oblige.

I give her nipple one last, hard suck and then tuck her breasts neatly back behind her clothes. I eye the slit up the right thigh of her dress, an easy access point to all that lies beneath. "When we sit for dinner, you're on my left. Understand?"

"Yes, Sir." She breathes it more than she says it, cheeks blushing.

God damn, she's beautiful.

"Meet me," I slip my hand through the slit in the dress and stroke her pussy through the lace, "by the elevator… when you're ready."

"Yes, sir."

She moans at my touch and bites her lip, body squirming against my hand.

I feel intoxicated from the control.

I remove my hand and suck the taste of her off of my fingers. She watches intently. I grip the curve of her ass hard and growl in her ear, "*…And ditch the panties.*"

50

Layla

The decor for this fundraiser gala is elegant, no doubt planned by an anal-retentive committee of prideful women known for having opulent taste.

Orion is in high demand tonight, getting pulled in every direction like a cricket in a cage of hungry leopard geckos. I must admit I've been thinking about lizards *far* too much tonight. I spent a good thirty minutes of my zoo trip sobbing my ass off in the Reptile Pavilion while Danny stood outside talking more to some buck-toothed alpaca than he did with me.

I watch Orion mingle from afar as I drift through the massive venue. Bundles of low sprawling flowers sit around barrel-shaped vases with lit floating candles on half the tables, while star-like metal sculptures adorn the center of the others. Light from the dim chandeliers above the dance floor makes the sapphire and amethyst-colored glitter tablecloths shine like gems. Each setting has a seat number, three glasses, a bread plate, and cobalt blue dishes on purple chargers. Rainbow-colored flatware is wrapped in a cloth napkin, each bearing various constellations. A small space-themed menu lies atop each dinner plate.

I keep hearing people mumble Orion's last name, catching bits and phrases as people chatter about Aspect Technologies and Alexander's personal planetarium, an anecdote attendees seem to find absolutely delightful.

A waiter walks by with a tray of champagne flutes, and I wave him down, taking two off the tray and mouthing him thanks.

This afternoon with Danny was worse than I could've imagined. I wanted to crawl into the cage with those depressed monkeys and have a complete breakdown. A glass of champagne… *or a few*… might help me smile at these strangers all night when all I want to do is fall apart.

I roll my shoulders back and walk toward Orion to give him one of the flutes. As soon as he notices me in the distance, he smiles. It seems to evaporate as soon as he sees the glasses in my hands.

Okay. Don't know what that's *about*…

When I reach him, I offer him a glass. He takes it and slides his other hand around me as if I somehow, on any planet, deserve to be the woman on his arm.

"Gentlemen, allow me to introduce to you the lovely Layla Whittaker," Orion points his champagne at me.

"Pleasure to meet you," one says while shaking my hand fervently. "Do you work for Aspect, too?"

I chuckle. "No, I'm afraid not. I work for a law firm in New Hampshire."

"Oh! What kind of law?"

As the men politely pry, I catch Orion staring at me with a smoldering intensity, the same secret look he'd flash me during family dinners back in New England. A fiery look that burns white-hot. A subtle expression that says he can't wait to get me alone. To be the recipient of such yearning and desire intoxicates me, an addictive drug I now crave. I can feel Orion ruining me by the day, setting an unattainable bar for other men.

Someone mentions the glamorous way the gala has been decorated, and Orion snaps back to the conversation. He introduces me to the others at the gathering: two astrophysicists, an aeronautical engineer, an astronomy professor at UT, and one of the former directors of the McDonald Observatory.

A man with a mic asks everyone to be seated, and everyone obliges. I sit to Orion's left, as per my earlier instructions.

"No more of this tonight if you want to play later," he says, leaning in close, tapping the flared base of my glass flute. There is a firmness to the warning. It comes as both a devastating blow and an odd relief. I wanted to drink -- *needed* to drink -- needed to drown my matriarchal drama in booze and bubbles. But this denial is wise, almost as if he senses I'd fall too far down the rabbit hole in this current state.

"*Yes, Sir,*" I reply in his ear.

"If you want to cum tonight back at the suite…" He slips his hand inside the slit of my dress and past the curve of my thigh until his fingers are at my bare entrance. I'm still wet from his touch at the hotel. *"Then not one peep."*

I swallow hard, glancing around the table chock-full of professors in formal wear, oblivious to the way my legs are spreading beneath the glittery table. He pretends to examine his menu as he presses inside of me, soaking it for a moment before making slippery circles around my clit. His eyes dart innocently to the man on stage, who seems to command the attention of everyone in the room except me.

I lean back, subtle and slow, pretending to decide on an entree. None of the well-educated men in our sphere suspect I'm being masturbated in public or that my legs are tense and shaking. Orion knows *exactly* how to touch me, how to make me quake with an almost effortless ease.

The man on stage drones on about the building they're raising funds for as my need for Orion deepens. I see the bulge in his lap pulse subtly every time he slips back inside, the visible evidence of his arousal an erotic turn-on.

As people start clapping, Orion's hand retracts to follow suit, and the tension in my body dissipates, unwinding the tightened coil in every rigid limb until I can move naturally once again.

This was only a sexual appetizer, a promise of what's to come back at the suite. The moment we get back can't *possibly* come fast enough.

51

Rainey Street creeps by as I French kiss Layla against the noisy leather of the limo, one hand roughly kneading her bare breast, her leg draped across my knee as I edge her pussy with the other. Her lips are an irritated red, tender and warm, softly accepting my tongue.

She is so fucking beautiful like this, aching for me, her body amenable to my every desire.

I drag her hips onto my lap, peeling the dress up to expose that perfect ass, to better fuck her with my fingers. The vehicle halts abruptly in front of a mechanical bubble-blower spewing soap into the loud night air.

"We're here," I whisper, kissing her deeply. She dismounts, tucking herself back into her dress, and I tip the driver an extra two hundred for his discretion.

A moment later, I've got her against the door to our suite, fumbling blindly for my key card as I grind against her, our bodies like a well-dressed mortar and pestle. The second the door beeps, I nearly rip the handle off and whisk her inside, pinning her against a hallway wall with a force that nearly knocks the air out of us both.

"Jesus Christ, Layla..."

"Mmmm. Say my name like that again," she laughs against my stubble, fingers clawing at my buttons with a frantic need, thighs cinched around my waist like a skin belt.

"Layla, Layla, Layla..." I press against her again, pinning her almost hard enough to bruise her ribs. "I fucking *want* you."

I nip at her lips with my teeth, holding her face in my hands. Her lids are heavy, skin reddened and soft, a look of utterly insatiable desire burning in her eyes.

I've never *needed* to be inside someone like this.

"Orion, I think I'm... ready." Her face blushes a new shade of magenta as she pants it into the night air, my mouth attacking the spot on her neck I know drives her wild.

"For what?" I cradle her face and thumb her agitated, beautiful bottom lip, so soft and pillowy.

"I... trust you," she confesses, her nose grazing the tip of mine.

"Yeah?"

"Mmm-hmm," she nods. "Yes, Sir."

"Trust me, how?"

A mischievous grin crawls up her fuchsia cheeks, and her feet slide to the floor. She twists until her chest is against the wall. She hikes up her gown, pressing the bare skin of her ass against my groin, her plug's gemstone unyielding against my throbbing hard-on.

"I trust you enough... to be my first."

I swipe the wheat-blonde hair from her ear. "I'm afraid I don't follow, Princess."

She cranes, and I lower so she can whisper it. *"I'll beg if I have to."*

The last of the blood in my cranium drains the second I realize she's referring to anal.

I feel weak, buzzing at the thought of it like I've had ten shots of adrenaline.

Just when I thought this woman couldn't be any fucking hotter...

The fantasy I've had of filling her, of feeling her muscles relax and unwind against me, her body vulnerable, accepting every inch of me, makes me feel *feral,* untamed.

"Are you certain, Princess?" I murmur. My demanding hands massage her breasts while her ass makes small circular revolutions against my crotch.

"Yes, Sir."

The second it is out of her mouth, my hand is in her hair, rough and domineering, a move that never fails to make her pussy soaking wet. She softens instantly. I walk her to the bedroom without a word, as still and pliable in my hand as a scruffed kitten

At the bed, I release her hair and grab her gown near the neckline. I tear it down the back with rough jerks instead of bothering with the zipper. It shreds, piercing the quiet with the most gratifying noise imaginable. I rip hard at the waistline, destroying the last of the glam apparel so her body is unencumbered, save for the thigh-highs and heels.

I hope that was one of Bambi's dresses.

If not, I'll fucking reimburse.

I pose her onto all fours, pert ass like a vivid dream, gemstone glinting with moonlight. The shades are wide open. I couldn't give a fuck about who can see.

I slap the insides of her thighs. "Spread wide for me, Princess."

"Yes, Sir." She submits as I strip. Her slit glistens, lacy bands of her thigh-highs choking her flesh in a way that makes me envious of every nylon fiber. As I shed my boxers, my engorged cock springs out, angry and overzealous, hard enough to hang a floor-length fur coat on.

I linger a moment, watching suspense consume her, the gift she's offering about to be wonderfully rewarded.

I tear open a condom from the leather bag on my nightstand and roll it on. I dig in again for the clamps and order her to her knees, facing me. The spikes of her heels dig into the bleach-white comforter. I suck and pinch each perky nipple, exciting it fully before squeezing a spring clamp onto each, tightening the tiny screws for a snug fit. She hisses as I tug the draped chain between them to test their hold. Their grip is perfect.

She stares, her eyes sparkling. I give the chain a tug upward, a harder one, this time for fun. Her breasts defy gravity, sweet little marionettes on strings.

"On all fours again," I command.

"Yes, Sir." She follows the order without question.

I bury myself into her pussy, groaning out as she takes all of my cock, the firm metal of the plug making every inch of the journey in so deliciously tight. I hook the chain with a bent finger, tugging back as I dive deep again. She moans, low and deep, like the wail of a lovelorn ghost as her body takes all of me, time and time again.

I feel the pressure start to build, her muscles gripping hard. Now that she's warmed up, I slide my cock out and caress her ass, kissing and biting the dewy skin there as I worship every curve.

I ease the plug out of her with care, mesmerized by her body's miraculous ability to accommodate and stretch. I toss it on the floor. It rolls against the windowed wall with a resounding *clang*.

I retrieve the lube from my bag, slathering it generously on her. I toss the container on the nightstand and position the head of my stiff cock at the entrance to her ass.

"You set the pace, Princess. Relax. You come back against me with that perfect little ass when you're ready. Take all the time you need."

"Yes, Sir," she says nervously, the bunched comforter dampening the sound of her voice.

I caress her back and grasp her hips, patiently applying measured, even pressure. I focus on my heartbeat, my breathing. Moments later, she starts to press against me, her ribs flexing hard beneath my fingers as she slowly starts to draw me inside.

"That's right." I grab her hips harder, resisting the dire, overwhelming desire to thrust. "Take my cock in your ass like a good girl."

"Yes, Sir." Another deep breath. She slides further, trying to relax in spite of the pain and pressure. I feel her open up, accepting the rest of the head. She pants into the covers at the sudden intensity of the stretch.

I tug the chain to give her another sensation to focus on, a distraction from the width of my crown. "Good girl. Hardest part is over," I coo. "Now take the rest of it, Princess. Take the rest of me inside."

She trembles and groans, a cathartic mix of pleasure and pain that I so deeply love to watch her experience.

I lean forward, gravity pulling me another glorious inch inside.

"*Jesus fucking Christ...*" I gasp, grateful she's entrusted me with this privilege. "You're taking my cock like *such* a good girl. Are you alright?"

A pause. Her voice shakes. "Yes... Sir."

"I want you to take all of me, Layla. Don't stop until I'm all the way in."

"Yes, Sir." I feel her breathe, her muscles trying to loosen, to welcome me. She slides back all the way, enveloping the rest of my cock with one controlled shove.

Jesus Christ, I feel like a fucking God.

Every neuron fires at once. I groan, my pelvis melding against her curves, my length buried inside. I stroke her hair and shower her with praise, allowing her time to catch her breath, to feel everything.

Despite sizing her up with the plugs every few days, my cock is still thicker than the largest of the three. This is an impressive feat.

I plant a tender kiss on her back. "Are you okay, Princess?"

"Yes… Sir." Her voice warbles.

"Do you need more time?"

"No, Sir." Her voice sounds far away and dreamy.

I scoop her stomach into my arms, and I reposition us carefully so that we are each on our sides. She follows my lead. I cradle her in my arms, stroking the curves of her clamped breasts with reverence. We lie like this, with me inside, until her body relaxes, until the pain subsides. I whisper in her ear and massage her clit until her breath grows ragged. I ask if she's ready for me to fuck her. She replies, without hesitation, "Yes, Sir."

Languidly, I draw back and thrust slowly, pulling all the way out the first few times to loosen her. Soon, we are writhing in unison, long strokes deep and unhurried.

As soon as my hand clasps onto her throat, she tightens and whimpers, the tell-tale sign she's nearing climax. She begs on a loop, soft and breathy, her strained voice dissipating in the darkness, "*Please, Sir… may I cum?*"

There's an increasing eagerness in each plea. She's so fucking close, but so am *I*, and tonight I want us to arrive together.

"No. Not yet, Princess."

I fuck deeper, harder, my strokes growing almost violent as my cock pistons. Soon, the hand around her neck releases, and I growl with so much urgency that I don't even recognize my voice. "F*uck, fuck… ask me again.*"

"*Please, Sir, may I cum?*"

"*Yes, Princess. Yes.*" I groan loudly and bite her shoulder.

Seconds later, she orgasms, her scream shredding through the quiet night. Her pulsing muscles milk me, plunging every stubborn drop of cum from my depths like an oil derrick. I pull out gingerly. We hiss in unison. I remove her clamps and toss them aside, clutching her sweat-drenched body protectively in my arms as our lungs heave.

She doesn't cry tonight. I suspect after the disastrous reunion with Danny, she's had enough of that for one day.

We don't speak. We just stare at one another while she lovingly strokes my hair.

This won't last forever.

But strangely, in the aftermath of tonight, a part of me genuinely wishes it *would*.

52

Layla

Orion shuffles into the suite's living room, groggy. He looks so sexy when he wakes up. Tousled red hair, muscles on display, boxers so low on his hips that I can see the grooves between the muscles. He rubs the sleep out of one of his green eyes with the heel of his hand.

"When did you get up?"

"Couple of hours ago." I motion with my mug toward the coffee maker. "Made java if you want some."

"Hours?" Orion waltzes toward me first, instead. He scoops me in his arm and plants a kiss on the top of my head before murmuring, "Good morning, beautiful."

I offer a smile and then go back to staring at the bottle of champagne that was sent to the room, propped lazily in a bucket of ice with a note laid against it. Condensation drips off it onto the table below. I fixate on the gold foil draped over the mushroom-shaped cork. Cristal. Cost a few hundred bucks, I'm sure. It was a gift from one of the coordinators of the fundraiser for our attendance and for Orion's generous donation.

And it *was* generous. There were a *lot* of zeros on that check he signed at the end of the night.

"Why'd you get up so early?" He settles onto the couch beside me and sets his steaming mug of coffee down on a coaster.

"I just… couldn't sleep much." I glance out the window, knowing that if I have to tell him why, I'll start crying again. And I can't have that. I just finally stopped.

"You okay? Is it something from… *last night*?" He asks it quietly, like the intimacy is some kind of secret.

"No, it's not."

"Talk to me."

I sigh long and deep and feel the itch of impending tears.

Here comes the rain again.

"It's… Danny, Alan, that whole… mess." My eyes drip again, a leaky faucet that no one can fix. I wrap myself tighter in the knitted blanket I found on the couch.

He rubs my back, strokes my hair, silent for a moment. "I'm sorry you're going through all of that."

His wording reminds me that I'm going through this alone, navigating the loss of my only son without anyone to help beyond the legal team I pay. Orion cares, but this isn't his problem.

"It took a lot of strength to do what you did yesterday."

"What?"

"To seek him out. To spend time with him. He can't deny that you're fighting for him. You're trying your damnedest to be there. He doesn't appreciate it now, but he will eventually."

"No, he won't," I say firmly, more angry than sad. "Alan has poisoned him. Danny's got parents with a stable job, he's got a new school, new friends. Even if I somehow get the mediator to see things from my side, I don't have anything to offer him anymore."

"He needs a mom."

"He's got Kayla." The tears flow harder now.

Orion draws a deep breath, lets it out slow and controlled. "Yeah, well, I think I failed him, too. Lunch with Alan didn't really go quite as I'd planned."

"What do you mean?" I turn and set my feet on his boxers. He massages one firmly without even thinking about. It's comforting.

"I guess I… should be honest with you. I tried to help." He shrugs. "It backfired."

"How… did you try to help?"

He studies me for a long time. "Please, don't be upset with me."

I'm on high alert now, a dog with its hackles up. "Okay, you're kind of starting to freak me out. Just… tell me."

His expression grows terse. "I asked him point-blank how much it would take to get him to share custody."

"How much what? Money?! Did you… try to… bribe him?"

He nods, apologetic, and I feel like my skin lights up, like a match dropped on gasoline.

"Orion, are you serious? W-why would you *do* that?!"

"I was trying to help! Growing up rich, you learn that everyone has a price. If it were a simple matter of money, it would be handled. You'd have your son back in your life, and my account wouldn't have even taken a dent." He motions to the huge penthouse suite around us. "As you can see, I have a surplus." He chews his lip for a moment as I stew in silence. Then, he says, quietly, "It would have been a small price to see you happy, Layla."

I want to feel all warm and fuzzy about that sentiment, but I just feel livid. "What did he *say*? Was it some astronomical number?" I wave my hands. "No. Scratch that. Don't tell me."

But he tells me anyway.

"He refused." He bobbles his head. "So, I went with my Plan B."

"What was that?"

"Layla… please don't be angry with me. Just… remember… I was trying to help."

"You telling me *not* to be angry instead of telling me what you did is actually *making* me angry."

"Fine," he sighs again. "A week ago, I had my Dad's PI firm do some digging. I wanted to know what was going on with him, and, also, frankly, with you."

"With *me*?! What the hell are you talking about? I've been nothing but honest with you since we met."

"Layla, I say this with no offense intended, but we come from different *worlds*. With the kind of money my family has, the people who come into my life always *want something*. There's always an *angle*. They need money or a favor or sway with law enforcement or political clout… I'm accosted by a barrage of open, grabbing hands." His eyes lock on mine. "But not you. When I met you, you didn't seem to *need* anything from me. You don't seem to *want* anything."

"That's because I *don't*. I just… I really *like* you, Orion. I like being around you. *With* you."

The admission hangs heavy in the air, a series of deeper declarations than I was prepared to make aloud. But it's just the tip of the iceberg for how I'm starting to feel about this man.

I let the emotions sit between us like a third person taking up space in the room, ones that seem to grow every time we kiss.

He makes me feel *safe*. No one has ever made me feel that way before. That's why this is all so confusing, why the anger about this overstep is suffocating me.

"The irony is that in a world of people who *want* things from me, the one person I want to *give* something to, I can't. I tried. And then I fucked it all up."

"Tell me the rest. What did the PI find?"

Orion looks away, his eyes darting to the foggy Austin skyline outside. "I asked them to look into you both. Just in case. In addition to some stuff about you, divorce decrees, and stuff about the accident, they also got… pictures."

"Of what?"

"Of… Alan. Ones of him doing some pretty lewd things with several other seemingly consenting adults."

"What were they doing?"

"Oh, Layla, please don't make me say it." He looks down. "They're gross, okay. Full stop. I don't want to talk about them. I just… I thought I could use them to get him to fold on the custody stuff. I was going to surprise you. Or maybe even let it seem like he had a change of heart. But… I was wrong. I botched it."

"You… tried to blackmail my ex-husband?"

"Layla… there's a letter," he blurts, his pained eyes rising to mine, as if he'd been trying to shield me from such a horrific declaration. My heart feels like it flatlines.

Please God, don't let it be what I think it is…

I don't say a word. I don't ask anything. Maybe I don't want to know. Maybe if we both stop talking right now, I can remain blissfully ignorant.

"Danny wrote a letter," he continues.

"Stop!" It comes out of my mouth as a command. The irony of this reversal is not lost on me.

He doesn't.

"He wrote a handwritten letter to the judge…"

"Stop!" I'm crying now, sobbing into my cupped hands.

"...Saying he wants to live with his father. Alan showed me a picture of it. He said the original has already been submitted to his attorney."

"Polaris!" I scream into my palms.

It's over. I don't stand a snowball's chance in hell of custody now, not with everything stacked against me.

"I'm so sorry, Layla." He touches my hair but I yank away from him, angry at the fucking world.

I try to control myself, wiping the tears on my sleeve. I stare into Orion's green eyes, sadder than I've ever seen them.

"I carried him in my womb. I fed him, clothed him, taught him the fucking alphabet. What the *fuck* did I do to him to deserve this?"

"I don't think it's you. He just wants to be with his dad. That's what he said in the letter."

"Oh, the fucking letter!"

"Layla, he's a boy. My mother, she loved me fiercely. She was always there when I needed her. But I had a different kind of bond with my dad. He had hobbies I enjoyed. He… gave me advice, taught me how to be a man, taught me how to work, how to manage an empire. It's just… a different kind of bond."

I don't want to hear any of this after the things I've sacrificed to be a mother. I don't want to hear that my cheating piece-of-shit ex is somehow more qualified to raise him because he has a prick. This is so unfair.

All the fighting, the money wasted on lawyers, the nights my stomach practically chewed a hole in itself…

It was all for fucking nothing.

"Layla, Danny will come around," Orion assures me. "A few more years and he'll be an adult. He'll want you in his life."

"No. You didn't see the way he was at the zoo. He was aloof and cruel. He didn't want to be anywhere near me. Might as well have been a three-hour torture session."

Orion sits in silence, devoid of any more optimistic wisdom to impart.

"You don't have children. You have no clue how it feels for your own flesh-and-blood to reject you."

"You're right. I don't," he says softly, a still pillar of calm that illustrates just how bad my boat is being rocked by this storm. I'm ready to capsize and drown in the churn.

It's all so fucking pointless.

I bolt forward for the bottle of champagne and peel the gold foil and wires off the cork.

He seems annoyed. "Layla, that isn't the solution to any of this."

"It'll sure as hell make me feel better."

"No, it won't."

"Don't fucking tell me how I feel."

"You'll be nice and numb to this for what? An hour? Two? Three? These problems are still going to be here when you sober up. Your son is still going to…"

Pop! The cork is so loud it scares us both. It ricochets off the walls, and I feel grateful that it didn't smash the window. The cost would bankrupt me.

Orion looks pissed.

"Hate me? Is that what you were going to say? My son is still going to hate me?" I chug the bubbly liquid. It bites back like a crisp seltzer.

"No. I was going to say that your son is still going to need his father right now!"

He grabs at the bottle in my hand. I whip it away. I feel like a child, one whose favorite stuffed bear is about to be donated to Goodwill to prove she doesn't need it anymore, but just like a kid with a stuffie, I feel comfort when I hold it.

"I'm an adult. I'll drink if I damn well please."

His lips purse, and he shifts a few inches away from me, as if his body is being repelled by mine.

"I know about your accident, or rather about the parts you conveniently omitted. Like how you refused to breathalyze, how you lost your license. You didn't blow because you were drinking, and you knew what the outcome was going to be. You left that part out of your story. I had to hear it from Alan, of all people."

I say nothing. I feel shame wash over me as I pick at the remnants of gold foil on the bottle neck.

"Layla, I have always been honest with you. And I always will, even if the truth is painful. So I need to tell you… your son mentions in his letter -- and I'm paraphrasing -- that you started right after the divorce. He said he doesn't feel comfortable being around you when you've been drinking. I'm sure you think Alan is the villain here and that he's poisoning your son. But I think you need to at least consider the possibility that that shit," he points to the bottle clutched in my hands, "isn't helping matters either. That bottle will *solve* nothing. Your problems will still be here long after it's empty." After a long silence, he glances out the window again. "Have you ever considered AA?"

I suddenly feel defective. Repulsive. Like he will never again look at me like he did last night.

There is pity in his eyes where there was once admiration and intrigue. The absence of those things makes my heart feel like it's breaking. It's like he's seeing me now for the first time, raw and completely exposed for the fraud that I feel like. Like he can't stand the sight of what's in front of him.

I have never wanted to exist less. If I could, I'd fold flat like an origami bird and disappear on the wind.

I know he's right, but the need to numb myself is too strong. I'm overstimulated, tired of crying.

I take another drink.

"Jesus, Layla!"

Orion rips the bottle from my hands. He's on his feet in a flash, heading toward the kitchenette. In the middle of the room, I lunge for it, grasping with a pathetic desperation, an all-new low. In a calculated flurry of movement, Orion coils me in his other arm. He thrusts the Cristal over the sink.

"No!" I scream, tangled in him, cinched like prey in the clutches of an anaconda. He's a powerhouse of controlled muscle, stronger than I'd even realized. I thrash. He squeezes tighter until he's dumped the remainder of the champagne down the drain.

Once the bottle's empty, he hurls it in the sink basin. It bounces, miraculously unbroken despite the sheer force. Abruptly, he releases me, his body readying for some kind of physical retaliation from me.

But all of the fight has left me. It snaked down that drain behind all the wasted Cristal.

I storm off to the bathroom, locking the door behind me. I bury my face in my hands and burst into tears. I hear him growl a string of obscenities before retreating to the bedroom. As I sit alone in silence, one horrible question loops around and around in my head.

What the fuck have I just done?

53

Orion

The flight back to Austin was dead-silent, the air alive, surging with frustrated energy. I never tore my eyes away from the rolling clouds outside, not even when I heard Layla order a vodka soda. Probably just to spite me, to remind herself that she can, that she is fiercely independent and can do as she pleases.

Pouring out the champagne was never about controlling her. Despite our sexual relationship being one based on domination… that isn't who I am outside of the bedroom. I have always admired her strength. Even on her knees, bound tight, she has always been the one with the power.

Dad's house has been just as quiet in the weeks that we've been back, avoiding eye contact whenever we pass in the halls. She's been having her own meals delivered so that she doesn't have to deal with me. The space between us is a spreading chasm, vast with no bridge currently under contract.

The strangest thing is that I miss her. *Fiercely*. The feeling started as a dull ache at first, but now feels sharper, more acutely painful as the distance grows.

I miss the private times we spent together, those deliciously sinful sessions where she gave herself to me, wholly and completely, submitting a level of trust I've never quite felt truly worthy of.

Yesterday, I took The Birdie home to grab more clothes, check the plants, collect the mail, and relax in a space where I didn't risk running into her at all. But part of her was already there, her scent ingrained in the fibers of my bed, in the tub where I bathed her tender skin in milk, on the living room couch where we ate stale Christmas cookies post-coitus, the waning moon our only witness.

And now… back here at Dad's house, there are memories of her in nearly every room.

Despite starting as a casual fling, part of me was convinced that once her job was done, I could still see her, feel her.

Idiotic, I know.

A knock at the office door rips me out of my lamentation. My stomach twists, hopeful Layla will enter, even if for something mundane or perfunctory. Perhaps she forgot the access code to the planetarium. Or maybe she needs a key to some chest in the observatory, and we can quest for it together, a journey long enough to offer the genuine apology that's been eating away at me. Long enough to tell her sorry for everything I fucked up in Austin with Alan and her son, for holding her prisoner as I drained that *stupid* bottle, for insinuating she should get in treatment.

None of it was my fucking business. Now pride prevents me from opening my mouth every time we coldly cross paths.

My heart sinks when I see that the person entering is Leo. It's the first time I've seen him since our fight. His face is healing. I feel like I should be experiencing more remorse for what I did. But he's just…

Kind of an asshole.

"Hey," he mutters. Normally, he struts with a confident swagger, but today he seems reserved. Afraid, almost. He settles into the chair across from me and sets a pile of envelopes on the Narcissus desk, one I vividly remember sullying a few weeks ago. It'll be transported to an auction house next week, according to the update Layla slid beneath my bedroom door during my last visit to Bethlehem.

"Grabbed the mail on my way in. Figured I'd save Wanda the trip to the box."

I nod curtly.

"What? You're not talking to me now?"

"Just surprised to see you, is all." I tap my fingers on the veneer between us. "How's the eye?"

Leo takes his glasses off to show me. Save for a slight ring of yellow around one eye and a small cut on the bridge of his nose, his face has pretty much gone back to normal.

"I take it I won't be getting a bill from Andromeda's plastic surgeon, then?" I say, a dry joke.

"Who taught you how to hit that hard?" Leo laughs. "Sure as hell wasn't Dad."

It wasn't. Dad was a pacifist. Always said *words were stronger than muscles*, a fact that makes me feel physically sick about restraining Layla that last morning in Austin. I should've never touched her. I should have given the bottle back and let her make her own decisions. I just hated the idea of her digging a deeper hole of despair. I wish I could convey that I only wanted to help her.

"Didn't dad push you to do karate and boxing in high school like he did me?"

Leo laughs. "Hell, no. He just sent me off to that stupid space camp every summer. Said I needed to socialize and deal with people more."

I laugh. Sounds about right. "And how'd *that* work out?"

"Exhibit A, I guess," he points to his eye. "Who knows, maybe if I'd have spent a little more time studying the planets and shit instead of trying to finger-bang Laura Tandy, I'd be better off."

We sit awkwardly for a moment before he speaks again.

"Thought I'd pop in. See if I can get an ETA on when this shit'll be all wrapped up."

"You in trouble?" My smile fades. It all makes a lot more sense in retrospect. "You are, aren't you? It's why you've been in such a hurry to liquidate."

Leo shrugs and sits in silence like he's trying to decide whether to admit his faults freely or lie to save his pride.

"I remember when I was right around fifteen, the money from your mom's inheritance got released to you. Seemed like it was gone in a month."

"It was." He grits his teeth. "I bought the stupid… fuckin'… *yacht*. Then, Stephen sunk it. Dad had to bail me out. He offered me a chance to come work at Aspect and climb my way up the corporate ladder like you ended up doing, but I thought I was such hot shit back then."

"Let's be real, Leo, you *still* think you're hot shit."

He nods. He'd be a fool to dispute it. He knows his ego is his worst enemy.

"I thought I didn't need Aspect or Dad. I burned a lot of bridges."

"I know. I was there with my popcorn, watching the mighty Leo fall in real time." My smile fades. "So, what's going on now? Why the hurry with the house? What the fuck is going on, Leo?"

"Same as always. Bad decisions. My buddy, Rob, made it big on those stupid penny stocks. Turned the money they'd invested into a fuckin' fortune. I was sure if fucking *Rob* could do it, so could I. Lost my ass. After the election, stocks tanked. Half of those fuckers flat-lined." He runs a hand through his dark hair and scoffs. "Plus, I'm still paying the first two wives' alimony. *Cunts*."

"And I'm sure all the drugs and shit add up, too." I raise an eyebrow at him.

"What?"

"I'm not an idiot, Leo. Back in your modelling days, it was coke. Then you went through that Adderall phase, remember? You were rail-thin at Aunt Kay's fourth wedding. One of the groomsmen outed you. Caught you crushing it up and snorting it off the bathroom sink. And now... dude, you're *definitely* still on something. Ketamine, if I had to take a guess. You've got that erratic Musk-chainsaw energy about you lately. You're always on whatever is fuckin' hip at the time."

"*Hip*? Did you just say *hip*?" He laughs. "So sorry I'm not a Boy Scout like you."

"I'm not gonna give you another loan I know damn well you're never gonna pay back. Trust me, you'll get the money from Dad's estate as soon as it's available. I just hope you don't squander it like you did your mom's. You don't have any more rich relatives who can die and leave you anything unless you start sucking-up to Aunt Kay."

"Meh, she's already got two kids that'll be fighting over that shit." He laughs and bobs an eyebrow. "What about *you*? You, uh, need someone to put down as a beneficiary on your life insurance?"

I laugh, hard and loud. Quite possibly the first time I've genuinely laughed with my brother in years.

"Leo, I'd sooner will my fortune to Kay's toothless Border Collie."

"Worth a shot." He shrugs and then points at the door. "How are… you two doing?"

"Who?"

"Don't play dumb."

I sink a little, deflated. "There's no *we*."

"You fuck it up?"

"Why would you assume that?"

"Because I've lived with you. Your *be-your-best-self* bullshit gets old sometimes. You like to act like you've got all the answers. And the worst part is that sometimes you *do*. It's honestly infuriating."

"It was a fling." Even saying the words aloud, brushing her off like that, makes me feel nauseous. Layla was more than just a fling. I actually cared about her as a human being, and we were so sexually compatible that it hurts. Touching her was like wielding fire in my bare hands.

Eager to change the subject, I reach into the desk drawer where I found Dad's flash drive. In it now sits the original and two duplicates I made. One for each Stone.

I slide one across the desk toward Leo, and he takes it, confused.

"What's this?"

"It's a flash drive, Dummy. You stick it in a port on your computer. It holds files."

"I know *what* it is, Numb-nuts. I meant what the fuck is on it?"

"Videos. I made a copy of one Dad had here in his desk in a pouch." I smile a little, recalling all of the clips on it.

"Anything good on it?"

I nod, a pang of emotion rattling me. "All of it, actually."

"There stuff from when we were kids on here?" He smiles a little.

"Yeah. All of us. Bambi, Aria. Stuff from our fishing trips. Skiing. Your Bar Mitzvah. Hanukkah… you name it."

Leo holds it up. "Thanks." Suddenly, his smile turns sour, and his lip quivers. I can't remember the last time I saw him choked up over anything.

"What?"

"It's just…"

We sit in silence for a moment before he speaks again.

"…I feel like I took him for granted a little." He sniffles, trying to stave off his emotions. It's the first time in so long I've seen Leo's humanity.

"I miss him," I say, my throat tightening.

"Wish I could give him shit about his stupid Patriots choking just shy of the Super Bowl this year."

"I've accidentally tried to call him three times. Every time, I don't remember he's gone til I get his voicemail."

A stilted silence.

"Remember that time when you fell into Lake Winnipesaukee?" I chuckle.

Leo laughs, embarrassed. "Oh God, yes. That day Dad got us those goddamn *leaches*."

"I'll never forget the look on your face when you went overboard. Dad tried to hand one to you, and you backed up over the edge like that thing was covered in ricin or something."

"They're blood-sucking freaks. Little squirmy nightmares."

"Dad couldn't stop laughing. He almost pissed himself. He had to hold out the net to pull you back in."

"Dude, it was freezing. I was wet the rest of the day. My *balls* got a fuckin' rash. That day was horrible."

As our laughter dies down, I finally say, "Well, it wasn't *all* horrible."

He becomes solemn, too, knowing that I mean *that at least our father was with us then.*

"I think Dad would like this," I say.

"What?"

"Us. Sitting together. Remembering the times we had with him."

"He always used to talk about mom. He'd say *as long as you don't stop remembering the dead, they're never really gone. They live on through you.*"

"He said the same about my mom, too." I nod.

"We're orphans now, you and I."

I rub something on the desk. "Maybe we'll be lucky. Maybe one day we will be dead and our sons'll be keeping us alive like this."

"I'd say we're missing two important variables in that equation."

"Eh, there's still time," I say with a shrug.

He cocks his head to the side. "Is that what you want? You want a legacy?"

I offer a subtle nod. "I think about all the things I did with Dad growing up. I'd be remiss if I said I didn't one day want to have that with a kid of my own."

"You wanna waggle a fuckin' *leech* at him until he falls off your boat?" He laughs.

I smile. "Well, I'll at least be smart enough not to *pay* for him to go finger-bang any of the Tandys."

"Hey, I don't appreciate the judgment. At the time, she was cute. At least I wasn't a celibate *priest*, like you. "

"Oh, I'm no priest." I chuckle. "Trust me."

I think about Layla.

I miss her.

She's right here *in this house*.

And I miss the hell out of her. So much that it fucking makes my chest ache.

"No, you just wear the Father Stone frock during your pervy little role play, I'm sure."

"What makes you think I'm a perv?"

He laughs loud. "Oh, *please*. These walls might be high, but they're *thin*." He points to the door again. "You like her, don't you?"

I don't reply.

"You *do*. I can see it all over your face. She really got under your skin."

I offer another slight nod, angry that I just entrusted Leo with anything truly personal. "Doesn't matter. It's over now."

"Want some advice from your big brother?"

"My twice-divorced bully half-brother, you mean? Nah, I'm all set."

"Fine. Suit yourself." He shrugs and stands, shaking the USB at me. "Thanks for this, Annie."

A moment later, he's gone and I'm left in shock. It is such a relief to put down our swords, even for one day, to enjoy a reprieve from decades of feuding. It feels just like the *dreidel* video, as though Dad once again brought the two of us together.

54

Layla

My driver pulls up to the Stone residence. I thank him and make my way up the long, slick path to the door. Once inside, I hang my coat. As I breeze toward the stairs, something catches my attention. Past the empty parlor, the dining room lights are on, the chandelier casting a hazy glow on the table, one with a bouquet of crimson peonies on it.

Nearby, Orion waves, a smile gracing his lips. In the two weeks I spent avoiding him, I have forgotten just how piercing his green eyes are.

His button-down shirt clings tightly to his arms. God, how I miss being wrapped up in them and held like the world is ending…

"Have you eaten?" His voice is gentle as he motions to the spread behind him with those firm hands of his. On the table sit plastic boxes of sushi and bowls of fried rice and soup. It all smells divine.

I shake my head. I was going to scavenge from my box of cheap groceries in the room, but the thought of eating canned ravioli for the fourth night in a row makes me want to go to bed hungry.

"Would you join me?"

"I don't think that's a great idea, Orion."

The truth is, I'm fucking embarrassed. Embarrassed by how child-like I behaved in Austin. My life felt like it was disintegrating. Being distanced from it now, I realize it really wasn't. Talking to so many other people over the last two weeks helped me gain some perspective on it all.

"Please," he says. "Don't make me beg."

"No." I smirk. "Usually, that's *my* job."

He pulls out a seat for me, and after a moment of reluctance, I sit. He slides me in toward the table, always so damned chivalrous.

He deserves a fucking queen.

He lowers himself into the chair next to me and slides some food between us.

"I must start tonight off with a slight confession."

"And what's that?"

"Well," he laughs nervously, staring down at his plate. Some red hair falls over his forehead, and all I want to do is touch it. "I've been ordering us dinner every night this week, but then before I can ask you to join me, I hear you leave the house to go out to dinner, or whatever, and I panic. I chicken out every damn time."

"Really?" That makes me smile. *Oh, if only he knew…*

"If you don't believe me, you can see for yourself. There's an absolute *pile* of leftovers stacking up in those fridges."

"That's very…" I want to say so many things: Sweet. Considerate. Unnecessary. Undeserved…

Instead, I just let it linger.

"I'm glad I caught you before you ate tonight. Hope you're hungry."

"Honestly, I'm starving." I use some chopsticks to pull a few pieces of a spicy salmon roll onto my plate. "And, since we are trading confessions here, I haven't been going to dinner. I had some microwavable stuff DoorDashed last week. I've just been eating that."

"Oh…" He seems confused. "What… you know what, never mind. It's none of my business."

I sit for a moment, letting him stew in this mystery a bit before pulling a small plastic coin out of my pocket. I slide it on the table between us.

My one-week chip.

Seven days of sobriety.

Seven gruelling days of self-reflection without being able to self-medicate the pain away. Seven long sleepless nights thinking about the mess I've made. In the hours after my custody mediation, I even had to call my sponsor so she could talk me out of my dark hole, all the while reminding me to take one minute of life at a time.

Those minutes turn into hours.

Those hours turn into days. And so on.

Everything Orion said that morning in Austin was the truth, as much as I didn't want to hear it. The alcohol *wasn't* helping. The pain was still there. Danny *still* needed his father. I was still alone when I was sober, whether I liked it or not.

"I'm proud of you," Orion says.

"Me, too."

His smile disappears, eyes on the vase full of peonies. "I'm sorry for what happened in Austin, for everything I said, and for trying to tell you what to do. I should've stayed out of it. You're an adult. If you wanted to drink, you had every right to. I should never have grabbed that shit away from you."

I hold up the chip.

"You did me a favor."

I eat a few pieces of my roll in silence, trying to choose my reply carefully.

"I'm sorry for how I reacted. I didn't want to hear it. I was being childish and stupid. I was hurt by Alan, by Danny... but that's still no excuse. Finding out about the letter felt like an arrow through the heart."

"Trust me, I wanted to *tell you* about it as much as you wanted to hear about it. Part of me knows how close I was to my Dad, and I could understand where Danny was coming from in wanting to be with *his*. But I also felt angry *for* you. You're a nurturing person. You have this kind, gentle way about you. It was upsetting to see that Danny was *choosing* to miss out on that."

"Thank you for saying that."

"It's true. It doesn't matter if I had a hunk of mirror in my arm, or was having a panic attack... you're always trying to comfort me. I wish there were more people in the world like you, Layla. I really do."

"I missed you. Since Austin, I *really* missed you." It feels like the words aren't enough, like I can't articulate what I really want to say, which is that… I think…

I think I've fallen for him.

And it's terrifying because…

I fucking blew it. So hard.

His hand slips over mine, rubs it softly. He's warm, and I suddenly remember how blissful it felt to wake up cuddled in bed with him.

"I miss *you*, Layla."

He leans in, cups my face, and kisses me, soft and slow. His fingers thread up into my hair, and my body lights up.

God, I have missed this.

As we separate, I feel hollow, like his affection was the only thing that gave me shape.

"I'm sorry. I shouldn't have done that," he says, forehead against my own.

"Done what?"

"Kissed you." He pulls away, gazes into my eyes.

"Don't be," I say, wishing he'd kiss me again. *Wishing he'd never stop.* "I know this thing with us was just a fling…"

He speaks softly in my ear, the tip of his nose tickling my temple. "Doesn't have to be."

"What do you mean?" I ask, loosening his tie as he drags his lips and teeth along my jawline.

"We could be *more*." He kisses my neck.

"Yeah?" My eyes flutter. I swallow hard.

"Do you *want* this to be more than a fling?"

Of course I do. "Yes, but…"

"*No but.* Just say yes."

I chuckle as he nibbles my earlobe. My voice grows breathy as I'm swept away in his current. "Orion, you're… *gorgeous*…" His hand roams, caressing every spot he knows I love. "Intelligent… sensitive…"

"Mmmm. *And how,*" he jokes, dragging my hand south so that I can feel how hard he is.

"… and, my God, you're hotter than the fucking sun."

"*Ten thousand Fahrenheit…*" He bites my neck and tightens his fingers in my hair.

"You're rich… and sexy… and successful."

"Mmm, don't stop. I love these compliments," he jokes, his voice vibrating my skin.

"Orion, I have nothing to offer you," I finally say. "I bring nothing to the table."

His head pulls away, and the hand in my hair loosens. The mood shifts.

His emerald eyes bore right into my soul, hurt that I could utter something so cruel.

"Layla Whittaker…" he studies my face. "You are… *everything.*"

It's three words… but the last one makes my breath hitch.

***

In the morning, I awaken in his arms, snuggled together in a cocoon made of a childhood comforter. He's already awake, watching me sleep on his bare chest.

388

"Good morning," he coos.

"Mmmm. Morning," I purr.

The muscles throughout my body ache from the strain of last night's intense lovemaking. Our bodies did everything in their power to make up for lost time.

"How long have you been up?"

"Twenty minutes. Maybe thirty. Just... thinking."

"About what?"

"About IC 1805 and IC 1848."

"You are *such* a nerd," I tease, laughing into his ribs.

"Guilty."

"Alright. I give. What are those numbers?"

"They're nebulas."

"What's a nebula?"

"It's like... a colorful emission in space."

"*And*...?"

"And... I was just noticing you have this scar on your arm. Looks just like the IC 1805 from this angle."

"Okayyyyy..." I look at it. "That's from my car accident."

"Here's the interesting part: My scar from a few weeks ago, where I shoulder-slammed the mirror... see this?" He twists his arm toward me to show me a blob-like scar with rough edges on his shoulder. "I just think it's funny."

"I don't get it. Why is it funny?"

"Because mine looks like Westerhout Five. IC 1848 is called the *Soul* Nebula."

"And?"

"And IC 1805," he rubs a finger on my scar, "is the *Heart* Nebula. In space, the emissions are near each other in the Cassiopeia constellation. They're... *together*."

He stares into my eyes with a soft smile. "Heart and soul."

I crane my neck up. "I've heard you say some really geeky space things before, but *that one* takes the cake."

Orion slinks down deep beneath the covers next to me, pressing his lips against mine, his tongue soft and sensual. His hands find my breasts. Even though I'm exhausted from last night, a few seconds of his skillful touch get me all fired up again. When I look at him, I feel like I just can't get enough.

"I have something for you. If you want it," he murmurs, tracing my collarbone to my sternum with a finger.

"What is it?"

He retrieves the box under his bed, the one full of dirty adult novelties that started it all. He pulls out the gold leash and holds the collar in his hands like it's a priceless crown.

"Layla, I have... *never* given a woman one of these before."

I sit up slowly, covering my chest with the bed sheet, a strange moment of modesty despite all my vulnerability. "Are you... asking what I think you're asking?"

"When I took your ex to lunch, he said you didn't work because he doesn't believe in spending his life with one woman. He spouted off all kinds of sleazy horseshit about men being genetically programmed to fuck a lot of women. He said spending his life with one person was an idea that scared the shit out of him. But I'm not Alan. Being intimate -- *truly* intimate -- with one woman… that's exactly what I want. One I can share my life with. One with whom I feel I *belong*, and that she belongs to me."

He hands the collar to me. I take it, this singular gift worth more than all of the high-end items in this manor.

"I don't have a plan, okay? I don't know if I want marriage and all that stuff. But… if you want to be with me, this would be a symbol. Something private, something for just us. And, I know this one's cheap. It would just be a placeholder until I got you a *proper* one, too. Something custom. Real gold. Not this cheesy plated stuff."

"Yes. I want it." I look him in the eyes and motion to both of us. "I want *this*. Whatever that looks like going forward."

"Good." He runs a hand through that gorgeous red hair and exhales, relieved. He never takes those green eyes off me.

"Can I try it on?"

"Of course. It's *yours*."

I drop the sheet and clasp the leather around my neck with a mile-wide grin. The gold links of the leash dangle between my breasts, the excess pooling in a cold coil in my lap. "How does it look?"

After a pause, Orion smiles. "Like it was *made* for you."

Epilogue

Orion

Layla growls, teeth bared, thighs splayed. She dangles there in midair, suspended in our sex swing, her freshly-pedicured toes curling in the nylon stirrups by my ears, arms struggling against the rope she's bound by. Her expression looks like hatred to the untrained eye, but I learned a long time ago that it means my cock's rubbing her G-spot just the way she likes.

Eleven months ago, I upgraded her collar. The old one was a cheap novelty by comparison. This one I had made just for her with tooled premium leather, a solid buckle with a padlock, and a chrome heart-shaped loop in the center. There's even a sterling silver-plated leash to match around here somewhere, among the ever-growing supply of toys we've amassed.

Layla cries out, legs trembling. After being together this long, I know how close I can get her to the edge. I can hear it in her subtle pitch change when she begs. I can feel it in the tendons in the backs of her thighs. Even the speed with which her smoky eyelids start to flutter betrays her.

I slow my thrusts. On the days I permit her to cum, I time our orgasm together, a skillful feat that fills me with pride no matter how many times we fuck.

Which, admittedly, is still frequent.

...Just one of many *things I love about this woman.*

Sex with her has morphed into something deeper as the months have gone on. My love for her has grown so fierce it fucking *hurts* sometimes.

For every occasion, large or small, I rain diamonds down on her like the atmosphere of Jupiter. But at the end of the day, behind closed doors, the gifts I offer don't mean a damned thing.

She just wants *me*.

And she *has* me.

Heart, soul, cock… every fucking inch I have to give.

"*May I… please… cum, Sir?*" she breathes.

I tug the chain of her nipple clamps, new ones that match the collar. "No, ma'am." I shake my head sternly. "Not yet."

I kneel and spread her with my fingers, tongue slithering through her slick folds. She whispers a stream of obscenities, a very good sign, I've come to learn. I power on a small bullet-sized vibrator and massage it against her clit. I adore the way it makes her judder and squirm when she's this close. Her head falls back, and she struggles to keep her breathing controlled.

I rise and slip back inside, her walls pulsing around me. I thrust steadily, well-aware I'm riding a fine line already, acutely aware she can't hold back much longer.

"Please, Sir. May I cum?" she asks again, so polite and meek despite the barrage of stimuli.

It's time.

"*Yes, Venus. You may.*" I thrust again with a grunt, so deep that I bottom out.

After the collar, the nickname Princess seemed too informal, too common for a Goddess such as her. One clear, starry night nearly a year ago, I showed her each planet through my telescope. She became enamored with Venus. I explained that for centuries, it had been a symbol of love, beauty, and fertility, and I think she felt especially drawn to it because of that.

I call her Venus for entirely different reasons. For one, if you don't count Earth's sun or moon, Venus is the brightest object in the night sky. Layla Whittaker has *always* stood out as being brighter than the rest.

Venus is also the hottest planet in our solar system. One look at Layla's nude form and any man will undoubtedly know why *that* one's applicable.

We howl unabashedly, necks taut, eyes tightly pinched, sweat beading down every extremity. The orgasm rocks us both and her warm depths greedily accept my cum as though it's the only thing that can quench the insatiable thirst inside her. I slide out, and my mouth claims hers with force and gratitude.

Twenty minutes later, we are in bed, her untied and naked, nestled in her usual spot in my arms. Toys washed. Rope-burned arms lotioned. Swing untangled. Bindings neatly coiled, hanging on the pegboard. The door to our tiny dungeon locked.

The lights from our Christmas tree cast a soft glow from the living room, a scant amount of gift boxes beneath, one of which contains an engagement ring. It is the last one I'll have her open come Christmas morning.

"What's that one?" I ask, pointing.

"Easy. Little Dipper." She chuckles, staring up at the image I've projected on our ceiling, a star formation.

"I see someone has been doing her homework." I smile. It pleases me how much of an interest she's shown in astronomy, especially over the last six months. The other night, when she was able to point out the Dark Horse Nebula with the telescope out in the woods, you could have knocked me over with a feather.

Dad would have loved her.

I wish they could have met, but I am grateful that his loss -- a year ago tomorrow -- is what brought her into my life. So rarely do we ever get such a positive from a negative.

And now I never want to let her go...

"Give me a harder one. Not, like, *super* hard... but no more softballs."

"Okay, shut your eyes."

She does. I lean over, careful not to unplug the cord to the tiny projector, and scroll through my phone to another image I took a while back, a slightly more difficult constellation.

Capricornus. Not a softball, but it's no Vulpecula or Draco either.

"Okay."

Her eyes bolt open, and her head swivels toward me. "Oh, *come on*."

"What?"

"I said no softballs."

"What is it?" I laugh, trying to figure out whether she's stalling for time or if she really got it that fast.

"Easy. Horned Goat. Capricorn." She scoffs.

"Jesus. Okay. Color *me* impressed." I wave at her. "Fine. Shut 'em. And don't start getting cocky."

This time, I pull up an image of The Charioteer. A fastball, if anything.

"If you get this one, I'll buy you another car."

She laughs, opens her eyes, and studies it.

"The… Eagle?"

"Nope."

"Okay, you stumped me with that one."

"Auriga. The Charioteer."

"Fuck! I always forget about that one." She studies it for a long time and smiles at me. "Alright, I've got one for you."

I laugh.

"No, seriously. I'm pretty sure I can stump you. It's one I just learned about yesterday."

"I highly doubt you'll stump me, but I encourage you to try." I laugh. I've lived and breathed outer space since I was a boy. The chances are ridiculously small.

She unplugs my phone and shoves the cable into hers. The projector displays her lock screen, a photo of the whole group of us in Austin this last summer. Alan, Kayla, Danny, Layla, and I each hold our corrugated signs, variants of "We suck" and "Better luck next time" after a timed heist-themed escape room kicked our asses. It was a worthwhile visit, one in which her son's indifference and anger softened a little. She'd been sober six months by then and gotten her license back.

I was grateful Alan allowed her to see Danny, even after he'd been awarded full custody. It barely took any buttering up to get him to agree to the meeting. Fogo's chiaroscuro really *does* go a long way with that man.

"Close your eyes. No peeking."

"Sure," I murmur, closing them. I have a feeling it's going to be The Serpent Bearer. The lost thirteenth zodiac, as some call it.

"Allllllright. Open them."

When my lids rise, I'm instantly perplexed. The black-and-white photo is of poor quality. Blurred comet-like stars appear to freckle a blotchy night sky.

"Uhhhh. Where did you get this image?"

I don't want to admit defeat, but I can't make out a single constellation in the mess of specks and nebula-looking blobs. I crane my head to the side to view it from another angle.

"I know. Honestly, it's not the best photo," she admits.

"No kidding."

"Here. Maybe you'll get it if I rotate it one-eighty for you." She taps a button and rotates it twice, and I'm just as confused as before. Maybe more.

She stares at me with an expectant grin.

"I…"

"Here. What if I invert it?"

"Invert it?" What the hell is she talking about?

"Yeah, the colors."

"It's black-and-white? What's there to invert?"

She slides the image left, and a new version of it appears, the tones swapped. Now there are black specks on a white sky with seemingly gaseous swaths of gray throughout the center.

"Is this a stock photo? Or something from a website?"

"No."

"Layla, where did you get this photo?"

"From Dr. Sparks."

I search the depths of my memory for an astrophysicist or astronomer with the last name of Sparks, coming up empty. Finally, I look at her, ready to cave. But the smile on her face tells me I'm in the wrong mental file altogether.

"Maybe if I show you the un-cropped version..."

She slides the image to the left, and the next one displayed is fully zoomed out, speckles and dots all over the upside-down cone of light, framed by jet black. At the top is writing: Whittaker, Layla. Yesterday's date. On the side are a lot of letters and numbers, all starting with the term "1. Trim."

First trimester.

My eyes widen, the image burning proof that my life will never be the same as it was five short minutes ago.

Layla has tears welling in her eyes, ones of joy. Mine look the same, distorting the woman I love through a wall of liquid.

"Sparks says I'm about six to seven weeks along."

I feel scared and overjoyed in equal measure. For a moment, I am floored. Frozen. Stuck in time. But soon, I manage to free myself, kissing her with elation, caressing her face as she coos, "You're going to be a father."

My heart feels full, my universe expanding.

"They don't look like much yet. Mostly black voids."

"*They*?" I ask, looking back up at the ultrasound on the ceiling. Sure enough, two amorphous shadows. This revelation sucks the breath right out of my lungs.

She settles against my chest and stares up like she's admiring the sky. "I know it's a little early for names, but I don't hate Castor and Pollux if they both turn out to be boys."

The instant she utters the reference to the twins in the Gemini constellation, I realize I've met my perfect match. Wherever my parents are, in whatever far reaches of the universe they might still exist -- in spirit or energy -- I know they're feeling just as proud as I am.

About the Author

Odessa is an award-winning filmmaker and a cancer survivor who spent over a decade working in the film industry. However, storytelling has always had a spell over her.

Born in Wyoming and spending most of her adult life in Florida and Louisiana, she now lives on the beach in New England with her boyfriend. When she isn't writing, she's usually tending to her massive vegetable garden or kayak fishing.

Odessa Alba is a romance pen name (an easy way to keep her genre fiction separate for readers.) She has published several horror novels under her real name, Erica Summers, and writes cozy mysteries under the pen name Trixie Fairdale.

A Note From The Ogres

Even though this book was proofread thoroughly by professionals, beta readers, and ARC readers… mistakes happen. We want our readers to have the best experience possible. If you spot any spelling, grammatical, or formatting errors, please feel free to reach out to us at:

Rustyogrepublishing@gmail.com

Reviews

If you could take the time to leave an honest review after you've read this book, we would greatly appreciate it. We respect your time and promise it doesn't have to be long and eloquent. Even a few words will do!

As a small publishing house, every review helps others determine if this book is right for them and greatly increases our chances of being discovered by someone else who might enjoy it.

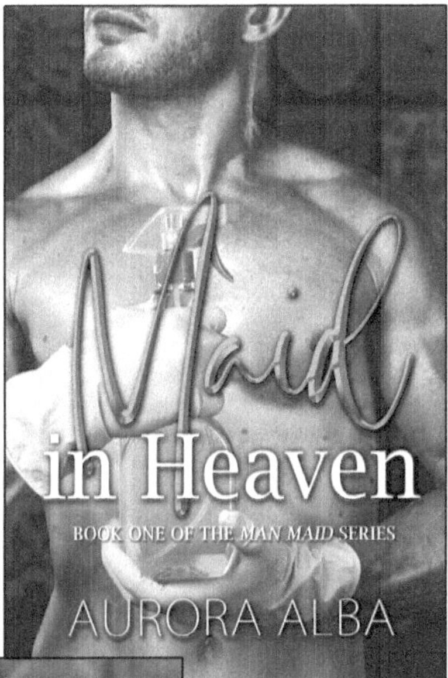

Maid
in Heaven
BOOK ONE OF THE MAN MAID SERIES
AURORA ALBA

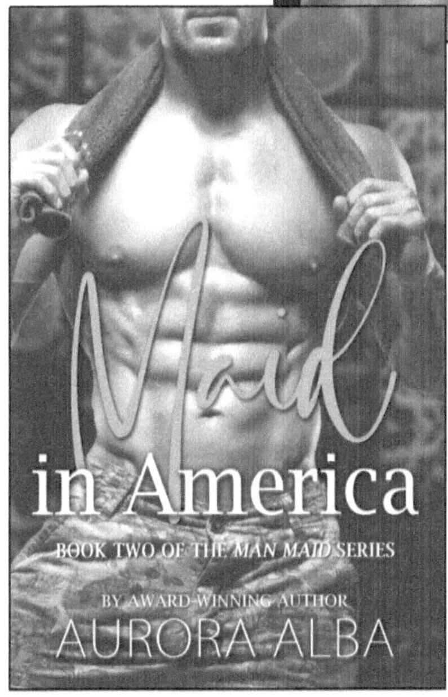

Maid
in America
BOOK TWO OF THE MAN MAID SERIES
BY AWARD-WINNING AUTHOR
AURORA ALBA

The
Billionaire's
Assistant
Odessa Alba
A NEW ENGLAND BILLIONAIRES BOOK

Rumspringa
Odessa Alba
A NEW ENGLAND BILLIONAIRES BOOK

The Ugly Sweater
PARTY
A FORCED PROXIMITY ROMANCE NOVELLA
AURORA ALBA &
ODESSA ALBA